Ungifted

J.D. Ruffin

3Aussies Press

Thank you for joining us on the Kingdom War journey. As a special thank you, I'd like to give you a free copy of *The Rise of Irina*. Just tell me where to send it.

Chapter One

High Chancellor Danai Thorn strode through the massive bronze doors of the Temple of the One. At midnight, the Temple should have been deserted, but one lone supplicant rested on her knees with her forehead reverently touching the cold stone floor.

He loomed over the praying woman. When she didn't turn, he barked, "Out, now! The Temple is closed."

The woman's head wheeled around, a scowl creasing her weathered face. "This holy place is never closed, and I am in prayer."

He thrust out his palm, called to his Gift, and a ball of brilliant azure flame blazed to life above his palm. The woman tumbled back and scurried away before gaining her feet and racing out of the building, casting a frightened glance over her shoulder as she crossed the threshold.

Silly, pious fool. If she only knew The One she actually worshiped, Thorn thought.

He dismissed his flame and stalked the length of the Temple's nave, taking in every corner of the grand hall. Normally brightly lit, only a few candles still flickered, casting eerie shadows that hid nearly as much as their light revealed. Enormous colorful tapestries hung on the walls, depicting The One as an ambiguous ball of light comforting some commoner or healing the lame. Thorn's favorite was viewed by many, even some priests, as a garish misrepresentation of their benevolent, loving god. It depicted troops locked in a bloody battle on a field littered with the dead and dying. The familiar light of the One shone near the front line, urging *their* side to victory. Few knew that tapestry was older than the Temple, even older than the people's false god.

But Thorn knew.

He climbed the few steps that led to a marble altar, then walked around it toward the door leading to the building's eastern end. He knelt, lifted an ancient rug, and found the ring he sought. After a final check for witnesses, he lifted the trap door, summoned another flame, and descended into the catacombs.

The walls of the narrow hall he entered were adorned with golden plaques engraved with the names and honorifics of long-dead Kings and Queens. The marble walls, with their golden monikers, were smooth and well maintained, somehow both stately and humble in their simplicity.

The end of the corridor held a set of double doors etched with the Phoenix, the universal symbol of magic. Fist-sized rubies set into the eyes of the Phoenix glowed and gained intensity with each step Thorn took in their direction. When he arrived to stand before the doors, the rubies flared to brilliance.

He extinguished his flame and placed his palm against the breast of the Phoenix.

"E vesh Irina," he whispered.

Irina, take my life.

The ruby eyes pulsed, and Thorn heard a click. He gripped the handles and pulled, the doors swinging easily on their ancient hinges.

What opened before him stole his breath.

The large perfectly square room was brightly lit by dozens of braziers with magical flames dancing above silvery bowls. A semicircular knee-high wall stretched nearly the width of the room. Ten water-filled paces spanned the area between the wall and a set of marble steps that led to a landing of polished marble whose colors swirled and churned like an angry ocean. A sarcophagus of unmarred gold rested atop the swirling sea.

Intricate carved panels on the wall behind the golden coffin reminded Thorn of a massive headboard towering over its slumbering guest. Of the three pieces, the left and right we made of snowy marble and arched inward, mimicking a profile view of two praying supplicants facing each other. In contrast, the center piece's ebony surface towered above the others, rising nearly to the ceiling. Golden script etched in the inky stone shimmered, as if freshly hewn, as it had for more than a thousand years.

Thorn crossed the lake, ascended its shore, and stood before the monolith. Transfixed, fought to shake his head free of its paralyzing lure as he sensed the stone assessing his presence.

Nothing moved.

Nothing breathed.

Nothing mattered but the stone.

After a moment of disquiet, tension evaporated, and Thorn again stood before a simple monument. He traced its glittering script with his fingers. The Prophecy had lived in his memory for most of his eleven centuries of life but gained power in his heart each time he stood before its golden text.

Seven Scattered as lands shattered.
Bind the Heir. Make diamonds bleed.
Speak the Words.
E vesh Irina.

Chapter Two

Declan made it fifty paces before turning to watch Keelan and the team disappear into the woods.

He studied the map of the surrounding mountains Atikus had scrawled for him and was amazed at the Mage's perfect recall. Atikus had even included large boulders with unique shapes to use as landmarks, noting them in fine script on the edge of the page. Declan's destination, a mystical gate that would transport him to the isle of Rea Utu, was drawn as a small archway with odd symbols crawling up and down each side.

He smiled, thinking of the old Mage. Atikus said he hadn't visited the gate—or even the mountains—in over twenty years, yet he drew a better map than any Declan recalled seeing before.

"What am I supposed to do when I get there?" he thought aloud.

Kingdom scouts were scouring the forests lining the border, possibly preparing for an assault by the armies camped beyond the mountains. Melucia's military was weak, offering little hope of defending against the might of the Kingdom's forces.

Atikus had practically begged Declan to seek aid, describing the town of Rea Utu and its inhabitants, but giving little guidance on how Declan was supposed to find The Keeper and the magical well. No one even knew if the Keeper could help, but the Mage insisted that they had to try, and Declan was the only person alive who could make the journey.

That was the strangest part, the part that made old resentment rise to the surface. Declan, the one without a Gift, the one magic had rejected, was the *only* one who could run off to some mystical island, meet with the holy magic man, and save the world using his secret well?

It sounded ridiculous. At least, it would have if it had come from anyone other than Atikus.

"Can't worry about any of that now."

He folded the map and stuffed it in his coat pocket, then rechecked his pack and headed west.

There were only a few hours of daylight before the sun slipped beyond the peaks, cloaking the forested slopes in shadows, so he found a small clearing among a stand of pine and made camp for the night. Once his tent was tethered securely, he gathered loose branches and made a fire. There was something about the scent of a fire when it was first lit that made him smile.

He dug through his pack and settled on a dinner of dried beef and apples. He was used to sparse rations, but couldn't stop images of roasted meats dripping with fat and an ocean of peppery buttered vegetables from invading his mind.

He crawled into his tent and had barely closed his eyes when a sudden movement outside pricked his senses. Without stirring, he peeked through the open flap. What he saw made a smile crease his face. He lifted his head, careful to avoid spooking his visitor.

Standing on his pack not two paces away was a fuzzy baby owl. The feathers around its legs shone a pale gold and puffed out to resemble a mummer's pantaloons, but its head was hooded in charcoal plumes with a splash of white that rose to form white brows. Declan couldn't help grinning at its massive black eyes with golden rings that never wavered in their piercing glare.

As he leaned forward, the owl began hopping up and down on his pack, peeping urgently.

"Hi there, little guy."

He sat up and faced the bird with his legs crossed. The peeping and hopping accelerated, so he reached down to where the last of dinner's dried meat lay wrapped in a cloth and tore off a piece, slowly reaching it out.

The owl froze.

It swiveled its head to the right, then to the left, then back to the right.

In a blink, it darted forward, snatched the meat out of his hand, and raced back to its perch on his pack where it began tearing and swallowing.

"Quick little guy, aren't ya?"

The owl stopped ripping long enough to peep a piece of its little mind in his direction before resuming its meal.

Declan was stunned. "Uh, OK. So . . . what was that all about? You don't like the meat?"

The owl focused on dinner, ignoring Declan.

"So that's not it. Hmm. You're not a little *guy*, are you?"

The owl dropped the meat and hopped a few times. *Blink, blink.*

I'm losing my mind in these woods.

"Alright. Sorry about that . . . uh . . . miss."

He watched the fascinating creature devour her last bite, then settled back into his bedroll. The owl hopped off the pack and edged closer, then scurried back a step. She did this several times, each new attempt traveling a bit closer. Finally, when he thought she might run away into the safety of the forest, the golden blur darted from the pack and hopped onto his legs.

He froze.

She pecked and scratched, then settled into place and began cleaning her feathers. Preening complete, she nuzzled deeper into the crevice between his shins and closed her eyes, emitting a long whirring sound that reminded him of a cat's satisfied *purr*.

He couldn't think of anything that wouldn't disturb his new friend, so he settled back and closed his eyes.

Declan woke the next morning to the pattering of the owl on his chest. As his eyes adjusted to the light of the new day, the undersized ball of fluff glared at him.

"Good morning, Miss Owl."

The bird hopped twice and blinked.

"OK, OK. I'm getting up." He leaned forward, and the owl hopped off his chest and resumed her stare.

He chuckled. "Persistent little thing. I bet you're hungry. Let's see if I have any more of that meat you liked so much."

He dug into his pack and held out another piece of meat. She snatched it from his fingers and ran to the other side of the fire. While she ate, he made quick work of his own breakfast, then began breaking down the campsite.

The owl hopped to the edge of the clearing and bounded on top of his pack, watching his every move. Satisfied everything was in good order, he turned toward her.

"Miss Owl, it's been a pleasure, but I really need to get moving."

As he knelt to lift his pack, the owl scampered up his arm and into the hood of his cloak. He craned his head and laughed as she gently pecked his earlobe.

"Where I'm going, you can't follow, little one, but I suppose you can ride back there a while. It'll be nice to have someone to keep me company in these lonely woods."

She peeped twice and nuzzled his neck before settling into the deepest part of his hood.

As they hiked, brisk wind whipped through the trees, but the sun shone, and they made good progress down one mountain and up the next. Each time they stopped to rest or eat, the owl waited until Declan fished more dried meat out of his bag, then peeped happily as she shredded it to bits. When the bird finished her meal, she clambered up Declan's arm and back into the warmth of his hood.

As the sun began her descent behind the mountains, the sounds of someone approaching halted their progress. Declan found a hiding place among some fallen logs and nocked his bow. The owl stirred, poking her fuzzy head out of his hood, but remained quiet.

Tense moments passed before three men in blue Kingdom tunics stomped through leaves and over limbs with confident indifference. They were spaced roughly fifty paces apart and, scanned as they trekked. Each carried a loaded crossbow that moved to either side with their gaze.

As the search line passed Declan's hiding place, one of the men stopped and held up a fist. His head swiveled as he inhaled deeply. The others paused and watched their partner's familiar routine. A moment later, he shook his head and signaled for the team to continue forward.

Like most Rangers, Declan was skilled with his bow and was confident he could take down two of the men before they could fire a shot, and, while he liked the idea of thinning the enemy's ranks, his mission was to reach the gate, not hunt scouts, so he and the owl kept their heads down until several minutes after the uniformed men vanished.

"I'm afraid Atikus and Keelan were right. The Kingdom is up to a lot more than just guarding the woods. I've really got a bad feeling about all this."

A muffled peep sounded from inside his hood.

They were cautious in their advance from that point forward, stopping periodically to listen and watch for threats. It slowed their progress but seemed prudent after nearly running headlong into a team of scouts.

As darkness fell on the second day, they came upon a huge rock formation that reminded him of a giant hand giving a thumbs up to the world. It looked natural enough, and the boulders were far too large and heavy for men to move, but Declan couldn't shake the feeling they were *arranged* in that formation somehow.

He rechecked the map and his pulse quickened. This was the last major landmark Atikus had drawn. He scanned the area and found a trail leading from the base of the rocks up the mountain. The heavily obscured trail hadn't been used in a very long time and ran nearly straight up the mountain rather than winding back and forth, making the ascent both physically challenging and dangerously steep.

They were roughly halfway up the mountain when Declan felt the firmness of stone under his feet. He knelt to discover ancient steps buried and worn by centuries of disuse—but there was no mistake—someone had built a stairway that mirrored the path on the map. As he peered closer at the first step, the baby owl hopped out of his hood and onto the stone, peeping in rapid succession while hopping and flapping her wings. Declan cocked his head as she turned and scrambled up the path, peeping all the way.

"What the . . ." was all Declan got out before she disappeared from view. He straightened sore legs and started up the stairs after the owl.

He stopped counting steps after thirty, realizing this would be a long climb, but was pleasantly surprised when the path ended abruptly. The entrance into the mountainside looked more like the crack on an egg than an intentional opening. The owl's peeping echoed from within and a strange, shimmering glow shone faintly through the opening. When he didn't enter immediately, the peeping became more rapid and insistent.

"Yes, dear. I'm coming."

I'm being henpecked by an owl. Now I know *I'm losing my mind.*

He squeezed through the crack and was stunned to see it open into a wide chamber that was well lit by braziers mounted on tall stands scattered throughout. He walked to one of the silver basins and marveled at his reflection in the polished metal. Cerulean flames blazed above each bowl, dancing with warmth and light.

At the far end of the alcove sat a round table. A silver pitcher and three crystal glasses rested on its wooden surface. Declan was again shocked to see the pitcher nearly full of garnet liquid, and barely a hint of dust on either the table or pitcher. Curious, he poured a small amount into one of the glasses. The nutty, hearty aroma of well-aged grapes tickled his nose. Fascination conquered caution, and he took a sip.

"Sweet Sprits! That might be the best wine I've ever tasted."

The owl peeped to his left, and he turned to find her standing in front of a large metal arch. The far wall was visible through the structure's center. Flowing script in a language he didn't understand covered the silvery face and shimmered faintly. At the apex, a small but unmistakable etching of the Phoenix glowed brighter than any of the lettering.

The owl peeped a few more times and cocked her head. He reluctantly set his glass on the table, then moved to inspect the arch. As he traced his fingers across the script, he felt a tingling sensation, as if the arch was somehow alive. Encouraged, he placed his palm across a section of the writing and gripped the archway.

Nothing happened.

He stepped back a few paces, scanning gate again. "OK, I'm here. How to I make this thing work?"

He walked around to the back, finding no seam or break in the gleaming surface. The script appeared to be a continuation of whatever was etched on the front, and he couldn't find any unusual symbols or raised areas that might offer some guidance to the gate's operation.

Without thinking, he stretched his hand through the archway.

Still nothing.

The owl peeped up at him twice.

"I'm trying. I just don't know what to do now."

Frustrated, he walked back to the table, sat, and poured a full glass of the wine. As he set the pitcher back down, he noticed that it didn't seem to be any emptier, despite having nearly a quarter of its contents drained into his glass. He grabbed the pitcher's handle again and filled the other two glasses.

The pitcher remained full of the aromatic liquid.

He sipped his wine while watching the owl. She stood by the archway and stared back at him, never moving. As he finished the glass, he realized the gnawing hunger he'd felt when they entered the cavern had vanished.

"Wine that never runs out and satisfies hunger? What is this place?"

The owl peeped a few times in reply.

He grinned down at his little companion. "I'm all ears if you have any new ideas. Sitting here with a good wine is the best I've got at the moment."

She swiveled her head left, then right, then turned and darted through the gateway. As she crossed through the arch, a veil of shimmering light flared into existence, and she vanished as the last of her tail feathers crossed the veil. A second later, the quicksilver winked out, leaving Declan openmouthed, glass halfway to his lips.

He downed the last of his wine, unwilling to waste a drop, and approached the archway. Gathering his courage, he marched purposefully through the gate and smacked into the wall on the other side, tumbling backward onto the floor. He stood, then retreated for another glass of wine.

At least that *works.*

As he drained the last of his wine, his arm prickled. He glanced down to watched in amazement as the cuts and scrapes he'd received on their journey slowly closed and vanished. Before he could process what was happening, his arm was completely healed.

He pushed back from the table and flexed. His back and legs no longer ached.

Holy Spirits of Utu!

Realizing the power in the pitcher, he grabbed one of his water skins, emptied it, and carefully replaced it with wine.

"There's nothing like having a Healer in your pack."

As he was returning the pitcher to the table, the veil shimmered again, and the owl hopped through. Her tiny brow furrowed as she scurried to grip Declan's pant leg in her beak, tugging in the direction of the archway.

"Little one, it wouldn't let me through. I don't know how to make it work."

She let go, peeped a few times, then resumed her tugging.

He barked a laugh. "Alright, I'm coming."

He knelt and scratched the owl's head, which she returned with an affectionate nuzzle, before pulling free and mounting his arm to perch on his shoulder. He slung his pack over his other shoulder and walked to stand before the arch. The wall-bouncing incident had taught him caution, so he stepped slowly this time. As soon as the owl on his shoulder crossed the arch's threshold, the veil shimmered into existence. He drew in a deep breath, inched forward, and vanished from the mountainside alcove.

Chapter Three

Declan blinked several times to clear the flares from his eyes left by the brilliance of the gate's shimmering veil. Dizziness threatened to steal his footing, but his hand found the cool rim of the gate, and he braced himself until the feelings cleared. When he was stable enough to open his eyes, he was shocked to find himself in a small grotto almost exactly like the one he'd just left, complete with a table, three chairs, a pitcher, and glasses. He turned to inspect the gate and found its writing to be identical to the one he'd seen in the Melucian mountains. He traced its lettering with his fingers, just as he'd done before.

He'd nearly forgotten his feathered companion until the owl peeped, then scampered down his arm and hopped to the floor. She scurried to the opening, another crack in another egg, then turned and glared at Declan.

He resisted the urge to roll his eyes. "Can you give me a minute? If Atikus was right, we just traveled over three hundred leagues and across a narrow sea. My head is spinning."

The owl peeped twice, tottered over to the table, and pecked at one of the chair legs.

"What?" Declan cocked his head in disbelief as the owl offered her wisdom for his recovery. He was pleased to find the pitcher full of the same flavorful wine and filled his glass to the brim. The owl peeped a reprimand and pecked his boot.

"It's magical wine. I'm duty bound to drink it. You want me to get the most out of this journey, don't you?" he joked as he took a satisfying sip. "Besides, now that you mention it, I don't remember feeling anything bad after drinking that other wine. Imagine that—all the wine I can drink without ever getting a hangover. I may never leave this place!"

The owl pulled at his pant leg, so he reached down and let her hop onto his hand, then hop off when it reached the tabletop. She fussed at the table's wood for a second before settling in, resuming her stare at Declan.

"Sure wish I knew what was going on in that little head of yours," he said as he took another sip.

Peep. Peep-peep. She hopped over to an empty glass and pecked at it before turning back to Declan.

"Uh, really? You sure about that? I didn't know owls drank wine."

She pecked at the glass again.

He shook his head and poured a small amount from the pitcher, then tilted the glass so she could reach the ruby liquid. Her beak disappeared for a second, then resurfaced as she smacked it together a couple of times, a tiny pink tongue poking out to clean off the last drops.

He scratched her head, and she squinted and nuzzled his hand.

It had only been a few days since the owl had happened into his campsite, but he was growing attached to the creature. She'd already made him smile and laugh more than he could remember recently, and there was something special about her, something powerful and unique. As crazy as it sounded, she seemed to understand him and respond when he asked questions. Then there was their trip through the gate. He'd done everything he could think to activate the portal, but only when *she* was on his shoulder did it allow passage.

Special is an understatement.

In his heart, he understood, but the thought flew away every time his conscious mind tried to grasp it.

He peered out of the crack in the wall at complete darkness. Even the moon was hiding, refusing her light and guidance.

"We could use a night's rest, little one, and this cave is safer and more comfortable than the forest floor," he said as he moved to retrieve his bedroll.

Peep.

As he poured one last glass of wine, the owl gave him a sharp couple of peeps.

"Hey! I might have something scratched, strained, or broken. You don't want me dying in my sleep, do you?"

When he finally stretched out, the owl hopped from near his legs, onto his chest. This time, rather than settle, she glanced around, tottered up to his shoulder, then bounded onto his forehead and into his long wavy hair. She scratched and pecked a moment, then dug herself in and stilled. In seconds, he heard her familiar hum of satisfaction.

Declan smiled, content with the world in an oddly magical—somehow perfect—moment in time.

The next morning, they ate the last of the dried fruit and crusty bread, which Declan gladly washed down with more wine. When he finally stood and grabbed his pack, the owl jumped and peeped until he lowered his hand to allow her to her nest in his hood.

Atikus's map was a perfectly detailed rendering of the mountains in Melucia but offered nothing of the island of Rea Utu. The Mage had instructed him to search the town for someone who could direct him to the Keeper but urged caution when revealing his destination.

How am I supposed to do both?

With more questions than answers, he squeezed out of the cave's narrow entrance to find the surrounding landscape remarkably similar, yet completely different from that of the mountains of his homeland.

These peaks rose taller and their edges appeared more jagged. They were cloaked in trees, but not the pine, oak, or other firs he was used to. Towering palms of every variety blanketed the land in all directions. They poked out of cracks and clung to impossible ledges. While the trees back home were taller and thicker, the palms of this island swayed and bent gracefully with the ever-present breeze. The foliage atop the trees allowed far more light through the canopy than in the forests of Melucia, which encouraged shorter palms and other plants to blanket the forest floor.

There goes my easy hike down, Declan thought, realizing that he'd have to hack his way through.

He scanned the horizon and was rewarded with an incredible sight. From the height of the peak on which he stood, he could see a handful of surrounding mountains, but also the entire eastern side of the island nestled into the arms of the Great Sea. The rising sun scattered hues of yellow, orange, and red across the crystal blue ocean. He'd always thought of the mountains in his homeland as the most beautiful, serene place in the world, but nothing had prepared him for the majesty of the isles.

The owl poked her head out of the hood and hopped onto his shoulder. She nuzzled into the bend of his neck as they shared the morning view.

Coo-purr.

In the distance, he could see the dots of huts and smoke trails of a village.

As he took his first steps, his feet struck stone similar to the stairs he'd climbed the day before. They appeared as unused and worn as those in Melucia, somehow even more weathered by time and the tropical climate. Thankfully, they wound down the mountain, twisting and turning in ways that made the trek less steep.

By the time they reached the bottom of the mountain Declan struggled to breathe in the heavy island air. The sun bore down mercilessly, and sweat soaked through his shirt and cloak. He stopped and packed his cloak away, reducing to a thin, long-sleeved white shirt that billowed in the ocean breeze. His wide-rimmed Ranger hat shielded the sun from his eyes as he donned it for the first time in weeks.

During his change, the owl hopped out and began exploring the island floor. She was captivated by the sandy carpet, pecking and scratching, making it scatter in every direction. A moment later, she darted into the underbrush, returning with a small lizard in her beak, gazing up at Declan.

He guessed they had six or seven leagues of hiking before they would reach the town. The land before them was lush, a mixture of sandy patches and vibrant green fauna. The path stopped at the base of the mountain, and Declan feared the hike would be slow in the thick underbrush.

"Little one, standing here won't get us there any quicker. It'll take us all day and probably some of tomorrow to reach the town." The owl peeped and dutifully accepted his outstretched arm.

The day grew hotter and more humid, as the cawing of gulls and crashing of waves filled Declan with an odd peace he'd only found in the mountains—but it was different here, somehow rawer and more natural. That didn't make sense, as the mountains of his home were equally natural and untouched, but something about the island felt more . . . untamed.

He loved it.

The sun moved slower in the island sky than it had over Melucia but finally slipped behind the mountains, leaving a stunning image of a dying flame above the peaks. They found a small patch of sand and made camp for the night.

As he gazed at the stars, his mind wandered to his last days with Atikus and Keelan. He hadn't meant to sound so bitter, to even talk about his pent-up frustration, but something in the easy way the Mage and Keelan interacted, in his brother's calm, commanding presence, propelled long-held resentments to the fore.

In their youth, Declan couldn't get enough of his big brother, following him everywhere, watching him train with Guardsmen, even imitating how he'd wave his arms when he got excited telling a story. He'd idolized Keelan.

When did that change?

At sixteen, Keelan graduated from the Guild Academy and joined the Guard. Declan remembered standing on the step of the Mages' Quarters, a ten-year-old boy, watching his brother cross beneath the Guild's arch for the last time. Atikus stood by his side, his large, wrinkles hand on his slender shoulder, ready to comfort and guide his last adopted son.

In the years that followed, Declan remained one of the most popular figures throughout the complex, Mage or student, but through it all, that feeling of abandonment and loneliness shrouded his thoughts. First his parents, whom he'd never really known, then Declan, the brother who had become his world. A seed of anger and pain planted itself within him, only to surface fully matured over the last few days.

Declan felt completely adrift.

He'd joined the Rangers to get away—to get *far* away. He liked the job well enough, but his green cloak represented more than just a chance to serve; it was an escape. Escape from the expectations of the Mages, escape from those ridiculous golden collars and the piteous looks of the people wearing them, and escape from all the talk of "the great Keelan Rea" and his steady stream of accomplishments, all of which underscored Declan's utter failure to even find a path, much less success.

That failure weighed like millstone about his neck, immeasurably heavy, unmoving, and unforgiving. He'd felt that weight since he was a boy; but now, a man of the revered Melucian Rangers, he still couldn't shake its grip.

No one even *saw* Declan, much less cared if he existed. His dreams were often filled with scenes of boys in the Academy, their collars glittering and jibes stabbing, as he fought back tears and flipped confrontations with a joke or an easy smile. He'd learned how to wield that smile like a weapon, fending off the hurtful attacks, but those attacks still bit deeply.

In his darkest, most private moments in the mountains, as he stared out at the vastness of nature, his mind wandered again to the idea of escape—escape from his pain and from the constant nagging of that little voice in his head that chided him for being lost, from the dread of expectation each time he returned to civilization, and escape from the pity in the eyes of every Gifted person he met. It would be easy to walk off the edge of the world, to never be seen or heard from again, to never hurt again.

But he wasn't even brave enough to free himself.

He glanced down at the little owl, her tiny chest rising and falling with each breath, and the pain, frustration, and anger . . . evaporated. He didn't understand the effect she had on him, but couldn't look at her and feel anything but happiness and peace.

His mind returned to the present, to the journey ahead, to the Keeper and their quest for his magical aid—assuming he had any to give. It still seemed ironic that he, the Mute among the team, had been sent in search of a *magical* solution. He supposed his skills learned in the Ranger corps made sense for a mission such as this—and it would free Keelan to continue his search for the missing Healer—but why not Atikus, or Sil, or anyone else with a Gift?

There was so much he just didn't understand.

And yet, for the first time in his life, a small voice within whispered,

This *is your path.*

Despite the heat, he shivered. There was a sense of rightness to the voice he couldn't quite grasp, but he knew it was true and breathed deeply at the realization. Finally, boy who'd spent his life escaping was headed *toward* something.

The sun climbed above the ocean early the next morning. When Declan was slow to stir, his feathered companion leapt onto his chest and began hopping and peeping.

"Alright, I'm getting up," he said, peering at her through blurry eyes.

She stopped hopping but gave him one last peep before jumping down and scampering off into the foliage.

Declan stowed his bed roll and rummaged through his pack, realizing the handful of nuts he'd found was the last of his rations. He chased them with a few swallows of wine from the cave, and suddenly felt awake and full.

The owl returned with another lizard, this one twice the size of the last. She strutted up to Declan and tossed it at his feet.

"Uh . . . no thanks. Those nuts really filled me up."

She peered up at him, then back to the lizard, then back up at him again, finally deciding to take her meal a few paces away and enjoy it by herself.

A little after noon, the pair finally reached the edge of the village, entering through the back of several buildings that lined the main road. They passed a farrier and blacksmith, an old man and woman spinning pottery, and several small shops selling fruits, vegetables and fish. One shop offered jewelry made from shells, pearls, and other ocean-dwelling creatures.

As they turned onto a wide, gravel-strewn road, they were greeted by the village's lone inn, a two-story wooden box painted in cheerful sky blue. Yellow lettering scrawled across a wooden sign nailed above the door that read, "The Dancing Gull."

If not for the fish netting, rods, and other oceanic decoration, Declan might've thought they'd stepped into any in inside the borders of Melucia. Only two of the tables held patrons, one old couple whose skin had been baked to a crisp by the island sun, and a trio of burly men in overalls. An unusually tall, thin man with richly dark skin stood behind the bar wearing a bored expression as he wiped a mug with a dingy rag. His hair was a wiry black jumble that sprouted nearly a hand in every direction, accenting his already soaring height.

As Declan strode through the room toward the bar, everyone stopped eating and stared. He couldn't decide if he'd drawn every by because he was an obvious stranger to the village, due to the tiny woodland owl perched on his shoulder, or the paleness of his skin. Their gazes weren't hostile, but there was a keen wariness in their eyes. Declan had felt like an outsider his entire life, but this was a different sort of insolation.

The musical lilt of the tall bartender's speech smiled in Declan's ear. "Welcome t' the Gull. What can I do for ya, my friend?"

"What's good for lunch?"

"Ya must be new t' the Isle. We have fish, or ya might try the fish, and on the morrow, we have fish." The man laughed, though his broad smile failed to reach his eyes.

Declan flashed a smile. "Well, I guess I'll try the fish. Would you mind putting a small piece of raw fish on the side for my friend?"

"Of course, of course. Never seen a little bird like t'at on the island before."

"We've traveled far together," Declan said simply.

The barkeep resumed wiping the mug. "What brings you t' our island, my friend?"

Declan knew this question would come quickly but was surprised when the bartender asked so openly. His head remained bowed toward the mug, but he looked up at Declan out of the top of his eyes, intent on the answer to come.

"We're here looking for help with some . . . *family troubles* back home. My, um, uncle . . . sent me to ask for guidance," Declan fumbled.

The man continued cleaning, his eyes never straying from Declan's. "And who on our island would be helpin' a family on the mainland?"

"Well . . . uh . . . I don't know exactly."

The man set the mug in front of Declan and stared at him for a long moment before filling it with ale. "Gonna be hard for somebody t' help ya if ya don't know who you're askin'."

Declan nodded and raised the mug to his lips. The owl hopped off his shoulder onto the bar and stared up at the tall man who looked down and laughed again. This time warmth rippled through his smile.

"Curious little t'ing," he said before disappearing through a door behind the bar.

As soon as the bartender left the room, the other patrons, who had been watching and listening with undisguised interest, resumed their meals. Declan turned as the trio of men huddled and whispered across their table. One stood and exited the inn, leaving the other two to finish their meals. For a moment, Declan thought they were trying a little too hard not to look in his direction as they ate.

This is starting to get really uncomfortable.

Turning back to the bar, Declan took another sip of his ale and was rewarded with a light, fruity flavor unlike any of the dark ale he enjoyed back home.

Sometime later, the innkeeper returned with a steaming pile of flaky white fish and a bowl of fried fruit that Declan thought looked like miniature bananas, then set a smaller plate containing a piece of raw fish before the owl.

"That fish is nearly as big as you are, little one," Declan laughed as she struggled to pull it away. She promptly dropped the fish out of her beak, looked at him, and gave a harsh peep that made him laugh harder.

Neither noticed the bartender following their exchange when the man spoke with obvious surprise. "T' bird understands ya."

Declan nodded through laughter. "It sure looks that way sometimes."

The pair was halfway through their meal when the main door opened and three more men in fishing overalls entered. When Declan turned, he recognized the one in the middle as the man who'd left earlier.

"Ya need t' come wit' us, *mainlander*," the man spat the last word with obvious contempt.

Declan finished chewing his bite before raising both palms in a gesture of surrender. "Easy, friends. We came here for help, not trouble."

"Your kind always brings trouble. Now get up. Yer comin' wit' us, one way or the other."

Declan kept his hands raised and stood slowly. The owl hopped onto his arm and raced up his shoulder, where she peeped angrily at the men.

The barkeep surprised everyone, placing both hands on the bar to brace himself and hopping over to stand between Declan and the men. "Take him to Larinda."

The fisherman cocked his head and asked, "Why do we honor t'is man wit' his strange bird? He needs t' leave the Isle before somet'in' bad happens."

"It's not him. *It's the bird*. Larinda need t' see the bird," the barkeep said, never breaking eye contact with the burly fisherman.

The brows of the fishermen rose as they gaped at the tall man. Declan had no idea what was going on, but thought the barkeep was trying to help and didn't interrupt. Even the owl quieted, swiveling her head from the bartender to the men.

The men huddled and whispered for a long moment before turning back and nodding. The one who'd spoken before took a step toward the barkeep. "As ya say. Larinda will decide what's t' be done."

The bartender turned to Declan and stared at the owl on his shoulder, then whispered without moving his eyes from the bird. "Go wit' these men. They will take ya t' Larinda. Ya will be safe 'til she decides what t' do wit' ya."

Declan held the man's gaze a moment, then nodded, grabbed his pack, and followed the fishermen out the door.

The two men still eating at their table rose and joined the escort party, trailing behind Declan and the owl. The road ended at the steps to a small rectangular hut held aloft by thick stilts. To either side were rings of smaller, oval huts that reminded Declan of eggs poking halfway out of the ground in a strange symmetry he was sure held some deeper meaning to the locals. Beyond the outer ring, he two large docks stretched like wooden fingers over the crystal blue waters. Small fishing boats dotted the shoreline, there were no larger ships the docks were clearly built to accommodate.

As they climbed the steps, Declan noted its construction differed from the other structures he'd seen as they entered the village. The roof, walls, and floors were made of several layers of tightly lashed bamboo. Blanketing the bamboo roof were large interlocking tiles he was used to seeing on Melucian houses. As they entered, he realized the bamboo structure surrounded an oval courtyard that took up most of interior.

The men had to prod Declan to continue walking as he stopped in the doorway to gawk at the tropical paradise of the courtyard. Flowers and palms of every variety filled the area with sweet scents and brilliant colors, lining a cobblestone path that led from the door to a clearing at one end of the garden where several chairs and small tables lay scattered about.

In the center of the tables and chairs sat a high-backed bamboo chair that reminded Declan of the seats of power used by the Triad back home. A frail-looking woman with wiry gray hair and luminous brown eyes lounged comfortably. Her skin was dark and rich—and was losing its battle with wrinkles and creases thanks to years baking beneath the island's sun. As they approached, the woman's eyes passed over Declan, fixing instead on the owl perched on his shoulder.

The men brought Declan within a few paces of the woman, offering no bow or other gesture of obeisance, but it was clear who was in charge in this village. The elder returned her gaze to Declan and scowled.

One of the men leaned near Declan's ear and whispered in a quiet, dark voice, "Ya stand before Larinda, Mother of t'is Isle. Don't move from t'at spot and show respect, and she might let ya leave in one piece."

The woman's voice carried the rasp of age, but the steel of one accustomed to being obeyed. "Who are ya and why are ya disturbin' our peaceful shores?"

Declan offered a deep bow in the mainland style. "I am Declan Rea, a Ranger of Melucia. Arch Mage Velius Quin and Mage Atikus Danai sent me in search of aid."

Larinda's scowl deepened. "Ya've seen our village. What kinda help ya see we have t' give ya? We want no part in mainlander foolishness."

Declan sucked in a breath. He'd played this conversation in his mind a hundred times over the past few days, but it never went like this. He didn't know if he could trust this woman but didn't see any other options.

Here we go . . .

"I seek the Keeper's aid."

Everyone—and everything—froze. The wind gently blowing flowers and palms stilled. The sounds of the waves crashing and the gulls cawing vanished. In a blink, nothing existed except the old woman, Declan, and the owl. She rose from her seat and planted her fists on her hips.

"What do ya know of t' Keeper?" she asked with eyebrows raised.

Before he could respond, the owl peeped several times and hopped from Declan's shoulder onto one of the cushioned chairs, then bounded to the floor near Larinda's feet and began tugging at her linen trousers. Larinda, startled by the sudden movement, gawked as the owl released her pants and uttered a stream of peeps. The old woman sat back on her throne, mouth agape and eyes wide. The tension that had built only moments ago dispersed and sounds of the ocean filled the courtyard again.

"Dear Spirits of t' Deep!"

She covered her mouth and stared down as the owl climbed her leg and perched on her lap. The bird peeped again several times, and the woman broke into childlike laughter, tears falling to her cheeks.

"Yes, dear one, it's good t' see ya again after so long!" Larinda stroked the owl's head affectionately.

"Ya done right t' bring 'em t' me," she said to the men behind Declan. "Now, leave us alone t' talk a while. We'll be fine."

They glanced at each other, then back to Larinda, who made a shooing motion with her hands. "I said go. What ya waitin' for?"

Larinda motioned to Declan as the men retreated. "Drag t'at chair over here. We need t' talk."

Declan's head spun, but he did as he was told. He sat and watched in silence as the old woman fussed over the owl. There was a familiarity—no, *an intimacy*—to their interaction. He could see it in the bird as much as in Larinda. They were gentle and affectionate, as only those who'd lived a lifetime together could be.

"How . . . How's this possible? You *know* her?" Declan couldn't take the silence any longer.

Larinda continued stroking the owl, never looking up, a broad smile creasing her weathered face. "Young man, I'd know t'is beautiful Spirit anywhere."

Declan's jaw dropped.

Larinda looked up. "When did she bond wit' ya?"

"Bond? I don't know what you're talking about. Wait . . . you said 'after so long' a minute ago. She can't be more than a month or two old. How could you know her?"

The woman laughed again, a rough yet joyful sound. "You really don't know, do ya? She's Órlaith, t' Golden Princess. She has always been and will always be, so long as magic flows through our world.

"Ranger Declan Rea, I don't know why, but t' Daughter of Magic has chosen you for her Bond-Mate."

Chapter Four

It took nearly a day for Keelan and his team to wind their way down the mountain and locate a decent spot to set up camp roughly a half mile from the perimeter of the Kingdom's military that sprawled from Huntcliff across the base of the mountains. Neatly arranged tents lined newly established walkways and dirt roads. The sun was setting, making countless campfires visible as they twinkled into existence for leagues in every direction like new stars in the darkening night sky. Sil pointed to heavy fortifications built along the edges of the camp, indicating the army's intention to settle in for the winter.

Three soldiers, two armed with swords, one with a bow, passed within a few hundred paces of their hiding place. The soldiers appeared bored and rarely looked beyond their own conversation, which was loud enough to be heard echoing off the mountainside.

"They don't seem too worried about intruders, but one of us should still keep watch throughout the night. Let's eat a bite, and I'll take the first shift," Keelan said. The others nodded and began rummaging through their packs.

The Kingdom patrols continued at regular intervals through the night, and while the soldiers changed, the loud, bored mannerisms remained consistent with each new team.

The next morning, as they broke down camp, Keelan quietly asked, "Sil, think you can find another feathered friend to scout for us? I'd like to know how far this camp extends. I don't see any way through, so we'll have to take the long way around."

"Shouldn't be a problem. Let's go up the next mountain, away from the picket line. I should have more luck finding birds up there. I need to be fairly close to make the initial connection."

Sil spotted a nest in a tall pine, and a moment after the team halted, one of the dusty-brown birds drifted to the ground and landed on the ground before her. After a few minutes of mental instruction, it launched it self through the forest canopy and over the sprawling tent city.

Sil sat on the ground and crossed her legs, then fixed her eyes on some distant point in the woods. Declan and Atikus watched in silence from a few paces away. silent to allow her to concentrate.

Atikus opened his mouth to break the silence, but Sil suddenly rose and shook her head clear of the magical vision.

"The encampment isn't as large as we'd first thought, extending the tent rows another league or so to the southwest, but I sent the bird further west along the King's Road and found an endless line of pikemen, archers, and others headed east. The further she went, the hazier the vision became, but I think there was a line of siege weapons at the far end of one column."

Atikus turned to Keelan. "That fits with what we thought before. They're not planning to attack before winter, but they're definitely preparing for an offensive when the spring thaw comes."

"We've sent warning, and Declan is finding aid. We're not scouts or part of the army. Our focus now has to be finding the Healer and bringing her home safely, hopefully figuring out why she was taken." Keelan waited for Atikus or Sil to object, but they simply nodded. "Sil, if we stay up here, halfway up this mountain, do you think we'll be well disguised enough from the camp below? I'd rather not waste the time climbing higher if we can avoid it,"

"Yeah, pretty sure we'll be ok. When I was scouting through the bird's eyes, the trees were pretty thick. As long as we don't make any crazy noises or rapid motions, we should be fine."

"Alright, let's get on with this. It'll take us the rest of the day to get across the next two mountains. Based on what you described, that should put us well south of the army's perimeter. We can cut through the countryside from there," Keelan said.

Leaves littered the forest floor as the autumn months surrendered to winter. Keelan worried that the thinning canopy might make spotting them easier as they wound their way around the military encampment, but the day passed without incident. They continued hiking half a league past the southern edge of the camp but decided to wait until the next day to leave the mountain cover, making camp among the trees.

"Keelan, where are we headed?" Sil asked. "We lost the Healer's trail days ago and have no way of knowing where those men are taking her, or if they made it through the military camp. For all we know, the Kingdom forces turned them back at the border."

Keelan leaned back against his pack. "Atikus, any thoughts? I don't know the Kingdom's geography well."

"The King's Road forks about a thirty leagues past Huntcliff. One fork continues around lake to the town of Cradle, then through the Spires toward the capital.

The other goes through a village called Irina's Seat, then shoots south to toward the coast. They were probably a day ahead of us when we ran into that patrol near the border. If they didn't stop in Huntcliff, a slow-moving cart would probably take a week to get to the fork, maybe a day or two more. That would put them roughly a third of the way to the fork on the King's Road right now."

Atikus paced and muttered to himself, then stopped and turned, "Sil, any chance you could send a bird that far? You might be able to spot them on the road."

She whistled quietly. "It would be difficult that far away, but I guess it's possible. I've never tried anything like that. I'd need to pair with a much stronger bird . . . something like a hawk. They can fly higher and have better sight than the songbirds we've been using."

"Atikus, could you lend Sil magical strength or something, like what the Mages did with the scrying back in Saltstone? Would that extend the range?" Keelan asked.

"Hmm . . . maybe. That could work," Atikus said.

"Once I've bonded, I can plant an idea in the bird's mind, like following those men, and won't have to maintain the concentrated connection. The bird will stay on task until we get too far apart or something else breaks the bond. That would let us keep moving and simply check in periodically. Do you think that would work with us linked?" she asked the Mage.

Atikus nodded. "It should. I wouldn't be guiding your Gift; you would be in control. All I would offer is additional magic, more strength to power your bond with the bird."

Keelan perked up. "I saw several hawks when we were higher up the other day. Climbing this mountain to find one would take us in the opposite direction and put us further behind. Do you really think this could work?"

"I don't know. I think so, but that's a long way to stretch a bond, even with Atikus's added strength. On the other hand, without something like this, how would we even know where to start?" Sil asked.

"She's right, Keelan. We're hiking blind," Atikus said.

"I don't love this, but can't think of a better idea," Keelan conceded. "Let's get some rest and start early in the morning."

Morning came quickly the next day, though the sleepy sun took his time rising over the mountains. Keelan led the team on a winding trek. A small stream trickled nearby in its rocky bed. Flashes of silver darted in and out of the rocks as she Sil to refill her skin with the crystal-clear water.

By the time they reached a clearing two-thirds of the way up the mountain, the sun had started his descent. Atikus tossed his pack on the ground and slumped against a large boulder.

"I'm too old for all this hiking," the Mage said as he rubbed his neck.

"Guess it's a good thing we'll be stuck here a while. Sil, what do you need us to do?" Keelan asked.

"Nothing, really. I just need to look around, see if I can spot anything flying up here. It doesn't take a second to bond once I've found the right bird."

Another hour passed before Sil pointed toward a small moving dot in the distance. They watched as it came closer and resolved into a majestic golden eagle, wings spread wide as it glided toward the peak. Sil sat, crossed her legs, and closed her eyes. A heartbeat later, the massive bird burst into the clearing and settled before Sil, shook itself, then stretched its tawny wings to their full twelve-hand span before tucking them and cocking its head in her direction.

Sil reached a hand toward the eagle's head and received a nuzzle in her palm. There was a heartbeat of eye contact between them, then the bird took flight and vanished from view.

"That was better than I'd hoped. Eagles are highly intelligent and have excellent eyesight. It'll take him more than an hour to get within range of the search area, so we can start back down." Sil stood and dusted off her breeches. "If we can't locate them before it gets dark, we'll have to wait until tomorrow. Eagles have keen day vision, but they can barely see what's right in front of their beak at night."

"That might be the most incredible thing I've ever seen. That eagle was huge." Keelan gawked at Sil while Atikus grunted in agreement. A light flush colored her cheeks as she shrugged.

The trek back down the mountain was much easier than the climb. The sky was filled with orange brilliance when Keelan called a halt and Sil contacted the eagle again, this time with Atikus's hand holding hers to provide a steady flow of additional magic. She opened her eyes after a few moments, wobbly from the disorienting view several leagues in the air. Atikus braced her with a hand.

"That was amazing. I've never bonded with an eagle before, and this one likes to fly high and fast. Spirits, it felt like I was really there." Her childlike smile was infectious, and Atikus grinned.

"The extra trickle of magic can be euphoric, too. You were channeling a lot of power, probably more than you realized," Atikus said.

She wiped the grin from her face and restored her Guard's tenor. "We spotted a cart that matched the description, complete with two men wearing dark clothing. Details weren't great, probably more due to the strain from the distant bond than the eagle's vision, but I'm fairly confident they were our kidnappers."

"Where were they in relation to Huntcliff? Could you tell?" Keelan asked.

"Yeah. They weren't as far along as Atikus thought. Probably seven leagues from Huntcliff. Distance is really hard to make out through a bond, though."

"That's the first good news we've had in a while. Based on what you described, they'd have another four or five days before reaching the fork, right?"

Atikus nodded, then turned to Sil. "Could you see anything of the troops headed toward Huntcliff? If we can get a sense of numbers, I'll contact the Arch Mage tomorrow."

"I saw long columns headed east. The eagle didn't go low enough to get any sense of numbers or composition, but we can definitely do that tomorrow. With his vision, I should be able to get you a solid estimate."

As they settled in for another night on the mountain, Keelan thought through the days to come. They'd have to cut across a lot of open ground before reaching the road. On foot, that would probably take a week. From there, he hoped they could buy horses and make better time.

They were packing for another long day when Keelan asked Sil to look in on the robed men through the eagle's eyes again to make sure they remained on the same track. The others continued their packing while she settled into her cross-legged position and closed her eyes. More than a dozen minutes passed before she stirred again, surprised to see Atikus and Keelan watching impatiently on the ground beside her.

"We were starting to get worried. You haven't taken that long before." Keelan placed a steadying hand on her shoulder as the vision faded and her head swirled.

"The eagle flew north to rest for the night, almost to the coast. We had to fly back down and then locate the cart. They traveled a lot faster than before. I doubt they stopped for the night based on where we found them. At this rate, they may reach the fork within a couple of days."

Keelan released out a heavy sigh. "So much for our good news. We may have to take some extra risks and find horses along the way. What about troop movements?"

"No real change in the troops. There's still a long line coming in, but they're in no hurry. It was weird to see how they left the road to let the robed men's cart through. It almost looked like they were afraid of them, but from the sky, who knows?"

"The Children are a tiny cult, but they have an almost mythical reputation. We think of them as a story to scare children, but folks in the Kingdom still fear the legend of their power following the Kingdom War," Atikus said.

"That might explain how they made it through the border so easily. Wish we had a few of those robes. Might clear some of the challenges from *our* path." Keelan's wheels were turning. "Unless either of you has a better idea, I still think we have to move across the open land toward Rutin. We'll probably make it halfway by the time the cart reaches the crossroads, but that would get us past the army and in position to pursue them."

By mid-morning, the team had made it to the bottom of the mountain and into the vast, open land of the Kingdom's eastern edge. To the south and west, the grassland stretched for many leagues, empty and undisturbed. Soft rolling hills carpeted in emerald were adorned with yellow and pink flowers that thrived in the cool near-winter days. No wildlife stirred, save flocks soaring overhead toward their winter retreat.

Several leagues to the northeast, the haze of the army marred the chromatic sky. They had walked more than six leagues when the sun finally set, and Atikus was showing his exhaustion. Keelan, determined to put more distance between them and the camp, suggested they rest for a short time but then continue traveling into the evening.

Five hours later, the old Mage could walk no further and insisted the team make camp for the night and was snoring before Sil could even offer him something to eat. She smiled and covered him with a blanket before getting herself settled.

As Keelan gazed at the stars in the crisp night sky, his mind drifted to Tiana in her pale blue smock. He could see her bright eyes and warm smile. His vision shifted to her empty, ransacked infirmary and his own smile vanished. Standing in the foyer, he stared at the tapestry adorning the wall, the last vestige of her father still present in her practice. An unfamiliar moisture bloomed in his eyes as he thought of his failure to protect her, his failure to bring her home.

He welcomed sleep, hoping it would rescue him from the waking visions that pained his heart, but soon learned that visions of the Healer haunted his dreams as well.

Chapter Five

The Queen reached across and gently gripped her husband's hand. The Council had been haggling over preparations for hours, and tensions were running high.

"You're doing the right thing," The Queen stroked his hand.

Alfred raised her hand to his lips. He had been staring at the same empty spot on the council table for a while, barely hearing the heated discussion among his advisors. He maintained his stare and whispered, "I hope you're right, Issy, but this whole thing makes me sick. Going to war again? After our fathers kept the peace for a thousand years? This is all we'll be remembered for."

"They took *our daughter*! For all we know, Jess may be dead. If an attack on the royal family isn't cause for war, what is?" she hissed.

He squeezed her hand affectionately. "We *think* they took her. All we have is supposition and circumstance. I just wish we had proof so my conscience could settle."

The King rose from his throne and the debate ceased. Alfred paced around the table, again not looking at anything in particular as his counselors watched.

"High Sheriff, what news from your men on the search for the Princess?"

The lawman man with shoulder-length dusty-brown hair stood and faced the King. "Your Majesty, I have men in every town and village across the Kingdom searching for her. The Princess's likeness is posted on virtually every street corner in the land. We will know when she surfaces again."

"But you've heard nothing since she was taken from the King's Road two days ago?"

"No, Your Majesty," the Sheriff said, bowing his head. "Several of my men were in pursuit and had maintained visual contact since she left Spoke but lost her when she crested a hill and made the Bend. The team said it was as if she simply vanished. They fanned out and scoured the area for miles over the next few days, but found nothing.

"Your Majesty, the Kingdom is vast, but there are only so many places to hide, especially with all the troop movements underway. We'll find her."

"And your boy? Was he still with her?" The Queen's words dripped with venom.

"Yes, my Queen. The team saw them fleeing together."

The King stopped that argument before it could start. "We'll deal with Danym later, *after* they are returned safely. Keep us informed, Sheriff. I need to think about all of this. Get something to eat and we'll reconvene in one hour."

As the counselors rose and filed out of the throne room, Isabel caught High Chancellor Thorn's eye and motioned for him to follow. They wound their way through the hallways, finally entering the Queen's private study. She closed and locked the door behind them. "Where is she, Danai? I can't See her anymore. My Gift has been blind to her presence since she was taken."

"I don't know, Your Majesty. As the Sheriff said, the constables tried to catch the pair midway between Spoke and Cradle. The whistler they fired to mark their location prompted a chase, and then they simply vanished. My Mages have tried to scry for her using the items you gave us, but they failed. It's as if someone—or something—is blocking our Gifts."

The Queen sank into one of the leather chairs facing the fire. "I've heard of Enchanted devices that do exactly that. Those I personally Enchanted for the King offer privacy from eavesdropping and some other magical protections, but I've never tried to shield a *person* from detection. That would take an incredibly powerful Gift."

"Your Majesty, I am unaware of any other Enchanters in the Kingdom. You are the only one."

"We need more evidence of Melucian provocation. The King is wavering on a preemptive strike, and I refuse to let Jess's kidnapping stop our plans," she said.

"Perhaps this is exactly what we need. If we could find evidence of a foreign Enchanter, some device of Melucian origin, the King would shed all doubt, but my people inside Melucia's Guild have gone quiet. The Triad knows we're mobilizing."

The Queen thought for a long moment, then stood and turned toward Thorn. "Danai, if I could perform the Enchantment on an object, would your Mages be able to trace it back to me?"

He hesitated. "I don't think so. Enchanting is such a rare Gift that few understand how it works, much less how to probe an Enchanted item, but . . . is it worth the risk? Discovery of your involvement would spell disaster for you . . . and the King."

"We cannot fail, Danai. I *will* unite this continent under our rule, one way or the other. If any of your Mages becomes suspicious, deal with them. Understood?"

He didn't flinch, only bowed. "Of course, Your Majesty."

"Now, leave me. I need to think . . . and try to locate Jess again."

Thorn bowed again and backed out of the room, closing the door behind him.

Isabel strode to the far side where a set of dusty law books consumed the shelves. She pulled volume twelve halfway off the shelf, then three, then nine. A loud click sounded, then pulled volume nineteen, which served as a handle, opening the entire second and third shelves on hinges, revealing a large alcove containing more books, vials, and a few velvet bags. Isabel scanned the books, settling on an ancient tome whose faded cover was falling apart. She returned to her chair by the fire and spent the next thirty minutes leafing through pages of washed-out script and diagrams.

Two quiet raps at the door startled her.

"Your Majesty, the Council is reconvening," Thorn whispered from the other side.

"Tell the King I will join you shortly."

"Yes, Your Majesty." She waited until Thorn's footfalls faded, then returned her attention to the text.

The long–dead language used in the book she held made her search more challenging. There were too many letters in each word—and far too few vowels. Added to that, she counted no less than ten different accent marks above, below, and across various letters.

Another ten minutes of searching rewarded the Queen with her prize. The top of the page read, *Clżnfërdnķĭn*, roughly translated as "Sight Blind." The steps outlined in the formula were surprisingly simple, though some of the items required were rare and would pose a challenge—at least, for anyone who wasn't a Queen.

Isabel smiled and set the book down on a side table, then walked back to the hidden compartment and retrieved one of the velvet pouches. She pulled the silken cord and removed an ornate seal used to embed a crest into wax, one her spies had stolen years ago to prove their proficiency and deep access within Melucia's leadership. She turned it upside down and admired the workmanship required to craft the intricate quill, the symbol of the vaunted Melucian Merchants' Guild. At the time it was stolen, Isabel thought it little more than a prize, a trophy reminding her of the incredible reach of the Crown. Now, she saw it in a very different light—as the tiny pebble that would finally tip the balance and start her avalanche.

Yes, this will work quite nicely.

Chapter Six

Declan laughed, causing Órlaith and the old woman to glare in his direction.

"What do ya find funny, young man?"

"This is *insane*. She's just a baby owl I found in the woods back home. Besides, I'm not even Gifted; why would some ancient magical being choose me for anything?" He ran the fingers of both hands through his hair.

The woman stared at Declan so long he thought she might've fallen asleep with her eyes open. She seemed to stare *through* his chest. Órlaith mirrored her, making the quiet moments even more uncomfortable.

"What? What are you staring at?" he finally asked, unable to take the silent scrutiny.

"Bond-Mate, ya are a child wandering in the wild wit' no clue where ya need t' go. Ya t'ink of Magic as a tool, some dead t'ing to use, but it's alive. Magic *knows* and *sees* and *grows*. The Daughter is wise and chose ya t' be her champion. Do not be a fool and laugh at what ya don't understand." The woman suddenly stood and placed Órlaith back on his shoulder, offering a small bow as she stepped back a pace.

Órlaith nuzzled his neck.

Declan fumbled to recover. "Mother, I meant no disrespect. This is a lot to take in, and I don't have time to learn all about magic. I came here looking for the Keeper because my people are in danger. I don't know how long we have before a powerful enemy invades, but there's no time to waste. Will you help me find him or not?" He was beginning to sweat through his shirt—and not from the tropical heat pouring through the garden.

Larinda regarded him a moment longer, then nodded. "I can't refuse the Daughter and her Bond-Mate, but I don't speak for t' Keeper. He may choose t' help—or he may not. Come wit' me. What I have t' tell ya can't be said out here."

She turned and led them down a narrow path, stopping before a wall. When reached up and placed her palm on a stylized carving of a flower, it began glowing softly, then a section of the wall shimmered out of existence. She strode through the opening into a room only large enough to hold two chairs and a small table. She took her seat and motioned for Declan to do the same, then placed a finger on the wall and lamps belched azure flame, casting a warm light throughout the space. The opening transformed back into a wall as soon as the magical flames appeared.

When she glanced up, Declan was staring, open-mouthed.

She cackled. "Told ya there was much ya don't understand, child! Ya t'ink islanders don't know how t' do basic magic? We live simple lives, but we serve the Phoenix herself. Magic is all around ya, boy."

Órlaith peeped in Declan's ear, then hopped down onto his lap where she fidgeted a few times before settling and closing her eyes. He peered down and smiled at the fuzzy creature who seemed to trust him completely. *Only the Spirits know why.*

Larinda cleared her throat to get his attention, then waved her palm across the air between them. Declan nearly jumped out of his chair when a window opened, revealing a lifelike map of the island. He reached out to touch it, but his hand passed *through* the illusion. When he removed his hand, the image reformed before his eyes.

"That's . . . remarkable," was all he could manage.

"Pshaw! 'Tis magic, child." The woman waved her hand at him and laughed again.

She drew a symbol in the air with her finger and the image scattered, then resolved into a close-up view of the mountains to the southwest of the village.

Declan leaned in. He could see the trees waving in the wind, birds taking flight, every detail.

"It really is a window," Declan muttered to himself.

Larinda pointed to a nearly-invisible path near the base of the southernmost mountain. "This will take ya t' the Keeper. His hut is halfway up."

The image shifted with her words, and a log cabin came into view. An old man with dark leathery skin wearing a white robe sat in a chair on the front porch.

"That's him. Show him respect, and ya might learn somet'ing. Show him anyt'ing else, and ya might not come back," she said with one eyebrow raised. "It'll take ya all day t' get t' the trail, so ya best start now."

Declan was a stunned at the sudden dismissal, but he put Órlaith back on his shoulder and started to stand.

The woman's hand clamped across his forearm.

She held him transfixed with her gaze for a long moment before releasing his arm and reached up to place her palm against his chest. "Child, I See the Light in ya. If ya want t' learn anyt'ing, look inside. *See* the Light."

Larinda's gentle touch struck something deep within him, and dropped his pack to wrapped the old woman in a tight embrace, lifting her off her feet. She giggled like a child and returned the hug with a strength and warmth that broadened his smile. When they separated, a tear escaped her ancient eyes, and a smile creased her lips.

With a touch of her palm against the wall, the opening to the room shimmered into existence again. Declan grabbed his pack and stepped out, glancing back one last time to find the woman had vanished, leaving a cloud of twinkling light in her wake that winked out before his eyes.

Declan shielded his eyes as he stepped through the outer door of Larinda's home into the blazing island sun. A gangly man who looked no more than twenty stood at the base of the steps with a pack slung across his back.

"Mother Larinda sent me t' guide ya. I have food and water for the trip." The man tapped the pack on his shoulder.

"Thank you. I'm glad to have a guide—and some company for a change." Órlaith peeped in his ear and pecked his earlobe. "Sorry, little one, I didn't mean . . . uh . . . sorry."

The man's eyes widened at the exchange. Larinda may have asked for the man's aid, but she clearly hadn't told him much about his charges. Declan remembered

Atikus's warning about keeping his mission to himself and decided not to reveal anything to his new guide.

"I'm Declan, and this is Órlaith." He scratched the owl's head and earned a coo-purr.

"I'm Sabu," the man said, touching his palm to his chest and dipping his head in the island greeting. "I have horses for us at the stables. There's plenty of light today t' get ya t' the mountain. Come."

They walked a block, then left the road to pass by several small buildings before finally reaching a stable. Two horses waited, one pure white, the other solid black. Sabu mounted the white horse, as the black stallion's intelligent eyes followed Declan's every move, shifting between man and owl. Órlaith's presence peaked the horse's interest. Declan reached his hand toward the animal's nose and was surprised when the horse met him halfway, closing his eyes and pressing his head into his new rider's palm.

Sabu watched the exchange and whistled. "Never seen Novi take t' anyone like that."

"I'm a Ranger; always had a thing with animals. Can't really explain it."

Sabu smiled. "Yer Light burns bright, Ranger Declan."

Declan eyed Sabu, surprised by the second reference to "his Light" that day. He placed Órlaith on Novi's neck, then mounted and moved the owl to his shoulder.

As they trotted out of the stable, Declan turned to his guide. "What do you mean when you talk about my 'Light?'"

Sabu laughed, a deep melodic rumble. "Can you not see the sun when you look up, Ranger?"

He kicked his horse into a canter and said no more.

Declan whispered to Órlaith, "What have we gotten into, little one? I don't understand a thing these people say." The owl made a sound he'd never heard from her, something he swore was a laugh.

It's official. I'm insane.

Less than an hour had passed when the sun began his descent over the far side of the island. Declan spotted the beginning of trail. When they were within a few paces of the first stone, he noticed the trail's stone slabs were tightly interlocked and appeared untouched by nature. Around the path was a wilderness of untended flora, but no flower or root intruded on the smooth stones.

Sabu stopped. "Ranger Declan, I can go no further. Somewhere nearby is the Sacred Path. Find t'at and follow it."

Declan cocked his head and pointed down. "The stones begin there. Can't you see it?"

Sabu followed Declan's hand and shook his head, confused. "Not'ing but dirt and grass."

This trip just gets stranger by the minute, Declan thought.

"The Mother didn't tell me what ya seek, but ya must be blessed to follow the Sacred Path. Phoenix guide your Way." As he said his last words, he again placed his palm on his chest and bowed, this time dipping low and holding it for several seconds.

Those words were new.

Declan mirrored the gesture with a little less depth and duration, but Sabu appeared pleased anyway. He gave one last head nod before turning back toward town.

Now alone, Declan dismounted and offered Órlaith a piece of dried meat. As he chewed his own, he ambled around the area, trying to get his bearings. Tall palms swayed overhead in the ever-present ocean breeze while squatty thick-leaved varieties clung to the mountain's floor. Other than the perfectly clean stone path, nothing seemed unusual or out of place. Declan savored the peace and beauty of the isle.

He downed the last of his meal and turned to Novi. "The trail doesn't look very steep, winding back and forth. Let's try taking you with us."

He grabbed the horse's reins and turned toward the path, but the beast resisted. When Declan pulled harder, the horse whinnied and yanked his strong head back, tugging the leather straps out of Declan's hands.

Órlaith pecked at his earlobe again and peeped several times.

"Huh. Alright, I guess you don't want to go with us. Let me get the packs off your back so you can head back to town."

Novi quieted and let Declan remove the packs, shoving a slobbery tongue in his ear. Once the packs were clear of his back, Novi danced a couple steps backwards, still facing Declan, locked eyes, and offered a deep bow, bending his front right knee.

What the . . . ?

As the horse turned and trotted back toward the village, Declan thought he heard Larinda's amused cackle resonating through the trees in the mountain. He couldn't help but laugh and shake his head again.

"Little one, looks like it's time to move forward."

Órlaith peeped her agreement from her shoulder-perch.

He took a casual couple of steps before his foot hit the first stone. As soon as it struck, the world spun around him. For a moment, everything went completely black, then a face appeared before his mind's eye.

"Declan Rea, Ranger of the Empire of Melucia, son of Kelså and Årtem Rea," a sonorous voice boomed, sending leaves rattling and Declan staggering back.

The words reverberated through his chest and nearly drove him to his knees. The man's deeply lined face, sunken cheeks, and piercing brown eyes were all made darker by the brilliant white of his bushy brows, mustache, and chest-length beard. The pure white robe draped about his slim shoulders shimmered in the sunlight, and the golden cloth wrapped many times around his head was unlike any headwear Declan had ever seen.

Declan swayed as the scene in his mind overwhelming his senses.

"You seek with blind eyes, Child of Magic!" the voice echoed against the mountainside.

"Child of—What's happening? I can't brea—" Declan gasped and fell to his knees, hand wrapped around his throat. He tried to suck in air, but nothing happened. His chest seized, and flashes of light flooded his vision.

Órlaith peeped again and again, hopping from his shoulder to the ground in front of him. When he didn't respond, a golden brilliance shimmered around the owl, and the plumes of her chest and belly twinkled like golden flames. Declan's eyes widened in shock as he struggled to breathe and she grew brighter and brighter. Órlaith opened her beak, and a stream of azure mist flowed from her tiny maw into his mouth. His chest swelled with the intake of Órlaith's magical breath, and the last thing he remembered before the world went dark was lying on his back, staring up at the little bird as she watched from atop his chest, peeping and . . . *glowing*.

Declan's eyes crawled open.

Everything hurt.

He tried to sit up, but a wave of dizziness and nausea forced him prone. He worked to clear his vision as he blinked up at the star-filled sky.

"You're awake!" the excited voice of a perky young girl said from several paces away.

Declan ignored his queasiness and raised his head. Aside from the lush island palms, the land was empty around him.

He was *sure* he'd heard someone.

He edged onto his elbows before lifting himself to a sitting position and was relieved when the nausea didn't return. He glanced around again and found the area just as dark and bare as before.

"What are you looking for?" the girl's voice said.

He wheeled around a little too quickly and was punished by another wave of dizziness. "Who's there?"

"I am, silly. You fell down."

He held his head and swiveled.

Still nothing.

Órlaith hopped onto his lap, and stroked her head and smiled at her coo-purr.

"I love when you scratch with your fingernails."

Declan threw himself backward and his eyes flew wide as the bird's beak moved with the sounds of the child's voice. He'd moved so suddenly, she had to scamper back a few paces to avoid being thrown off.

He braced himself with his hands on the ground, prompting her to look up and say, "Done that fast? I really like the scratches."

"Spirits, I've lost it. I've *finally* gone mad." He rubbed his eyes, then returned his gaze to the owl. "Órlaith?"

"Actually, I prefer *Órla*. Órlaith sounds so stuffy and formal."

"How . . . are you talking?"

"Well, I open my beak and my thoughts make sounds, pretty much the same way you do it—and you talk *a lot*, mostly to yourself. That makes you look crazy. You know that, right?" She giggled.

"But . . . Órla . . . I can . . . *understand* you now. You're not just peeping."

"Peeping? That sounds gross. Like pooping. Why would anyone peep? Unless they *really* had to go." She giggled again.

Declan leaned back on his elbows again and tried to remember the moments before he'd blacked out. He'd stepped on the path, there was an old man shouting something, and he couldn't breathe . . . then Órla glowed and breathed something into him.

That had to be it.

"What did you *do* to me? What was that glowing mist?"

"I don't know. You couldn't get air, so I gave you some of mine. I was really scared."

He rubbed his chest. It still burned when he breathed.

As he struggled to his feet, he noticed they rested about ten paces from the first stone of the path. Whatever happened must've thrown him back. That explained some of the sharp pains in his legs, buttocks, and back.

He reached back, placing his hands on his lower back to stretch, when a glow flared from behind. He jumped forward and his hand flew to the knife hanging from his belt. He spun around, knife extended, finding nothing but empty grass.

This just keeps getting better.

"Did you see that?" he asked Órla.

"See what?"

"The blue light? You didn't see it?"

"Oh, sure. You mean that light that came out of your hands? I saw that. What were you doing?"

He leaned forward to dig his waterskin from a pack and realized that his back no longer hurt. In fact, *nothing* hurt anymore—and the burning in his lungs was gone.

He took a sip of the magical wine and tried to think. As he stood, Larinda's voice whispered through the trees as if carried by the wind.

Follow yer path. Trust yer Light.

Declan whirled around, but the old woman was nowhere to be seen.

"Whacha looking for?"

"Larinda. Didn't you hear her just now?"

"Nope. Nobody's talking except you. I'm used to that. Did I mention you talk a lot?"

"Yes, you said that. Thanks for the reminder," he scowled.

"You're welcome. You forget things sometimes, too," she said cheerfully, ignoring his sarcasm.

Midnight had passed, leaving the mountain shrouded in milky darkness, illuminated only by the moon that loomed larger than he remembered. He turned back to the path and shivered at the thought of touching it again but didn't see any other option.

"It'll be ok this time," Órla said, as she scurried onto the first stone.

He blew out a breath. "You sure? That last time wasn't fun—and I don't want to see what that old man would do if he got *really* angry."

She nodded. "Yep. It'll be ok. Just breathe—and do that thing with your hair again. It's cute."

"What?" he chuckled as he pulled his hand out of his hair.

He tossed his pack over his shoulder, offered Órla a hand, then walked to the first step, taking a series of deep breaths before placing his foot on it. This time, the stone flared brightly as he made contact, then gradually faded until it returned to its dull gray with only a hint of a glow.

The old man didn't return.

No one bellowed or shouted.

Nothing hurt.

Whew!

The second step was the same as the first—bright flare fading to gray with a slight glow. They continued up the path for thirty minutes, winding back and forth as it led them gently up the mountainside. They rounded a sharp switchback, and a clearing came into view. The cottage Declan had seen in Larinda's window also appeared. The old man sat on the porch exactly as before.

The man's head rose, "Declan, you made it."

"I had to help him. You scared the breath out of him," Órla said before Declan could speak.

The old man chuckled and stood, leaning heavily on a wooden cane carved with intricate vines along its length and topped with a polished, gnarled knot larger than both his fists.

"Daughter, it warms this old man's heart to see you again." He then turned toward the door and waved to Declan. "Come, come. We have much to discuss."

Declan followed the man into the cabin, surprised to find the inside even simpler than the exterior. On the side opposite the door, a teapot squealed angrily from its hook over the fire. Aside from a small bed nested against the wall, a round table and simple wooden chairs, the cottage was bare.

"Please sit. I'll pour us some tea." The old man shuffled to the pot, leaning his cane against the wall beside the fireplace.

His hand glowed faintly as he grabbed the handle of the boiling pot and poured water into two large mugs. The shock on Declan's face prompted a deep, rumbling laugh. "Dear boy, close your mouth. You look like a hooked fish, staring with your mouth open like that."

"He's silly like that sometimes," Órla said, prompting the old man's laugh to swell and his eyes to crease.

Declan set his pack down and sat at the table. The man replaced the kettle and joined him, taking a long sip from his steaming mug while staring silently at Declan over its rim.

The moment stretched.

Declan sipped, then cleared his throat.

The man's head finally snapped up. "Ah . . . Forgive me, boy. I was lost in thought. What were you saying?"

"Declan is silly," Órla offered.

Declan shot her a glare. "Why don't we start with an introduction?"

"That's a grand idea. It's been years, maybe decades—or centuries—I can't remember—since my last visitor. Days and nights . . . they all blend together, and I am so *very* old."

The old man settled back into his chair and took another sip before staring at his tea in silence.

More long, awkward moments passed.

Órla hopped from Declan's shoulder onto the table and trotted to stand in front of the old man. "Keeper, please."

The man startled and peered down at the little owl. "Ah, yes, Daughter. Forgive me."

His gaze returned to Declan, and clarity entered his eyes for the first time since they'd met. "Young man, I am the Keeper of Magic. Perhaps you will know me by other names in days to come. I stand vigil against those who seek the Well. Why did you intrude on the Path?"

Declan was taken aback. "I was *sent* to find you, to ask for your help."

"And what help could an old man offer?"

"Honestly, I don't know. They sent someone who doesn't even have a Gift to find magical aid." He ran his hand through his hair and sighed deeply. "All I know is that the Arch Mage believes you can help us, and I was sent to ask, to beg if necessary."

Declan explained the situation on the border between Melucia and the Kingdom, their encounter with scouts in the mountains, and the tens of thousands of troops now camped within leagues of his homeland. The Keeper listened intently, peppering him with questions throughout, all signs of the doddering old man had vanished.

"Without help, many will die, and Melucia *will* fall, likely followed by the tribal lands to our east. The military power of the Kingdom far outweighs all the other nations combined."

The Keeper stood and turned toward the fire.

"It has been over a thousand years since one came to me seeking aid. Her pleas were genuine, and her need was great, so I granted her access to the Well. The evil she wrought using the power of her Light was terrible. If I live another thousand years, nothing will cause me more sadness or regret."

"I don't understand. A thousand years ago . . . would've been the time of the Kingdom War . . . and Irina. Are you saying she used power you gave her to start *that* war?" Declan couldn't believe what he was hearing.

"Yes . . . yes. Irina was her name. I can see her face even now. She seemed so frail and helpless." The man shrank before Declan's eyes. "She found a way to harness the power of the Well and bend it to her will. She would've succeeded had your Arch Mage not come to me quickly and told me of the war she was waging. I granted him access to the Well, only the second in millennia, and *By the Phoenix*, he raised the mountains that now form your border, killing many and halting the plague of war."

There wasn't a child alive in Melucia who couldn't recite some version of the legend of Irina and the Kingdom War, but Declan never expected to hear the tale from one who actually helped bring it about.

"Wait, you said *our* Arch Mage came to you for help back then? Arch Mage *Velius Quin*? He can't be more than thirty or forty years old!"

The Keeper laughed so hard he spilled his tea.

Declan gaped as the dark liquid evaporated in tiny flashes of light as it touched the pearlescent fabric of his robe.

"Oh, my dear Declan, Quin must be twelve or thirteen hundred years old by now. Magic does wonderful things for the complexion." He laughed again, and Declan couldn't suppress a smile.

"After Irina's . . . troubles, safeguards were put in place to ensure the Well is never abused again. You encountered the first of those protections when you touched the Path. Without the flow of magic, one cannot even see the stones."

Declan's head snapped around. "Wait. Then why could *I* see them? I don't have a Gift."

The Keeper placed a hand on Declan's arm as a fatherly smile brightened his face. "My boy, there is Light inside you brighter than any sun. Magic has always flowed within you—*through you*, actually—though you may not have known it. You have much to learn, but the question remains—are you *worthy* to be taught?"

Declan's childhood anger flared, and he tossed off the old man's hand in juvenile rebellion. "I don't know what you're talking about—any of it. I've never been good enough . . . or worthy . . . or *whatever* for magic. Magic never chose me, and it never will!"

The Keeper stared at him for a long moment, his expression a dark mask, then stood and held out his mug. "I'd like some more tea, please."

"Get it yourself." Declan spat.

Órla couldn't tottered to the edge of the table and caught Declan's eye. "Get the man his tea, *Bond-Mate*." Her serious, almost-adult tone caught him by surprise.

"Fine!"

Without thinking, Declan reached down and grabbed the scalding handle, yanking the kettle off its hook above the fire. A glow flared from his palm, gaining brightness the longer he gripped the metal. His eyes flew wide, but the Keeper simply held out his mug. Declan filled it, then returned the kettle to its hook.

He gawked at his palm as the glow faded. There should've been a line of angry, damaged flesh. He should've been in pain—a lot of pain.

Unmarred, healthy skin stared back.

This can't be real, he thought.

"Oh, it's real, my boy." He heard the Keeper's booming voice in his head.

He whirled around to find the old man smiling and sipping his tea.

"But . . . how? I'm Mute and—"

"Yay! Declan made blue Light again!" Órla hopped on the table, snapping both men out of the moment. She continued her dance while Declan remembered to breathe. He leaned against the table to steady himself.

Without warning, the Keeper reached across and pressed his index finger into Declan's forehead. "Now, let's put that silliness about you not having magic away. The real question is, what will you *do* with it?"

The world spun into complete darkness.

Declan opened his eyes and sucked in the earthy scent of pine, the scent of home. He rubbed his eyes and sat up.

Órla must've wandered off because he was alone on the mountain.

The mountain.

Pine?

This is the wrong mountain! Where am I?

He leapt to his feet and searched for the Keeper's cabin, or the Path, or anything that looked familiar.

An arrow whizzed by his head, followed by a loud *whack* as it embedded in a tree nearby. He threw himself to the ground and crawled to hide behind a large boulder. Men shouted in the distance, and the crunching of leaves and twigs grew louder.

Another arrow flew overhead.

Whack!

He scrambled to his knees, then his feet, bent behind the boulder's protection. His mind raced.

Run or die . . . Run or die . . . Run!

He bolted from his hiding place and ran in a snaking pattern through the trees.

More shouts sounded.

He ran faster.

He heard shouts to his right heading toward him, then an arrow flew from that direction.

Whack!

The forest opened to a clearing by a bubbling stream. Atikus, Keelan, and Sil sat on a log and glanced up as he broke through the trees. They were eating and drinking, as if on a picnic in the woods.

"Declan? What's wrong? Why are you running?" Keelan asked.

Declan was baffled and out of breath. How could he be back in the mountains with Keelan? None of this made any sense, but his Ranger instincts took control.

"Men shooting arrows. *Run!*" he shouted.

Keelan and Sil jumped to their feet and raced across the stream. Atikus gaped at Declan, unmoving.

"Atikus, *get up!* We have to go. They're right behind me." Another arrow flew by, as if called by his statement. *Whack!*

Atikus stood frozen, staring into the woods, as three men in Kingdom cloaks broke into the clearing, two with bows nocked and aimed at Atikus.

Time crawled as Declan the arrows slipped past the men's grips and took flight in a perfect line to the Mage's chest. They moved as though sailing through syrup, slowly, but never flinching from their deadly path. The third man drew a sword and stalked Declan, his steps exaggerated by the strangely warped time.

Declan screamed, "NO!"

Without thinking, he threw his arms forward, palms outward, facing the men. A shimmering wall of light formed in front of Atikus as the Mage turned and his eyes found Declan's.

The first arrow struck the wall, and the barrier flared as the arrow sizzled and fell to the ground in a pile of ash.

The third soldier swung his sword in a wide arc toward Declan's neck, forcing him to dive as the blade passed a hair's breadth overhead.

With his focus lost, the wall protecting Atikus vanished, and the second arrow slammed into the Mage's chest. Blood bloomed across his robe. He staggered, then fell to the ground.

Declan rolled away to distance himself from the swordsman, glancing back, expecting a deadly blow, but gaped at the empty forest. Atikus lay bleeding and shaking, but the soldiers had vanished, and there were no sounds of pursuit. In fact, there were no sounds at all, save the old Mage's moaning.

Declan threw himself to Atikus's side and tore open his robe. The arrow had caught in his chest without exiting through the other side, making it nearly impossible to remove short of tearing flesh or vital organs.

He had no idea what to do.

Panic set in.

"Declan, go. Leave me." The Mage's voice was a rasp.

"I can't leave you, Atikus. *I won't!* Stay with me!" Tears blurred his vision as he gripped his adopted father's shoulder.

Sil burst back into the clearing, breathing hard. "Declan, come quick. Keelan's down. You have to Heal him!"

Declan looked from Sil to Atikus. Blood consumed the ground beneath the Mage, spreading quickly in every direction. "Atikus, I don't know how to Heal. What do I do?"

Atikus stared up with glassy, unseeing eyes.

Declan shook him and screamed, but the Mage didn't stir. Tears flowed freely, and pain's claws tore into his heart.

"Declan!" Sil shouted.

The present slammed back into his mind, and he leapt from the Mage's now empty shell. "Take me to Keelan!"

They ran a short distance before reaching Keelan's prone body. It rested atop a river of blood, with two arrows jutting from his chest and one his leg.

His face was ash.

His chest was still.

Declan fell to the ground and searched for a pulse that refused be found. He grabbed his brother by the shoulders, screaming again, no longer caring if the enemy found them. A flood of tears flowed down his cheeks as he craned his head upward and screamed curses at the Spirits.

"Keelan, NO! Not you, Kee."

His last words escaped as a childlike whisper.

The world spun again.

Keelan and Sil disappeared.

The forest disappeared.

The tears remained.

Declan found himself in the midst of a battlefield. A sea of soldiers in emerald or navy lay broken and bleeding in every direction, hundreds, no *thousands*, probably more. No one moved, save those near death who crawled and clawed and moaned for mercy, for an end to their suffering and pain.

Great, black birds held court in this graveyard, feasting like kings of the underworld. Blood and mud mingled for leagues, smearing the once lustrous landscape with a putrid, inescapable bile.

Declan's stomach to revolted violently as Death's scent gripped his mind.

He scanned the field, recognizing the familiar outline of Saltstone only a few hundred paces away. An orange glow blazed from behind the walls, and thick smoke billowed into the sky. He staggered toward Melucia's capital, dazed, stumbling over one corpse, then the next.

The East Gate stood open, its massive doors splintered by a metal-tipped ram that still lay on the ground nearby. His breath caught as he entered the once-grand city, his home, now a shell of its former glory. Flame and ash clung to everything once good and just. Nearly half a million souls called Saltstone home, yet Declan couldn't find a single building spared by the flames and wanton destruction.

He had only taken a few steps when the world spun again and he found himself at the familiar arch that marked the entrance to the Mages' Guild. The decapitated Phoenix that once soared on the arch's capstone lay hacked to pieces on the ground. The fist-sized rubies that once flared brightly in greeting had been plucked from its sockets.

He stepped over the rubble into the only place he'd ever called home. Swaths of navy mixed with gray and scarlet as bodies of Mages and soldiers littered the courtyard, broken and bloody.

His fallen family.

His throat caught as he passed the body of a student who looked in his first years of training, a young boy who lay frozen in horror, a silent scream begging to escape widely parted lips.

Hope rose as he spotted the Guild's Tower looming ahead, protected by the vein of raw power flowing beneath its stones and still unmarred by the chaos. His heart seized again at the sight of a black pennant snapping in the wind at the Tower's peak, an accusing finger to those who had yet to yield to its dark purpose.

Declan fell to his knees, overwhelmed and overwrought.

His city, his home, *his family*. All were gone.

Sobs came in waves, and his vision blurred.

When his eyes opened, he was still on his knees, but in the center of town where five roads and a river met, Saltstone's hub once alive with the chatter and clatter of hooves on stone. Broken bodies lay everywhere, this time of Merchants, Guardsmen and others. He couldn't shut out the screams and wails of mothers torn from their children, of fathers broken nearby, unable to rise. As if a distant memory, he watched merciless men on horseback swing swords and axes into heads and necks and backs.

Anguish and anger gripped his soul.

Suddenly, nothing stirred.

There were no sounds.

Saltstone stood mute.

And then it hit him.

There *were* no people.

The broken and bleeding we gone. The moaning and crying had ceased. The streets and fields stood vacant and still.

Where is everyone?

This hadn't been an invasion; it was an annihilation.

A woman in a flowing black gown appeared where the five roads joined. She held aloft a staff of pure silver etched with symbols that glowed along its length. On her brow sat a crown inlaid with seven bloody jewels that pulsed in an odd, aortic rhythm.

The woman turned and pierced his soul with her gaze. She smiled, threw back her head, and her laughter echoed throughout the city-turned-tomb.

Her eyes snapped back to his, and she called out, "This is *your* doing, Declan. *Your* victory!"

She pointed the staff, and its symbols flared as hungry flame streaked from its end and slammed into his chest. Heat and pain crawled across his body, consuming everything it touched as Declan's consciousness dimmed to a writhing, anguished nothing.

He woke sometime later to the tickling of Órla's feet against his chest. He began to sob.

Órla nuzzled his neck and *whirred*, as if sharing his grief.

It was just a dream! Keelan and Atikus are alive! It wasn't real.

"It *wasn't* real," he muttered through sobs. "Please tell me it wasn't real."

"No. Not yet." The Keeper's deep voice shook him. "Life and death hinge on the humblest decisions, many we face without knowing the cascade we begin.

"The Phoenix demands honor, wisdom, and truth. You, Declan Rea, stand before the world with the power to shape and mold—and to destroy. Your Path, *your choice*, will reroute the river of time itself.

"You now stand before a fork in the Path, and you have seen where each road leads. One will save your people. The other is the end of everything. You alone must choose."

Declan peered up through wide, watery eyes. "What do you mean *I* must choose? Why do *I* have to do any of this?"

"I'm sorry, Declan, but there is no more time. If you cannot choose, or refuse, both visions will come true." The Keeper placed a candle no taller than his thumb on the table and lit it with a flick of his wrist. "When the flame dies, the future is fixed. Spirits guide you, son."

The Keeper vanished.

Órla vanished.

Declan stood and whirled around, but they were gone. He was alone with the quickly burning candle.

He closed his eyes and was suddenly five years old and standing in the yard of the Mages' Guild. Atikus stood behind him, tickling his ribs as he howled in laughter and his bladder threatened to betray him. Keelan raced into view and assaulted the Mage's ribs, the three falling to the ground in a pile of laughter, squeals, and tears. The tickling stopped in time to save his dignity. Keelan helped him to his feet, and wrapped his arms protectively around his younger brother's scrawny shoulders. Declan glanced up to catch the old Mage grinning down, pride swelling in his eyes.

The present returned, and he again sat alone in the cabin, staring at the tiny flame, wax barely fending off the flame from the table's surface.

Atikus had saved them when their parents died. Keelan was his protector, relentless, steady, unflinching. He'd resented his brother's success, that he was good at *everything* he tried, but they were brothers and he loved him.

Spirits, how long have I been running? Keelan always had my back—no matter what. I've been such a fool, so jealous, so . . . childish.

And now I'm told to sacrifice him? To pick between killing the only people who ever loved me and the whole world? What kind of choice is this?

The screams of Saltstone echoed in his mind. He could see and hear and smell her death.

Then the woman returned to his mind with her angry flame and his dying breath.

In one vision, he was surrounded by soldiers who would likely kill him—or worse—capture him. In the other, he died in a magical blaze alongside the rest of the country he loved.

He glanced down to find the candle's flame flickering, its wax exhausted. His anger, fear, and helplessness erupted as he screamed at the ceiling, "I DON'T WANT TO CHOOSE! I *WON'T* CHOOSE! TAKE *MY* LIFE INSTEAD!"

His voice fell to a whisper.

"Please, just take me instead."

A heartbeat passed, then his eyes closed as his body tumbled to the floor.

Chapter Seven

The Crown Princess of the Kingdom of Spires, future Queen of the most powerful nation in the known world, jarred awake with the realization that her hands and feet were bound, and she'd been tossed like a sack of grain onto the back of a horse. Her captors drove the horses, making her uncomfortable position nearly unbearable as both saddle and buckle dug into her stomach with each bounce. She tried to orient herself, to find some clue as to where they were headed, but her vision swam each time she tried to lift her head.

Another arrow streaked high in the night sky, the screech of its whistler and pop of its flare marked their location for pursuing troops. The masked men spurred their horses to greater speed, and the countryside flew by in a blur.

The moon was bright, casting an eerie glow across the landscape. Another whistler launched some distance to their right, as a second team closed in on their position.

Jess finally lifted her head to search the horizon for those giving chase, but the land was void.

When the horses slowed and began to falter, the robed men called out to each other in a strange, guttural language. Moments later, the man in the lead pointed to his left, and the team veered off the road. If she hadn't been tied to the back of the horse, Jess would've been thrown as the beast turned sharply and traversed the uneven land.

They entered a forested area, forced to slow to a trot in exchange for the disguise offered by thickening trees. The trade was rewarded an hour later when one of the men returned and reported seeing constables passing on the nearby road, completely missing their trail into the woods. The leader decided the group should stay hidden in the forest for a couple of days to let their trail cool off, so the men dismounted and began setting up camp.

Winter was now only weeks away, but the men refused to light a fire. Jess shivered in the darkness, bound and propped against a tree. She was tired and hungry and scared and sore. She was *everything* all at once. It was overwhelming. The drug they'd given her dulled her soreness—and her mind—but not her racing emotions.

As she tried to shake the fog, to remember what had happened, Danym's smile appeared in her mind. That smile had always made things better, made her smile. Then reality slammed into her mind: Danym was one of *them*. How was that even possible?

She vaguely remembered escaping from the Palace and Danym's help as they fled the capital. Her memories of the mountains were hazy, but the emotional rollercoaster they experienced in the town of Spoke was clear. Her mind sifted through disjointed memories: the men in masks chasing them, the horses racing up and around and down the winding mountain road, and the moment those horrible men had nearly stolen Danym from her in one frightful shot. She could still hear him moaning as the Healer removed the arrow and used his Gift to save his life. There was so much blood.

Then, in the middle of their desperate flight to freedom, they'd enjoyed a few hours of uneventful, blissful peace. They'd held hands across a table by a warm fire, surrounded by people laughing and eating. They talked of nothing and everything. He'd been so sweet and gentle. She'd gazed into his eyes and believed a new life was possible—a simple life without royalty or duty or her mother's insane expectations.

In a flash, her memory shifted from Danym's smiling eyes to those of the stranger wearing a wild raccoon mask. He towered over her, holding her down on the ground as another man appeared with a poisoned cloth. His eyes were grinning again, but not a smile of happiness or love. There was a distant, malevolent gleam, something she'd never seen in him before. That voice in the back of her mind whispered hope, hope that the racoon man wasn't actually *her* Danym.

But in her heart, she knew.

She *knew* it was him.

She would know those eyes anywhere.

Jess stirred. She was stretched out on the ground, and small rocks dug painfully into her legs and buttocks. Two of her captors sat quietly on pallets ten paces away. One of them caught her movement and turned.

"Are you hungry?" he asked in a raspy, inhuman voice.

She shook her head. "No, but I would like some water."

As he knelt, she peered up at Raccoon. No, *Danym*. She drank deeply and began to cry. He took the skin back, but remained knelt by her side.

He placed a hand on her shoulder, but she smacked it off with a flail of her arm and glared up at him, her eyes ablaze with anger and pain.

"Don't you dare!"

Raccoon closed his eyes, nodded, and turned.

"Wait," she whispered tentatively. "Where are you taking me? Danym, tell me what's going on. I'm scared."

Raccoon stared down, and she thought pity flitted across his eyes before he silently retrieved the skin and strode back to his pallet, leaving her staring at his back.

Something in her snapped and she screamed, "My father will take your head for this, Danym Wilfred! But not before my mother sees you flayed alive!"

Apparently, raccoons could laugh.

"I HATE YOU!" Jess grabbed a nearby rock and tried to hit Danym in the back, but the straps tying her wrists caused her stone to fall short.

She turned away and wept quietly.

Chapter Eight

Declan crumpled onto the ground, knees wrapped in his arms, head down. His stubborn sobs refused to subside. Suddenly, there was a hand on his shoulder and the soothing sound of a woman's voice. "Oh, my beautiful boy."

Declan lifted his head and was startled to find an ageless woman kneeling before him, strength and comfort flowing through her steel-gray eyes. Her face held no lines of age, a perfectly cast ebony porcelain, unmarred by time.

She lifted a hand and cupped his cheek. "I thought I'd never see you again. How you've grown, my Declan."

His eyes darted, taking in the surrounding cave as his mind tried to process what she'd said.

He stammered, "Where—what? *Who* are you?"

The woman's confident air faltered. Her eyes retreated to her feet before returning to his. "My name is Kelså Rea. Declan, I'm . . . your mother."

"My mother? Spirits, I'm in *another* vision. What this time?" He wiped the tears from his eyes and braced himself to stand.

She pressed her hand to his shoulder, holding him in his seated position. "No, Declan, this is real. There are no more visions. You passed the Keeper's test, offering yourself in sacrifice for others—for everyone. In choosing to die so others might live, you proved your heart worthy of the next steps along the Path. It wasn't one of the choices offered, but it was the *only* acceptable one."

Declan's head reeled.

He gazed at Kelså, afraid to move or speak. How could any of this be real? His mother died years ago, and here this woman, who looked nothing like him or Keelan, claimed to be returned to him?

Órla hopped into his lap. "I knew you'd make the right choice. You're a lot smarter than you look."

Despite everything, Declan laughed. "Uh . . . thanks . . . I think?"

"Anytime! Can you scratch my head while you talk?"

Tension drained away with the simple act of scratching the owl's knobby head.

He scanned about for the first time and realized they no longer say in the Keeper's cabin, but in a cavern. Two torches hung in rings on either side of the grotto, their smokeless flame dancing on ends that never appeared to char. On a small wooden table in the center of the room sat a pitcher and two glasses. At the opposite end, the cavern opened into a tunnel whose walls flickered with the same magical light.

"Come, sit. Have some wine and rest." Kelså poured silky liquid into each glass and sat. Her golden dress swirled and flowed as if alive.

Declan set Órla on the table and fell into the chair. He barely knew where to look or what to think. The past hours had taken him to the edge of the world, and had destroyed everything he knew and loved. Exhaustion warred with a frayed heart as he took a sip of the wine. His fatigue vanished, and the anguish in his soul eased.

"This is the same wine from the caves with the Gates, isn't it?"

"We do allow ourselves a few luxuries, my dear." Kelså offered a slight grin.

They sat in silence for a long moment as Declan finished his glass and poured a second.

Kelså drew in a breath, and her brow creased. "Declan . . . I know you've struggled with who you are, who you want to be, who you're *supposed* to be. I'm here . . . I'm here to help you now."

Simmering anger found its way to the surface. "How could you know that? How could you know *anything* about me?" He ran his fingers through his hair. "They told us you *died*, but I see that was a lie. You just *left us*. You want to help me understand *that*?"

Kelså looked away, stung.

To his eye, she was strong and powerful, yet suddenly appeared small and unsure.

"I'm sorry. I'm so sorry." Her voice was a whisper on the wind. "Leaving you and Keelan was the hardest thing I've ever done. There hasn't been a single day that passed without you in my mind and heart, but we had no choice. Please . . . you must believe me."

Fire blazed in his eyes, and he stood to put distance between them. "You *always* have a choice. Isn't that what that stupid test was all about? You *chose* to walk away from us. I was so young that I couldn't even picture you in my mind, couldn't remember a single moment with you or our father.

"But *Keelan*—he was old enough to remember *every-thing*. Whatever you did stripped him of your face, but he remembered having a mother. He spent years crying in his bed at night when he thought no one was watching, years telling me stories of you and father, desperate to recount every moment he'd ever spent with you so he wouldn't forget and lose you a second time. He thought Atikus lied when he'd said you died, and I think that made it worse for him. In his heart, he *knew* you were alive—and didn't care enough to stay."

Declan pressed his back against the cavern wall, and his anger poured out, a waterfall of emotion released from the dam built so long ago. "He spent his whole life trying to protect me—to protect everyone—but he couldn't protect himself. When the nights came, and he cried himself to sleep because he wasn't good enough or strong enough or … whatever … to keep *you* there, he couldn't save himself. That was *your* job, and you walked away from it."

The silence that followed was broken by a faint clink as Kelså removed a silver pendant from her neck and placed it on the table. Declan eyed the locket. She stood, then glanced at the locket and stepped away from the table, surrendering the space to her son.

When Declan didn't move, Órla put one talon on the bottom of the locket and pushed up with her beak, popping the pendant open. Living images shimmered into existence above the opened piece. Declan edged toward the table and stared in wonder as a baby with unruly blond hair squirmed.

He could *hear* its giggles.

The image shifted to a rust-topped toddler chasing a scruffy puppy. The sounds of the boy's infectious laughter and the puppy's tiny growls echoed in the cavern.

The final shift revealed the older boy, now over five hands tall, clinging to the back of a horse as a lean man with flaxen hair braced him with his hand.

"I didn't leave you; I took you with me, as much as I could," Kelså whispered as she returned to her seat and stared at the locket.

Declan's anger abated as his voice caught in his throat. "I . . . I still don't understand. *Why* did you leave?"

"Some things are larger than us, larger than everything. You talk of protecting Keelan, but what if *the world* cried out for protection? Could you turn your back on everything? On everyone?"

Frustration replaced anger. "So, tell me. Whatever this is, just say it. Stop with the riddles and tests and lies. I'm tired of . . . all of this." He waved his hand around the room.

Kelså's eyes pleaded.

He could *feel* her anguish and guilt, but also her love—intense, overwhelming love.

The feelings flowed through him, and visions flared in his mind. He watched a younger Kelså as she sat at the same table with her head buried in her arms, as sobs wrecked the peaceful silence of the cavern. A man in a golden robe stood beside her, his hand on her shoulder, as his tears flowed as freely as hers.

For the first time, he realized leaving may have caused his parents as much pain as it had their children. They had suffered, too. Immaturity and selfishness mocked him, and he knew, with certainty, the depth of his mother's love. His hand stretched across the table and grasped Kelså's, squeezing it gently. In that simple act, offering grace and comfort to his mother, Declan's heart cracked open.

From the ashes of his bitterness, a new man began to emerge.

Kelså sprang from her chair and wrapped her son in a tight embrace. It only took a second for him to return the hug, and for both of them to dissolve into tears.

Órla hopped up and down. "Aww! Me too! Me too!"

Declan and Kelså laughed together for the first time as he cradled Órla in his palm and Kelså scratched her knobby head. The ensuing *coo-purr* made their laughter grow.

When their joy subsided, and Órla's itch was properly scratched, Kelså patted Declan's arm and stepped back. "Let me take you to the Well and try to answer some of your questions."

"The Well?" Wonder crept into his voice. "As in *The Well?*"

Kelså laughed again. "There's the little boy I remember. Yes, *the* Well."

Órla perched on Declan's shoulder as they followed Kelså into the cavern's passage, a rough-hewn shaft lit faintly by the stones underfoot, similar to those of the Path leading up the mountain. Declan brushed his hand against the walls to find them jagged and cold, not at all the regal picture painted in his mind as a child of a great highland shrine to magic with grand columns of marble and gold.

Few had ever traveled this path.

The tunnel opened into a massive underground chamber, and Declan froze in the opening, mouth agape, unable to process what he was saw.

"I don't know what I expected, but it wasn't *this*."

The cavern covered more ground than the entire Guild Complex back in Saltstone—the *entire complex*, with all of its buildings. Translucent crystals crisscrossed every inch of the ceiling and walls, creating a spiderweb of crystalline strands that glowed faintly from within. The floor was a solid sheet of crystal that Declan first thought was ice waiting to crack under his weight. Beneath the glassy floor swirled a lake of shimmering liquid that rippled and flowed in ceaseless motion. Luminescent mist rose from the liquid trapped beneath the crystal.

Declan steadied himself as he realized the lake's churning reflected in each of the surrounding crystals, giving the room life and movement that threatened to overwhelm his senses.

At the center of the room, two rings of stairs knelt before a platform of the same crystal. Kelså strode toward the platform. Her shoes made a strange clinking sound with each step, and the imprisoned mist reached for her as she passed over it. She was halfway to the center before she realized Declan hadn't followed.

Órla whispered in his ear, "Um, Declan, why's she laughing at you? I mean, you are kinda funny sometimes, but—"

"It's quite safe, my *brave* Ranger. Come on," Kelså called out with mirth in her voice.

Declan blew out the breath he'd been holding and took a tentative first step. The mist lunged toward his foot, and he leapt back. Kelså's laughter was punctuated with snorts that bounded throughout the cavern.

Órla giggled.

Declan gathered his wounded pride and marched into the room—not confidently, but not as tentatively as before. It was hard to know where to look: At the swirling blue mass or the sentient mist that clawed for his feet? At the reflections as they danced, bouncing off one crystal to another? Or at the platform he now faced that opened in its center to allow the mist to rise unhindered and crawl hungrily across his mother's form? She already looked ageless. With the mist, she was downright mystical.

"Ha. Mystical. Mist. I get it. That's funny."

Declan stumbled and fell to one knee.

Órla landed lightly and giggled again.

"Did you just say that in my head? Wait . . . did you hear me *thinking*???"

"Well, duh! Do you have other eternal spirits running around up there that I should know about? I can get jealous, you know."

"And now you're talking in my head. *Spirits!*" Declan scooted forward and sat on the first step, suddenly dizzy.

Kelså reached down and lifted the owl onto her lap, then scratched her tiny head.

"It's beautiful, isn't it?" Kelså waved a hand through the mist rising over the opening.

Declan turned and followed her gaze. "I don't understand any of this. When I left home, I didn't even have a Gift—wouldn't ever have one. Now I'm sitting in the heart of magic, an owl is listening to my thoughts, and mystical smoke is clinging to my arms. Yes, it's beautiful, but *really* creepy, and none of it make any sense."

Kelså smiled with her mother's heart. "Son, your connection to magic is waking, but your knowledge hasn't even stirred. Enjoy the journey and know two things for certain. First, everything is about to change. What you will learn about magic—and about yourself—will threaten everything you thought you knew before. Anyone who enters this chamber would face the same realization, but with your unique bond to Órla, I can't even guess where the Path may lead you. That's actually the second thing. No one truly knows where the Path will lead until the next stones. All we can do is take one step at a time."

She motioned to the seat next to hers. "Why don't we start with the question you asked before?"

When Declan rose and took his seat, mist crawled up legs and across his body. It tingled, and he could feel immense power coursing through him when he breathed in the vapor. One short breath was followed by a long, deep inhale, intoxicating his senses and swelling his chest. His eyes sparkled with azure light, and he felt somehow *whole*. He peered down at his reflection in the crystal platform and nearly fell out of the chair.

Kelså barked a laugh before covering her mouth, and he shot her an annoyed glare. She assumed a serious posture and tried to smother her smile.

"It does take getting used to, being magic," she said.

"You mean having magic?"

"No, I said what I meant. *Being* magic." She shifted so they were facing each other. "Declan, I know you grew up believing that magic is simply an instrument to be used. You were taught that those blessed with its touch have a single Gift, perhaps two if they're lucky, allowing a person to do very specific, useful things."

"That's right. That's how it works—isn't it?"

She breathed in deeply. "Magic is diff—Well, it's not like what—Goodness, you'd think after a thousand years I'd know how to explain this."

She stood and stared into the pool, then drew in a breath of mist. A blanket of calm enveloped her, and, as she spoke, her words took form as the mist swirling above the opening resolved into images.

"Thousands of years ago, magic permeated the world and everything in it. There were no Gifts as you know them, limiting magicians to a certain skill. People were born a Mage, able to wield its strength in full, or they weren't. Only a few in each generation would receive magic's call, and there were rarely more than twenty or thirty Mages living at a time—but into their hands was placed something both amazing and terrible: the power to shape and grow and heal—and to destroy.

"Mages were generally born with equal power. No one man or woman wielded enough to dominate the others. That didn't guarantee they'd use their power for good, but it did keep them in a sort of balance. Occasionally, one or two would try to assert their power over the others, but a swift, collective rebuke from the rest contained them.

"The Mages' Guild was actually born from this collective will, giving order to chaos, law to the lawless. Even the most willful Mages fell in line, fearing the power of the Guild's communal magic."

"That all sounds great, but why are people limited to a Gift now?"

"Declan! Don't interrupt your mother." Órla hopped a few times, mist bouncing around her, trying to keep up. "Kelså, please continue. This is a great story!"

Kelså smiled and inclined her head toward Órla.

The mist above the opening scattered and reformed, the image of Mages replaced by a tall woman in a golden gown with a gilded crown on her head.

"Then came Irina."

"*The* Irina?" Declan couldn't take his eyes off the magical mirage.

"Yes, dummy, *that* Irina. Now let her finish!" Órla swatted his arm with her wing.

He laughed. "Kinda bossy tonight, aren't ya, little one?"

Kelså cleared her throat and both their heads snapped up. "Yes, *that* Irina."

The image shifted to a seventeen-year-old girl. "She wasn't always evil. Both of her parents were physikers, the Mute form of a Healer. When her power manifested, she followed their path, choosing Healing as her passion, determined to save the world from disease and suffering. She studied the Healing arts, ignoring most other magical talents, and quickly became the most adept Healer of her time. She was adored and respected, nearly worshiped as some benevolent goddess descended from the heavens to save her people.

"A group of the other Mages became jealous of her popularity and fame. They feared her growing influence and believed her compassionate goodness to be an act, a ruse to win over the hapless masses and drive them to invest her with power to rule. By all accounts, she had been sincere, but the Mages believed otherwise and hatched a plot to take what she loved—to break her spirit.

"She was forced to watch as Mages appeared on her doorstep and slaughtered her parents. Her mother writhed in flame before her daughter's eyes. Irina was devastated and railed against the Mages and the evil they represented. Her anger raged, fueling her desire for revenge.

"Irina was the first to use Healing magic to actually harm another, stopping the heart of one of her rival Mages. She threw herself into the study of elemental magics, the powers of fire, earth, water, and air. Those who opposed her burst into flame at her whim or drowned while drinking a glass of water. She purged every Mage from the land now known as the Kingdom of Spires, killing or forcing them into exile. Every taste of power left her starved for more."

The mist-fueled image morphed again, this time revealing brutal battlefields covered in broken bodies and blood. Flames fell from the sky. Men ran and screamed and died.

Kelså's voice darkened. "She cowed the leaders of a fractured land, uniting them for the first time beneath her banner, declaring war on all who sought to be free. You were taught stories of the Kingdom War that followed, chivalrous tales of men on horseback fighting for honor and freedom, but what I recall was damnation itself born to life. Death rode beneath Irina's banner."

The cavern fell silent.

Even the mist quelled at Kelså's memory.

"You know of Arch Mage Quin's role in Irina's defeat. He was young then, but the Phoenix answered his call, and we were saved." Her voice faltered. "We lost *so many* in that war."

She drifted into memory, her voice a rasp when she spoke again. "What followed is known by only two people alive today, Velius Quin and me. Declan, you may *never* reveal what I tell you now, not to anyone, for any reason. Do you understand?"

He nodded, unable to speak.

"While the mountains still burned, Quin gathered the Mages who had survived. There were only a handful of us left. He led us through the Gate in the mountains and sealed us in this cavern, declaring none would leave until we found a solution, a way to prevent another Irina from ever threatening the world again.

"After an eternity of debate, a plan finally formed. We would reshape magic itself, stripping godlike power from the few while granting unique abilities to the many. The world would be safe from any one person bent on total control, while enriching millions of lives through a single-talent Gift."

Declan leaned back in his chair and released the breath he had been holding. "So . . . you *created* Gifts?"

She nodded slowly, her gaze still distant. "Son, there's more. Reshaping magic required a terrible sacrifice. All of us, the last living Mages, poured our power into the Well to affect that change. All but two were consumed, and the life of the last was forfeit."

"Wait. Quin is still Arch Mage. That makes you the one that was forfeit. What does that even mean?"

"For the plan to endure beyond our generation, one of us had to offer ourselves to magic, to become its protector, its Keeper. Declan, *I* am the Keeper of Magic. I gave my life to guard the Well and tend the flow of Gifts to humanity."

Declan's mouth opened, then closed. He could barely believe what she'd said.

"Wait . . . I'm confused . . . *You're the Keeper?*"

She nodded again.

His eyes widened. "But . . . Who was the old man in the hut then? The one who gave me the test?"

"The old man you saw was an illusion, part of elaborate magical security measures designed to frighten away intruders and protect the Well. He isn't real."

She sucked in another breath and sat, taking Declan's hand in hers. "Declan, in a thousand years, I have only left this island once, to deliver you and Keelan to the Mages in Saltstone. Within days of leaving these shores, I could feel the power that sustains my life begin to fail."

"And if you died, magic . . ." his words hung in the air.

A thought struck and he leaned forward. "Hold on. You delivered us to Saltstone? And you had never left the island? We were born *here*? Keelan told me stories about our childhood, about you and father. He never mentioned a cave or magical lake or any of this. And what about our father?"

Sadness mingled with something deeper as her eyes drifted into the past once more. "I met your father thirty years ago. Arch Mage Quin sent him as an envoy to Mother Larinda. He had just concluded an audience with her when he stumbled down the stairs and knocked me off my feet—literally *and* figuratively." She smiled distantly. "He was tall, with broad shoulders and a strong jaw—and golden hair that fell to his neck. He had this smile . . . The power of the Well couldn't compare to the magic in your father's smile. He was *such* a good man."

Her eyes revealed as much as her words, and Declan let her savor the memories in silence.

"You and Keelan were born here—down in the village, actually. Larinda delivered each of you and became a godmother to you both. Hardly a day passed that one of you wasn't distracting her from her duties—usually *Keelan*, for the record. For some unknown reason, that boy loved to run naked through her home. He thought it was hilarious to escape after a bath and streak through the garden."

"Wait. Keelan was funny? You've got to be talking about a different brother," he said.

"Oh, no. Keelan was *something* as a child."

She stood and walked to the Well, peering down at the swirling liquid. "Your father died a few years after we gave you to the Mages. I was here, tending the Well, when Larinda strode into the cavern. She is the only person on the island who knows what this cave contains, but I was still startled to see her. The look on her face . . . her eyes were so red and clouded. Your father had taken a boat to study some plant or fish. He was always studying something. The weather turned dark and waves churned. Men on shore lost sight of his boat before anyone could cry for help. For one born of such magic, he died a simple, useless death."

Declan stood and placed a hand on her shoulder. She met his eyes as tears clouded her own.

"He was *such* a good man. So kind and gentle. I see him in you, Declan, especially his smile."

He squeezed her shoulder but couldn't stop a question from escaping. "Why doesn't Keelan remember any of this? He remembers you and our father, experiences *with* you, but nothing of this place or any of the people here. At least, he's never said anything about them."

She sighed deeply. "The magic of the Well would make many covet its power. Part of the spell used to transform magic, the spell that also made me the Keeper, includes protections for this island, the Path, and the Well itself. You met the illusionary Keeper and his test. Another more powerful thread in that spell wipes any memory of this place from those who enter this chamber. Keelan doesn't remember this place because the Well took those memories from him when he left the island. What memories he has of your father and me . . . well, I had to leave him *something* of us."

Declan staggered back a step, horror written in his features. "So, I won't remember you when I leave? Or this place?"

"No. You'll remember what I teach you about magic and how to use your Light, but you will have no memory of me, the Keeper, or the Path." She stepped forward and took his hand again. "Declan, there was never a day you and Keelan weren't in my thoughts. Leaving you broke my heart, but duty is a privilege that exacts a price. To save this world, I gave up my own. *Your* duty demands the same."

He'd never known his mother; and now, when he'd crossed the continent and an ocean to find her, she would be stripped from his mind again? He pressed hands to his eyes and tried to stop the tears.

Kelså steered the conversation back to magic. Family and memories would have to wait. She knelt and slowly waved her hand over Well's opening, and words shimmered into existence, glittering golden letters etched in the swirling liquid below.

Seven Scattered as lands shattered.
Bind the Heir. Make diamonds bleed.
Speak the Words.
E vesh Irina.

"Declan, this is a prophecy, or some kind of instruction, from the time after Irina's death. It foretells her return and a renewed quest for power and vengeance. It doesn't say how or when she is supposed to return, but

Quin and I fear the cycle of her resurrection has already begun. If successful, we believe she would wield unrivaled power, reclaiming her magic from before our spell, possibly with the power to undo all of our protections."

She paused to let the implications of that future sink in.

"Wait. You're saying magic could be wiped out for everyone but her? *Everyone*?" He struggled to wrap his mind around the idea.

She nodded. "If our spell vanished, so would the Gift. She would remain the only true Mage in the world. Millions would become her slaves—or die."

"What about you? You're sustained by the Well's magic?"

"I would vanish as well."

She drew a breath of mist and held it for a long moment before letting it out, as if smoking a savory pipe. "Magic always seeks balance. Quin and I always believed it would provide something—or *someone*—to counter Irina's terrible potential should she rise once more."

She glanced into the mist, then back into Declan's eyes. "Órla, the Golden Princess and the Daughter of Magic, bonded with and speaks to you. Magic's breath flows through you. You are the son of the Keeper, Crown Prince in the royal line of magic itself."

Her eyes glistened with moisture and pride. "My beautiful son, this is going to be hard to believe, but

I think *you* are that balance, the special weapon magic invested with the power to counter Irina."

Chapter Nine

The next two days of hiking across the countryside were brutal, as the trio pushed to make up ground. Everyone was tired and sore but knew what was at stake and kept complaints to themselves—save Atikus, who was always hungry, musing about steaming potatoes, roasted pork, or other aromatic cuisine. Thankfully, the late fall weather remained clear and cool, perfect for a journey on foot, and Sil's eagle kept a close eye on Tiana and her captors, who'd made it past the fork and were now headed toward Irina's Seat.

Mid-morning of the third day, the town of Rutin came into view. The town served as a trading center for every kind of grain and livestock raised throughout the heartland of the Kingdom. Farms surrounding the town spread for a hundred leagues in all directions and filled tables in every corner of the country. Most of the people who lived in the area were farmers and wanted peace, a simple chance to raise a family, and to give something back to the land that offered them so much. They were good, honest folk who said what they thought and didn't mind a startled look when they did. A change in season stirred the town far more than a change of King or Queen, and politics rarely entered their minds. Still, patriotic pride flowed in their veins.

As the team entered town, they heard the shouts and jeers of hundreds coming from its center. Keelan led them down the winding roads past houses and shops toward the commotion. They stopped when the buildings opened into a central courtyard centered around a massive stone statue of some long-ago King. A red-faced man in green-and-gold livery stood on the base of the statue, waving his arms and shouting angrily to the men and women encircling him. Most wore aged, homespun clothes and wide-brimmed straw hats. The man had the crowd whipped into a frenzy and seemed intent on pushing them for more.

". . . our daughters and sons! And now we have *undeniable proof* that they've kidnapped *our own Crown Princess*, Jessia Vester!"

The man waited while the crowd gasped in anger and surprise.

"I say again, our men found *undeniable evidence* that a member of Melucia's Triad *directly* ordered the kidnapping of the Crown Princess. His *personal* seal was found on the road where the Princess was taken—and there's only one place that could've come from!"

"MELUCIA!" the crowd roared.

"For hundreds of years, the Melucians have grown fat off the hard work of our people. Look around. *You*—and your neighbors—are the hardworking men and women of the Kingdom. You feed not just our land, but *theirs*, too. You break your back so they can live like kings, and now they want more? Is that right?"

"No!"

"Are you going to let them continue stealing from your table?"

"NO!"

"It was bad enough that they thought to take our children, our precious *Gifted*, now they attack our royal family, the beating heart of the Kingdom itself! Can we let this treachery stand?"

"NO!"

"Can we let them go unpunished?"

"NO!"

"The King agrees and calls his people to rise! He calls *you* to take up arms and march! Together we'll teach those imperial bastards what happens when you strike at our heart—at the Spires!"

"We'll show 'em!" one man shouted.

Another yelled, "Kill them bastards! Make 'em pay!"

The speaker nodded and raised a defiant fist. "Heralds stand in squares just like this one all over our Kingdom, gathering men to fight for *our* King—to fight for *our* Kingdom!

"People of Rutin, *join your brothers and sisters!* Tell your family, your friends, your neighbors! JOIN US AND FIGHT!"

The crowd exploded. Chants of "Death to Melucia!" and "FIGHT! FIGHT! FIGHT!" thrummed through the courtyard long after the speaker stepped down from the statue.

Many in the crowd waved flyers. Sil looked down and found many more littering the courtyard and stuffed one in her pocket. Keelan led them along a road that skirted the courtyard until he found a large wooden building marked *Inn*.

A large notice board towered over the entrance, and two sheets pinned to the cork caught Keelan's eye. One had "REWARD!" scrawled in large lettering across its masthead and described four kidnappings that had occurred over the past few months. It described how constables believed the cases to be connected, possibly perpetrated by the same criminal or group. Brief descriptions of the four victims, along with an artist's sketch of each, filled the page. A generous reward was offered for information leading to the return of the victims.

The title on the second post made his breath catch. "JOIN THE KING! JOIN THE WAR!" it cried. Another artist's sketch of a teenage girl wearing a tiara consumed the center of the page. The rest of the sheet described the kidnapping of the Princess and vague references to the "hard evidence" obtained by investigators. Melucia's Triad was to blame. Like the liveried herald in the square had said, volunteers were being recruited in every town and village throughout the Kingdom to join the war effort.

Keelan turned to the others. "Stay quiet. I'll get us a couple rooms, and then we can talk."

The bartender eyed Keelan with caution, likely more from his towering size than any suspicion of Melucian ties. At more than eighteen hands, he drew a sideways look from most people he met. The man barkeep disappeared through a door behind the bar, returning a few minutes later with a tiny woman whose head barely reached Keelan's chest. Undeterred by his height, she squared up with Keelan, hands planted on wide hips, and met his gaze. After a bit of haggling, her manner softened, coins were exchanged, and she motioned for the others to follow her through a long hallway to their rooms.

Sil waited a few minutes before leaving her room to join Atikus and Keelan. No one knew they were in town, but it never hurt to be cautious.

"That was a fine welcome." Atikus said with a weak smile.

"I guess we know why troops are headed toward the border, but *the Triad* involved in a kidnapping? *Five* kidnappings, if you believe the flyers? That doesn't make any sense." Keelan sat on the corner of the bed as Sil took a seat at a writing desk against the wall.

"The man in the courtyard was wearing the green and gold of the royal house. Whatever's happening, it has the King's approval. This is *his* war," Atikus said.

"I wonder if they even know that we've had two kidnappings of our own," Sil said.

Atikus paced by the door. "They won't care at this point. If they're publicly blaming the Triad for their missing people, they'll say our kidnappings were part of the Triad's plot somehow. They'll use that to make us look even more sinister. 'We even did this to our own'—whatever 'this' is."

Sil unfolded the flyer she'd stuffed in her pocket and handed it to Keelan. It was a duplicate of the one Keelan had seen on the notice board.

"From the looks of this, they're recruiting volunteers from all over the Kingdom. The flame's already lit, and I doubt there's any snuffing it now," she said.

The three stared at the flyer for a long moment before Keelan broke the silence. "We can't control any of that. Our mission was to save our Healer, and that hasn't changed. We'll have to be a lot more careful when moving through towns and should probably get some new cloths to blend in better, but we stay the course.

"Sil, you should check on the cart; make sure they're still headed to Irina's Seat. Atikus, contact the Arch Mage and report what we've learned. I'll see about getting some new clothes."

An hour later, Keelan returned with an armful of clothes, which he unceremoniously dumped on the bed in front of Atikus. "Well, that was fun. I'm glad we thought to swap out our Melucian quills for crowns before crossing the mountains. If I'd dropped coins on the counter with the Merchants' Quill, I'm not sure I'd have made it back. The mob is roaming the streets, still raging."

Atikus shook his head. "I still don't understand what's behind all of this. Surely the King knows the Triad would never stoop to kidnapping, especially not the Crown Princess of our most important trading partner. We're missing a significant piece, maybe a few of them."

"I don't know, but I do know we can't win this war. Before all this recruiting, the Kingdom already had a standing army large enough to crush us. Now, we'll be lucky to last more than a month or two when they roll over the mountains." Keelan picked his new clothes out of the pile and began changing. "Were you able to get a message to the Arch Mage?"

He nodded absently as he picked through the clothes. "I'm confident he received the information. I just wish we could communicate both ways. He could help us figure out what to do over here."

"We know what to do. We follow the Healer."

Atikus eyed Keelan. "Son, this is a lot bigger than one missing girl. Our whole way of life is about to be attacked, probably destroyed."

"I understand that, but there's nothing we can do to stop—wait a minute. Can you contact Declan? You sent him for magical help, right?"

"Hmm . . . I can try. Where he's going, my telepathy might not work." Keelan's head snapped up at that, concern flooding his eyes. "Besides, he wouldn't be able to answer. All I could do is send a message about our situation and hope it helps him."

Keelan turned back to lacing his boots. The trousers he'd bought were an inch too short for his insanely tall frame, but the rough-spun tan shirt fit decently. He got to his feet and headed for the door.

"Get changed. We need to get some supper in the common room before it gets too late. I'll take meet you down there in a few minutes."

Keelan stopped in the door, Atikus's chuckle grabbing his attention. "Do I want to know what's behind that grin?"

"Oh, I was just thinking how command suits you, even when you're ordering an old Mage around his own clothes." Atikus coughed a laugh as his eyes sparkled.

"Sorry. Didn't mean to give orders. This whole thing's got my head spinning."

Atikus took a few steps toward Keelan and put a hand on his shoulder. "Allow a man to be proud of his son."

Keelan was dumbstruck, but the tight embrace that followed stunned the Mage even more. When they pulled apart, Atikus's broad smile lingered long after Keelan had left the room.

The common room was nearly empty throughout most of their meal, and the evening passed without incident. Atikus was in his element, entertaining Sil with stories of "little Keelan" and his brother "Declan the Terrible" from their early years in the Guild. Sil spent most of the night laughing while Keelan dreamed of ways to squeeze his massive frame under the table. Despite the embarrassment of his adopted father's tales, Keelan's heart was full for the first time in ages when they left the common room to get some rest.

The next morning, Sil joined the men in their room again, and Keelan explained how he'd bought horses for each of them, stating he hoped they could beat the masked men to Irina's Seat, assuming that was their final destination. They slipped out of the inn while the sun still slumbered, walked a few blocks to the stables, and trotted up the road.

As they passed the last few buildings of Rutin, Keelan reined in his horse. A few paces off the road, where any traveler could see, hung a straw man in a Melucian navy cloak, mounted high on a tall pole. He wore a hat with a makeshift Merchants' Guild Quill pinned to its brim. A dozen knives and arrows protruded from his body, and many more holes hinted at the game that was played the night before. Maybe they'd just been venting anger, but Keelan thought it looked more like practicing for their vengeance to come.

Chapter Ten

It only took a day of pacing around the palace and worrying about Jess for the King and Queen to decide it was time to head east. Alfred was determined to be nearby when she was found, which meant loading half the palace onto carts and carriages and traveling over the Spires as winter sank her teeth into the mountains.

The King's excuse to his advisors was that he wanted to review the troops and encourage recruitment in the towns "across the heartland." No one believed him, but they couldn't blame a frantic father for wanting to do something—*anything*—to feel closer to his missing daughter. Besides, the normally affable King had become unbearable in Council meetings, randomly eviscerating advisors with unusually sharp critiques. Many around that table had served this King for years or decades, and none had seen him behave in such a reckless manner before. It would be good to get him out of the palace for a while.

Prince Justin and his younger brother Kendall pleaded with their mother to join the retinue. Justin argued that Jess didn't trust their parents, but she trusted him. If she was found, and negotiation was required, he would be the best member of the royal family to win her back into the fold. Kendall just wanted to see the mountains and what was on the other side. He'd never been on an extended trip, and the whole thing sounded like a grand adventure. In the end, Isabel agreed to bring Justin but couldn't justify taking nine-year-old Kendall.

The story of Jess's kidnapping was now well-known throughout the capital as the Chancellor's mice scurried in the shadows, squeaking the tale as often—and as dramatically—as possible. His network of entertainers and innkeepers made certain some version of the tale was told or sung or read in every common room throughout Fontaine.

Recruitment flyers bearing the likeness of the Princess were plastered on virtually every street corner. The Chancellor even had a pack of graffiti artists splash images of the Princess on buildings, alongside calls for revenge. She might not have been the princess they'd hoped for, but she was *their* princess.

In a matter of weeks, her visage morphed from a petulant teenage girl people feared would one day rule, to a revered, near-goddess stolen by the minions of foreign dark lords. By the time the entourage left the palace, much of the populace believed Melucia was growing thirty-hand-tall monsters and were stealing children to feed them.

The parade of royal vehicles, surrounded by mounted guards in sharp emerald cloaks with golden trim, lumbered through the city to the raucous cheers of thousands. Chancellor Thorn had tipped Isabel off to the "impromptu send-off" he'd carefully orchestrated, but Alfred was caught unawares. His eyes brimmed with pride as he waved to the unending throng, overwhelmed by the outpouring of support for their monarch. When trumpeters played the royal fanfare as the caravan reached the edge of town, Isabel caught Thorn's eye and offered a discrete wink.

He really has outdone himself this time, She thought.

Ten carriages, twenty-three carts, and two-hundred mounted royal guardsmen snaked their way through the Spires like some sprawling centipede whose rear never quite kept up with its head. The first snows had coated the mountaintops, but thankfully, the King's Road remained clear. The trip to Spoke on the eastern base of the range would normally take a man on horseback a few days, but the slow-moving caravan crawled for more than a week before reaching the town.

The Queen insisted on one night in a real bed, so everything ground to a halt while the royal couple invaded the local inn. Chancellor Thorn had arranged for the inn to be cleared of guests long before the trip began. Alfred and Isabel were greeted in the common room by a line of serving girls and stable boys. At the head of the line, a round woman in a bright-yellow apron curtsied awkwardly.

"Your Majesties. Welcome. Please make my inn your home." She nearly passed out when Alfred took her hand and kissed it. Isabel stifled a laugh as one of the serving girls helped the woman sit to catch her breath.

The "royal suite" was smaller than most of the palace's broom closets, but Isabel didn't care. Rose-scented steam wafted off of water in a spacious iron tub and was all she could think about after so many nights on the cold, dusty road. Ignoring her ladies' knocks at the door, she tore off her clothes and had Alfred unlace the back of her corset before sinking low in the heavenly bath. The King pressed a kiss to her forehead then strode to the room next door, where another steaming bath awaited his arrival.

When he returned a half hour later, Isabel's pruny hand, still submerged in the cooling water, splashed in greeting.

"I've been thinking," she said. "At this pace, we won't get to Cradle for a month or more, longer if you stop along the way to review troops."

"That sounds about right."

She stood and wrapped a towel around her dripping body. "It's already been over a week since Jess was taken. If I have to wait another month to *do* something, I'm going to strangle somebody. I know, Wilfred's men have already scoured the area and probably interviewed every living person and farm animal within fifty leagues, but I want to see for myself. I can't just sit here and pretend anymore."

Alfred sat on the corner of the bed and began dressing for dinner. He buttoned his emerald coat, straightening its golden collar before peering up at Isabel. "Issy, I get it. I'm about to crawl out of my skin, too. I keep imagining what Jess must be going through and . . ." his voice broke.

It took a moment to gather himself. "Even if you and a few guards and left on horseback, you wouldn't get there for weeks, and I think you'd give the Captain heart failure if you left the safety of the small army protecting us. I want to do something—*anything*—but I don't know how to speed this trip up."

"I do. At least for one of us." She sat beside him and put a hand on his leg. "I Enchanted a medallion some time ago to allow me to Travel. It only works once and can only take me somewhere I know well enough to hold in my mind, but it will work. I could be in Cradle before you sat down to dinner tonight."

"Hmm . . . You say it will only work for one person?"

She nodded. "The medallion is on a silver chain I would wear for the trip."

"So, you would arrive in Spoke alone, with no guards? I don't like that. The people who took Jess are still out there, and for all we know, they could be in Spoke. I'm sure they would love a bigger prize, and there are only two people in the Kingdom who fit that description."

"I know," she said in a pleading voice. "But there are plenty of constables and troops in Spoke now. The whole country is gearing up for war. I could have one of our Telepaths contact the constables there and prepare an escort. I could make it safely. Please . . . *she's my little girl*. Alfred, I can't just sit here anymore."

Alfred wrapped his arms around her and pulled her close. The crown demanded he show strength, even when his own family was attacked. It was tearing him apart just as much as it was Isabel, but he didn't have the luxury of public displays—and neither did his Queen. He wanted to ease her pain, but the idea of letting her go off alone, unguarded, to do who knows what—*and in this state of mind*—it just didn't make sense. She could get hurt or kidnapped or worse.

He decided to give himself some time to think. "Issy, let's go have some dinner and think about this. If we can ensure your safety, I'll consider it."

He gave her another squeeze and stood to straighten his coat. "I'm heading down to the common room. Join me when you're ready. I heard a rumor the innkeeper stocked your favorite wine."

He gave her a tight smile and left.

As soon as the door closed, Isabel leapt from the bed and began to dress. She was furious. How *dare* he condescend to her like that. She was perfectly capable of Traveling on her own, with or without armed men lording over her every step. Spirits! Her Gifts were far stronger and more useful than his. Of course, Persuasion was important for a monarch, but he couldn't light someone on fire with his words. Just because he could barely pee without an attendant there to wipe up didn't mean she shared his weakness.

She threw her corset against the wall and watched it flop onto the bed. Her husband and ladies were downstairs, so things would have to fly freely tonight.

Let that show them ... literally. She chuckled to herself.

She opened her jewelry box in search of a country-inn-appropriate necklace. As she set the first few aside, too heavy with diamonds and other precious stones for this night, her hand brushed against a cold piece of metal at the bottom of the pile. She pried it out and held the medallion up to the light of the dresser's candle. Some kind of hunting bird, probably a falcon, was etched on the pendant's face. The piece glowed faintly and tickled her fingers. Without thinking, she slipped the thin chain around her neck, closed her eyes, and pictured the rolling hills outside of Spoke in her mind's eye.

When she opened her eyes, she stood alone on a dark, grassy mound. The medallion flared one last time before losing any hint of magic's touch.

Six robed figures entered the tomb. Five wore the traditional brown of the Children, complete with contorted masks depicting animals various species. The sixth was robed in scarlet, face covered by a mask of perfectly smooth, blank skin. There were no eye holes, yet the figure maneuvered the water and steps of the crypt with practiced ease. On the leader's head rested a golden crown banded by seven massive diamonds, five of which pulsed crimson as if tethered to some beating heart. Two thick braids of gold drooped from neck to waist.

As their leader passed, each of the robed figures bowed respectfully and muttered, "Vessel."

Ritual demanded this visit before each sacrifice. Only Irina herself knew who was worthy.

Vessel drifted across the shallow water and climbed the altar's steps in a single stride to stand before the golden tomb. Prophecy loomed from its ebony slate, and magical power crackled in the air. After a moment of reverent reflection, Vessel turned and motioned for the others to proceed.

Four of the robed figures began and placed lit candles at intervals along the outside edge of the water, then moved to the inner edge and repeated the process. The fifth, wearing the mask of a fox with the horns of a ram, approached Vessel with a ceremonial dagger proffered in outstretched hands. Vessel took the dagger, but Fox remained with arms extended and palms up. Fox muttered a few words, and the room flared with opalescent light. When the light faded, a lamb materialized in Fox's arms, squirming to get down. With one quick stroke, Vessel sliced the lamb's neck, then exchanged the dagger for the lamb and placed the bleeding corpse onto the tomb. Gold turned burgundy, then black.

When the tomb was coated in blood, Vessel lifted the lamb and handed it back to Fox, who placed it into the water and retreated to the other side where the other robed figures waited silently. The shimmering crystal pool began to bleed.

Vessel lifted the crown into the air and cried out, "E VESH IRINA!" then placed it on the middle of the bloody tomb. The candles flickered, and a torrent of wind whirled about the chamber. The crackling of magic became thunderous as a single bolt of lightning streaked from the prophecy to the crown. Thick, iridescent smoke rose in its wake.

No one moved.

No one breathed.

When the smoke dissipated, the ghostly image of a woman in a flowing gown towered above the tomb. Her sharp, angular nose jutted from an otherwise unremarkable face, and her eyes blazed.

"Why do you wake me, Vessel?" the woman demanded. Her voice sounded distant, the grating of gears not quite aligned yet still turning.

Vessel fell to her knees and pressed her forehead to the bloody marble floor. "Most Exalted Empress, we are your humble servants in all things. We come at your command. The Heir is finally ours."

The woman's eyes widened and a smile parted her lips. "Excellent. How long before you perform the final ritual?"

"Days, my Empress, perhaps a week. The King is rallying troops to invade our neighbor, so we must remain cautious to protect the Heir from prying eyes."

The woman nodded. "A thousand years I have waited, dreaming of a thousand ways to destroy this pitiful land and its feckless people. Days mean nothing. Protect the Heir. The fool king does my bidding, distracting those who would halt my return. Do not summon me again until the final ritual."

"Yes, Empress. As you command."

Lightning struck the crown again, and the woman vanished. The chamber became deathly still. Vessel rose, blood dripping from forehead to cheek. Beneath the blank skin of the mask, a ravenous smile emerged.

Days . . . only a few more days.

Chapter Eleven

Arch Mage Velius Quin sat with his hands crossed in his lap, watching the Ceryl Burner, the country's portly leader of the Merchants' Guild waddle nervously in circles around the chamber. The room, the heart of Melucia's government, contained three ornately carved, high-backed thrones. Each was adorned with plush velvet cushions and faced the others at room's center.

Those attending an audience before the body stood on a raised, eye-shaped platform at the center, and were forced to turn each time a different member of the Triad asked a question. It was designed to be uncomfortable—and succeeded with most visitors. An oculus in the domed ceiling shone milky light that encompassed the thrones and Eye, bathing the members of the Triad, while the rest of the room remained dim.

The gallery, one floor above, contained comfortable chairs for high-ranking spectators or government officials. On this day, the gallery stood empty.

General Titus Vre, leader of Melucia's armed forces, stood stiffly beside his seat as his glare bored holes into the poor messenger currently cowering from the Eye. Voluminous Mage's robes practically consumed the scrawny magician, who kept blotting sweat from his bony brow. He spun to face the Arch Mage when his master spoke again, nearly stumbling off the perch.

"Ceryl, please sit down. You're going to make our poor guest seasick." Quin grunted at the pacing Guild-master, then eyed the young Mage. "Now, Mage . . . Eric, was it?"

"Yes, sir . . . uh . . . Arch Mage. Eric."

"Mage Eric, walk us through one more time. This time, please just read the transcript of the message Atikus sent. You were in the chamber when I spoke his words to your pen, correct?"

"Yes, Arch Mage." He cleared his throat and wiped sweat from his brow again. "Mage Atikus Dani used Telepathy. You instructed me to transcribe his message as you spoke. Scribes are currently making additional copies for each member of the Triad, but I brought the original for your immediate review. With your permission—"

"Please proceed," Quin said.

Eric cleared his throat again and began to read from the parchment in his trembling hands.

"Our situation is more dire than previously thought. The Kingdom is rallying volunteers throughout the land to join in the war effort. They blame the kidnapping of four Gifted on Melucia, but the real catalyst for this invasion was the kidnapping of the Crown Princess, the fifth such act. The official story blames Guildmaster Burner and a coordinated Melucian plot to destroy the Kingdom's already thin magical line. They further claim that his personal seal was found at the site where the Princess was taken. Royal Speakers are whipping up crowds in town squares across the country, and flyers with the Princess's likeness call for the people to rise. Roads are clogged with lines of troops headed east. We've even seen siege engines among the caravans.

"All of this has the blessing of the King. There can be no doubt of the Kingdom's intention to invade come spring.

"As to our investigation, we found the Healer. Guard Sil Wesser bonded an eagle and is keeping watch. Her captors are on the road headed to Irina's Seat, and we believe she is still alive, concealed in the bottom of a cart. We are currently in Rutin but will leave for Irina's Seat before dawn.

"I will report again once we reach Irina's Seat."

"My Seal went missing a year or two ago. Servants scoured every inch of the building but never found it." Burner hurled his portly frame onto his throne.

"No doubt our little spy has been busy again." The Arch Mage sat back. "Ceryl, it's likely the spy is still working somewhere in the Merchants' Guild. We should redouble our efforts to root him out."

"Yes, yes. I've had my most trusted men on this for months. Any magical help your people could offer would be appreciated."

"Our only Truth Seer is sneaking his way through the Kingdom right now. I'll see what else we might offer." Quin thought a moment. "What about combating the story? Your trade network extends throughout the Kingdom. How can we use that to undermine their propaganda?"

"That's an interesting idea. If I could get word through their lines, we could make a dent in their story, at least get our version out there. Unfortunately, the border has been sealed for months. We haven't seen a single trade caravan return since summer," Ceryl said. "And if they're as angry as Atikus claims, I doubt even my closest traders will listen. They'll fear a traitor's justice for speaking against the King."

After a moment of thought, Quin turned to the General. "General Vre, please review our defensive status and strategy."

Vre gave Quin a pointed look, then shot a glance at the Mage still quavering on the Eye.

"Right. Mage Eric, thank you. You may leave." Eric bobbed his head toward the Arch Mage and skittered out of the room. Quin took a thumb-sized box out of his pocket, uttered a few words, and nodded to the others. "Speak freely now. The chamber is cloaked."

General Vre, ever the military man, stood with his back straight, hands clasped behind his back.

"By all accounts, the Kingdom's standing army boasts more than a hundred thousand well-trained archers, pikemen, and cavalry. If they're recruiting, we should add another fifty thousand, probably more. Their population is twice ours, and it sounds like they're motivated.

"As for our forces, the Rangers number a little over one thousand, and are divided between our western and eastern borders. Our army, currently stationed in three primary locations, numbers just over twenty-two thousand. If we're lucky, we could recruit another twenty or thirty thousand, but there wouldn't be enough time to train them before a spring assault. They would die quickly and barely slow the well-trained Kingdom forces. It would be a waste of lives.

"The Kingdom allied with the island tribes on Vint and Riz long ago. Their navies will make any counter by sea impossible. They'll also use them to blockade our ports, stifling trade and resupply.

"Unless you have some powerful magic up your sleeve, this isn't a fight we can win."

"Well, that was uplifting." Burner sniped. "What about the border nations? Surely they would offer aid."

Vre rolled his eyes. He despised the rotund trader and rarely hid it, especially in closed session. For reasons Quin never understood, the General believed Ceryl's constant happiness and annoying optimism to be a false veneer masking some greedy ploy to take over more of the nation's wealth. Never mind that *his job* was to grow trade and wealth for the merchants of the Empire—and he was good at it. Vre despised the man. Quin pursed his lips at the prospect of playing referee yet again.

"They're useless. They have no standing army, other than a weak constabulary that barely keeps order on their roads. Besides, they can't stop squabbling over fishing rights long enough to work together, even if it means their downfall. They'd probably surrender to the Kingdom before the first arrow was loosed," the General said.

Quin gripped and released his armrest. "We are significantly more powerful than the Kingdom where magic is concerned. Our Mages could hold off their army in the mountains for a few months, but they would eventually break. Here in the capital, where we have access to the Tower and its wellspring, our power is amplified, but most of our Gifts are peaceful, aimed at Healing, growing crops, or other mundane tasks. I believe we could defend Saltstone for a time, but not long.

"The gravest problem would be feeding the people throughout an extended siege. The rest of the nation would fall if we consolidated the army here, leaving Saltstone an island amidst a hostile sea. It would only be a matter of time before we were forced to surrender."

The Triad's Chamber was usually a blur of motion and commotion, but it fell silent as the three rulers stared blankly into the Eye.

It offered no wisdom.

Quin stood. "Gentlemen, I'd like to consult with my Mages, see if they can come up with options we've missed. In the meantime, Ceryl, check with your network. There have to be some who would be sympathetic. If nothing else, they may be willing to share intelligence from their side of the mountains. Our spy network is thin; your primary focus now is to strengthen it. Also, use your traders to contact the border nations and island tribes, anyone who can hold a spear or sword. I agree with the General on the status of our neighbors, but we have to try.

"General, we need immediate plans for a mass recruitment effort. Include options to draft any man, woman, or child of fighting age, then have your staff develop strategies for the defense of the western border. I'll have my Mages focus on defensive options in that region, as well. If we're going to bottle them up, the mountains will be our best hope. Once they get past Grove's Pass, the Empire *will* fall.

"Let's reconvene tomorrow at noon, lay everything out, and go from there."

Chapter Twelve

Declan's world tilted.

"You think *I'm* the hero who will save the world from the most powerful sorceress who ever lived? Me? Declan-without-a-Gift Rea?" He laughed at the sheer insanity of the idea.

Kelså nodded and crossed her hands in her lap.

Órla perked up, and Declan thought she . . . giggled? "It is kinda hard to think of you as heroic, especially with that puffy hair. I mean, really. What are you gonna do? Flick your curls at Irina?"

"Hey!" he said, right before flicking his hair in defiance.

Órla fell into a fit of odd, owlish laughter that made Kelså's composure finally crack. Declan's hands flew to his hips, making the two laugh even harder. He heard "teapot" through snorts, which inflamed the hilarity.

Somehow, the magic of his mother's laughter drew pain's poison from Declan's wounded soul, leaving him unburdened for the first time he could remember. A goofy, boyish grin replaced his indignation as Kelså reached up and wiped mirthful tears from his cheek. His heart soared at her touch—at *his mother's* touch. She startled when he stood, wrapped his strong arms around her, and lifted her off the ground, then held her close until the tears subsided.

Kelså reluctantly stepped back and captured Declan's eyes with her own. "No more of that 'I don't have a Gift' nonsense. You, Declan Rea, *are* a gift. Beyond any magic or power this world offers, *you* are my greatest gift."

Declan had never known the selfless, omnipotent power of a mother's love until that moment. He couldn't speak. He could barely stop the tears that clouded his vision again.

"You know, Some gifts can be returned, Kelså. This one keeps leaking!" Órla swiveled her head between Declan and his mother.

Kelså's barked out laughter as she reached to pick up the tiny owl. "Oh, no, little Daughter, this gift is perfect. He *will* save us all."

Declan sobered. "You say that with such confidence, but I don't even know how to use magic."

"Declan, everyone you know has one, maybe two abilities that showed up when they were young, and they learned how to use them mostly through trial and error. If the error wasn't fatal, they grew in their knowledge and skill. Some Gifts require training, but magic has a way of imprinting instructions on our brains, making it easier to comprehend. For most people, learning to master, or at least become competent in one Gift isn't terribly challenging.

"But you're different. I don't know all your magical abilities, but I suspect you'll be able to master many Gifts within each of the pillars. You will have to learn different ways of shaping and wielding your Light. Even your basic understanding of your own essence and how magic entwines itself will differ from anyone you've ever known. I know it's overwhelming, but I'm here to help you, to guide you."

Declan struggled through a cavernous yawn. He covered his mouth quickly, and his gaping eyes apologized for the weary slight.

"You've traveled a long way up the mountain, faced the Keeper's tests, and come to the Well to face your future. That's probably enough for one afternoon." She placed a hand on his arm. "Let me show you to your room. Are you hungry? Would you like anything before getting some rest?"

On cue, Declan's stomach roared. "I guess I am a little hungry."

"Alright, bring Órla and follow me. While you're getting settled in, I'll conjure up something to eat."

"Uhh . . . like . . . literally conjure up food?" He gawked.

She snorted. "Yes, like literally, with my all-powerful boiling pot and frying pan. Now, come on."

Declan watched Kelså turn and walk to the far side of the cave, opposite the entrance, where there was nothing but a solid wall of crystalline lattice. She didn't slow; she simply walked to the wall and placed a hand on one of the crystals, triggering an opening to shimmer before her.

"Coming?"

Declan woke to the thumping of Órla feet on his chest. When he reached up to wipe his bleary eyes, she let out an excited hoot.

"Finally! I thought you were going to sleep forever."

He leaned up onto his elbows. "No fear of that with you around."

"I know! I'm super helpful like that, right?"

"Yeah, *super*." He yawned and gave her head a scratch before standing and stretching his back.

He scanned the room, barely able to remember following Kelså through the winding maze of tunnels connecting the Well's cavern to his mother's living area. Unlike the corridors leading from the mountain's entrance to the Well, the walls here were smooth, more what he'd expect in some ritzy mansion in Saltstone than in a cave. He grazed his fingers across the stone and wondered at the combination of crystal lattice and granite. At his touch, filaments glowed faintly. The longer his fingers remained, the brighter they became, giving the room a pleasant, multi-hued light.

"So, Declan, I don't know how to tell you this, but you stink. Your mother asked me to . . . um . . . *gently* urge you to bathe and change into the clothes over there. She'll figure something out with your filthy forest garb." Órla covered her beak with a wing as if to hide from his stench.

He padded over to the table that sat opposite the bed and was surprised to find a wash basin filled with steaming water, soap, a stack of towels, and a neatly folded set of clothing, complete with leather shoes.

He soaked a wash cloth and pressed it against his face. How long had it been since he'd had a proper bath, or even washed his face? It felt amazing. He lathered up and watched the basin's water turn an unsettling murky brown.

"You really are disgusting. Don't you ever clean your feathers?" Órla squawked from across the room.

He smiled. "I'm doing it now, little one. Give me a couple of minutes, and we'll get something to eat. I'm starving."

He finished bathing and donned the black trousers and sky-blue shirt his mother had laid out, and was surprised to find an intricate silver pin attached to the shirt etched in the likeness of an owl taking flight, remarkably similar to the Melucian Rangers' pin on his uniform. He turned and offered Órla a bow.

"To your liking, Your Highness?"

"Finally! I thought you'd *never* address me properly. You may rise, Sir Stinky." She giggled and waved a dramatic wing in the air. "Now, be a good steed and pick me up. I'll show you to your mother. This place can be confusing at first."

"Hmm. If I didn't know better, I'd think you'd gotten a little heavier overnight." Declan stared down at Órla in his palm.

"You should never comment on a lady's weight, Declan. *Everybody* knows that!"

He chuckled and shook his head, then opened the door to find his mother standing there, knuckles poised to knock.

"Ready to hit me already?"

"Give her time. It shouldn't take long." Órla flapped.

"Very funny, you two. I came to see if you were up and hungry."

"Starving, actually." He looked past her, taking in the passage for the first time, then whistled. "This place keeps getting stranger and more impressive. I was so tired last night that I don't remember really seeing any of this."

Kelså turned to lead him through the tunnel. "These walls were formed thousands of years ago by the Phoenix herself. Her magical flame bore tunnels and caverns, melting stone and crystal to a glassy finish. Her breath infused this mountain and its minerals with magic, hence the light you see glowing through the crystals."

As the tunnel gradually rose, its sides remained smooth like those in his chamber, an intermingling of glowing crystal and ancient stone. The Well's chamber was already near the top of the mountain, making Declan wonder how much further upward they could go. They occasionally passed wooden doors in recessed grottos on the right or left, their rounded tops mirroring the circular nature of the tunnels. Declan drew breath and was surprised to taste a sweetness in the cave's air. In a strange way, it filled him with hope, revitalizing both his body and spirit.

I feel like I'm walking through a dream.

The tunnel ended abruptly at a rough wall, starkly different from the rest they'd just passed. Kelså placed her palm on one of the extruding crystals and was rewarded with the familiar liquid shimmer of an opening.

Through the portal, he could saw peaks of mountains across the island and, in the horizon, the undulating beauty of the ocean. The calls of distant gulls mixed with the whistling of the relentless mountain breeze. As a Ranger, he'd seen mountains from virtually every angle, and he loved the humble beauty of the peaks, but this was different. Tiny hairs on his neck spiked, and a chill trickled down his spine.

Kelså led them through the portal onto a landing. Savory meats, cheeses, and fruits had been carefully set on a table to their right. Declan's favorite wine sat in the center, waiting to Heal with its silky touch.

Declan's eyes widened as he glanced up from the table.

There were two concentric rings of stone pillars at the center of the landing. The outer stones were massive, standing more than twenty hands tall and three paces thick, and were the same glassy-smooth crystal and stone swirl from the cavern. The inner stones rose to Declan's waist and stood at intervals between those of the outer ring. One lonely stone stood in the center.

Declan walked around the stones and peered over the edge of the landing and spotted the path that led to the

Keeper's hut. "I walked up that trail. How could I not see these stones? They're incredible."

Kelså sat at the table and motioned for him to do the same. "If my memory is correct, you are only the sixth, maybe seventh person to *ever* see those stones. The magic of the Phoenix protects this place, and if she doesn't want you to see it, you won't."

Órla hopped onto the table and dragged a piece of meat from the platter. "Too much talking. Not enough eating."

Declan reached down to scratch her head and was rewarded with a peck of her sharp beak.

"Ow. What was that for?"

"I'm having a special moment over here." A stringy piece of the meat dangled from her maw.

Declan glanced up to find Kelså covering her mouth, eyes twinkling. He ignored her humor and dove into the table's fare. When his mother filled his glass with the magical wine, he stopped to savor the first sip, holding it in his mouth and inhaling the exotic aroma.

Peace.

That's what he felt in that moment.

He realized it was also what he'd felt in the caverns but hadn't comprehended it at the time.

Simple, blissful peace.

He let out a long sigh before attacking his meal.

Órla finished her meat, preened for a moment, then launched herself into the air and flew to rest on the stone pillar at the center of the ring.

"When did you learn to fly, little one?" Declan then turned to Kelså, his eyes once again wide. "She was just a few weeks old when I found her. I can't believe she's flying already."

"Time moves differently here, and she is part of this place. She will grow strong quickly. I expect she will be fully-grown by the time you leave." Kelså set her glass down and paused a moment, then spoke. "Declan, time will be different for you as well—in a good way, I hope. There is so much you have to learn. If I had to train you anywhere else in the world, the winter months would pass in a blink, and you wouldn't have acquired the skill to defeat the enemy. You've seen how long it can take someone to master a single Gift. Imagine trying to master two or three—or more.

"While you are here, days will pass and feel normal to you, but beyond this cavern, they will nearly cease to advance. Many months will pass here before a single week ends in Melucia."

Declan watched Órla preen on the pillar. "Will I age like she does? When I leave, will I be years or decades older?"

Kelså reached across the table and took his hand. "Son, look at me. How old do you think I am?"

He smirked. "Someone just scolded me for talking about a lady's weight. I think I'll stay away from the age question."

"About time you started listening to me!" Órla squawked.

Kelså grinned affectionately at the little owl. "I've lived on this mountain for nearly a thousand years and look the same as when I first arrived. There may be a new line on my forehead, but that's definitely another thing on the list you *never* mention to a lady." She cocked a playful, warning brow.

"When you leave here, those in the world will see you as you were before you came to the mountain. The temporal magic is so powerful it would take many centuries of 'mountain time' for them to notice even a slight difference."

Declan's shoulders relaxed a bit, but tension remained in his eyes, and his hand tangled in his hair. "Temporal magic, Gifts that aren't Gifts, me being . . . something. It's a lot to take in. Where do we even start?"

"We start in the same place any student would, with knowledge and study. Many believe magic is purely instinctually or emotionally driven, but that's not wholly accurate. Instinct and emotion play a role, but without knowledge, a Mage's potential is limited."

The baffled look on Declan's face almost made Kelså laugh. "All those years with Atikus and the Guild, and they never taught you *any* of this?"

"Not really. When I was little, they tried to teach me magical theory, but as the years passed, and a Gift failed to emerge, they decided my time was better spent studying more mundane topics. I was glad they stopped trying to teach me all the things I couldn't do. It was more frustrating than anything."

She pursed her lips. "Alright. Let me explain it a different way. You've been treated by a Healer, haven't you?"

"Of course. Never for anything serious, just a few deep cuts from sparring."

"That's actually a good example. Almost anyone with the Healing Gift could handle minor cuts like that, but let's say you broke a bone—or worse, had internal damage. A basic Healer who had never studied anatomy wouldn't be able to help you. A Healer has to visualize what they are Healing. If they had never seen a liver before, they couldn't visualize one accurately, and therefore, couldn't heal one. That's why Healers spend many years studying physical structures, such as human anatomy, before ever attempting to Heal anyone with more than a minor scrape. The basic knowledge of *intent*—what they want magic to accomplish—involves a lot more than hope for a certain result."

"I guess that makes sense." Declan's attention strayed to Órla. Her eyes were closed and her beak drooped.

Kelså waved a hand, making a ball of fire flare and explode. Declan nearly fell out of his chair.

"Son, you're going to have to *concentrate* to make this work. Healing is the most complicated of all the Gifts, so don't let that one scare you. I'm just using it as an example so you understand that knowledge is critical to expanding your power. As we get into the four pillars, I'll give you material to study before we start with practical application."

Órla, now wide awake thanks to Kelså's fire show, flapped back onto the table in front of Declan. "You've got this, Declan. Just remember, you're a lot smarter than you look."

Kelså barked a laugh that startled both Declan and Órla. "We'll skip the lecture on staying humble. I think she's got *that* well covered."

"Absolutely no worries there." His eye roll landed on the proud little owl who puffed out her chest.

"Alright, you two," Kelså took a deep breath. "I don't want you to think this will be all studying and no fun. Let's start with an exercise to help you find your Light. Everyone who can wield magic, whether one Gift or many, possesses this well of power within themselves. The first step in taking any action is grasping that Light, but you must learn to find it instinctively before you can shape it into action.

"Close your eyes and place one palm on the center of your chest, then focus on the pressure of your hand against your chest. Take a deep breath and continue focusing on that pressure. Feel ripples of sensation spreading out from your hand, but focus on its center, on your palm.

"Now, what do you see?"

Declan squeezed his eyes tighter, concentrating on his palm. "I don't see anything."

Kelså pursed her lips. "Keep your eyes closed. Keep concentrating on your palm."

She muttered a few words he didn't understand. Her index finger glowed, and she touched it to the back of his hand. Immediately, the glow traveled from her finger to his palm, then inward to his chest.

"Whoa! What was that?" His eyes flew open, and he started to lower his hand.

"Eyes shut! And don't move your hand. Now, what do you see?"

When he shut his eyes this time, his mind drifted to a dark space deep within himself. The sensation of being *within* was disconcerting, but also fascinating. The sound of his heart beating drummed in his ears, and he thought he could hear rivers of blood coursing through his veins and arteries.

"This is incredible. I can hear my own blood flowing!"

A pinprick of light twinkled faintly in the distance.

"I think I see something. It looks like a tiny dot of white . . . something."

"That's it. Keep concentrating but try to relax. Imagine yourself walking toward that dot. Getting closer. Can you see it getting bigger?" Her voice was deep and hypnotic.

"Yes. It's getting bigger."

"Breathe. *Slowly*. Take long, slow breaths and hold them before you exhale. Stay calm, focus, and walk forward," she whispered.

"It's growing so bright. It looks like a sun, pulsing, spitting flames in every direction. It looks . . . alive."

He could *hear* her smile. "It *is* alive. Keep walking. Tell me when you think you're close enough to touch it."

A heartbeat passed in silence. "I'm standing in front of it. It's . . . massive—and pure, bright white, but I can't feel any heat from it."

"It's not that kind of fire. Now, stay focused. Take your hand—the one that isn't on your chest—and reach out in front of you.—and do the same thing in your mind. Put your hand against the side of the flame and tell me what you feel."

"It's—*Spirits!* I don't even know how to describe it. It tingles and soothes at the same time. It feels like . . .

like tension in a bowstring pulled taut, not like the string itself, but the tension begging to be released. It *wants* me to release it."

Declan lost his concentration and his eyes flew open. Sweat fell from his brow.

Kelså took his hand again. "You just touched your magic, your Light. Now you need to learn to find it without my help. The stone circles over there create a focal point for the Well's power. Think of it like a magnifying glass for a Mage's work that should make your exercises a little easier. Go sit in the center next to the central pillar, and spend the afternoon finding your Light, then walking away from it. Don't get frustrated when it doesn't come right away. For now, don't touch it unless I'm here with you. I'll be back in a few hours to check on your progress."

She stood and placed a hand on his shoulder. "I really am proud of you, Declan."

"Thanks . . . mother."

His voice broke.

It felt so strange to call someone *that* word, but his heart filled at its sound, and Kelså's heavenly smile sent warmth through his body. He'd been wandering in the woods, lost, for so many years; and, somehow, on this faraway mountain on an island in the middle of nowhere, everything felt right.

He was at peace.

He was home.

At that thought, a spike of guilt pierced his idyllic moment. Throughout his childhood, he'd never been one to *deserve* parents or magic or . . . anything. He'd been a distant second to his older brother, and rightly so. Keelan was stronger, smarter, more committed to whatever he did, and Declan worshiped him. Doubt and shame clung to him, desperate to steal his moment of joy. He sat and put his elbows on the table, head in his hands.

"Umm, Declan, the Circle is over there." He looked up to see Órla pointing with a wing toward the stones.

"Sorry, little one. Just fighting old battles."

Órla's voice became deep and soothing, yet powerful. It filled the plateau and echoed off the mountainside. Declan bolted to his feet and took a step back from the table.

"Declan, you aren't who you've always believed. You are *so* much more. Accept it and walk into the Light. Become who Atikus—*and Keelan*—always knew you could be, who you are. Take your place in the Circle and claim your birthright, *Son of Magic*."

He stared at his little friend in awe. She shook her head, as if shaking off the persona that had taken control, then blinked up at him. "Well, move it, silly. Seems rude to keep magic waiting."

She took flight, landed on the central pillar, and stared back at him. He shook his head and smiled, then let his heart choose to take the first step, then another. Before he knew it, he was fully encircled and standing before Órla on her perch.

He reached down and gently stroked her head. "You're pretty amazing, Órla. I'm so lucky to have found you. Thank you."

"You *were* pretty lucky that day, but for the record, I found you. You were completely lost. So, you're welcome."

Declan shook his head—again—and laughed at how many times he'd done that lately.

He sat on the ground, crossed his legs, and closed his eyes. It felt strange, but he knew how important the proper mindset was from his training with sword forms and archery techniques. It always felt a little odd, stepping through the motions without a sword in your hands, but he knew shadowing was one of the best ways to create muscle memory.

It still felt weird.

Sounds of the forest and ocean filled his mind and put him at peace. He tried to focus with his eyes closed, to look inward, to see anything other than daydreams associated with the sounds around him. Nothing worked. Invariably, his mind wandered to the wind tickling his face, or the rustling of leaves. Thirty minutes passed before, frustrated, he opened his eyes and shook his head to find Órla staring down at him.

"I can hear your mind racing from over here. Until you learn to clear the clutter, you'll never see your Light."

He let out a deep sigh. "I'm trying. There's just so much going on—the wind, the trees, the ocean, the gulls. How am I ever supposed to concentrate through it all?

"Does your mind race when you shoot a bow?"

"Well, no. I have to shut everything out and focus on the target and my own breathing."

She cocked her head. "So do that, dummy."

He laughed. "You're a lot smarter than you look, little one."

"Oh, nice try. Everyone knows owls are majestic and wise. I look *incredibly* intelligent, which is a lot more than I can say about a certain Ranger I know. Now focus!"

Another laugh escaped. "Yes, dear."

The sun was beginning to set, and a kaleidoscope of shifting shades painted the island as the last of day's light fled behind the horizon.

Declan sat and crossed his legs again. He imagined himself standing and looking down the guard of his bow to a target in the distance. He felt the cold wood of the bow against his cheek, the texture of the string against his fingers, the light grip of the arrow. He took a few deep breaths and slowed his heart. In his mind, he pulled the bowstring until its tension matched his own strength, and he held. He breathed deeply again, letting out the exhale as slowly as possible.

Everything calmed. Everything stilled.

What was first a target in the distance transformed into a flicker. It swirled and flared, growing as he forced himself to walk toward it in his mind. He imagined setting his bow on the ground while keeping his eyes on the glowing ball. Another step closer. Then another. He remembered to breathe again, and the light flared brightly. He smiled inwardly at his success, and the Light flared again, as if buoyed by his joy. He laughed, and it blazed before him.

He stepped close enough to touch the flames with an outstretched hand and felt the Light coursing through him, yearning for his embrace. The power demanded to be shaped. It begged to be released—to be released *by him*.

In that moment, he knew for the first time that this was *his* Light.

His power.

As he reached out to touch the flame, a firm hand clamped on his shoulder, snapping his concentration.

The Light winked out.

Annoyed, he opened his eyes and turned to see his mother standing beside him.

"I was so close!"

She beamed. "I know, but you were about to do something you're not ready for, not without me here to guide you. You've made remarkable progress today. Earlier, you were afraid you'd fail; now you're so eager I'm having to hold you back."

Órla flapped to land on his shoulder. "Nice. Very nice."

"What, no sharp comment? You feeling ok?" He grinned at the owl.

"Success is so rare for you that I wanted to give you your moment. Moment's over."

"You two are something." Kelså laughed and helped Declan stand. "I think that's enough practical work for today. You have a few things to study later, but dinner's almost ready. Get cleaned up so we can eat before you hit the books."

On the way back to his room, Órla took Declan exploring, showing him what was behind the wooden doors he'd noticed earlier. Kelså lived in a small suite that included a bedroom, a sitting room with a fireplace, and a large bathing room with a massive copper tub.

They found another room contained a replica of the stone circles from the ledge, only smaller. At their center, rather than another pillar, was a seat made entirely of the glowing crystal. Around the base of the seat, symbols he remembered from his days in the Mages' Guild were inlaid in the smooth floor.

Only a few doors down from his room was a library. He thought it looked more like a temple, with ceilings that towered over forty hands and were brilliantly lit with the ever-present crystal lattice. Shelves containing thousands of volumes, many in languages Declan had never seen, covered every wall. As he strolled around the room and ran his fingers over the spines of various tomes, he was surprised to see the gilded titles of a few flare brightly at his touch.

Keelan would love this place, he thought.

When they were younger, he could barely pull Keelan away from his books. To Declan, books always seemed so dry and boring, especially when he could be outside playing or *doing* whatever the book just talked about, but Keelan loved learning. He'd tried to get Declan interested in reading, telling him stories of fantastic places and people. The stories were exciting, and having Keelan make voices was funny, but the idea of sitting all day and staring at paper made Declan want to crawl out of his own skin.

Who could do that?

And this whole adventure with the Keeper, and the Well, and *their mother* . . . Keelan would have loved every minute. He would've loved the challenge of learning magic, especially the book-learning, the part Declan dreaded. Kelså would've had to drag Keelan out of the library to get him to rest each night.

There had been so many strange things happening lately, and all so quickly, that Declan hadn't had time to think about his brother or Atikus much. Now that he was standing still, able to think, he realized how much he missed them.

Keelan had left to join the Guard years ago, and they really hadn't seen each other much since. Then, at sixteen, Declan joined the Rangers and was stationed at the border a hundred leagues from Saltstone. He'd had all the time in the world to think out there in the lonely woods, yet family never really crossed his mind. Why were their images now haunting him? Now that he was so far away, unable to just hop on a horse and visit, why did he wish he could do just that?

"I guess *why* doesn't really matter. I just miss them." The words tumbled out before he realized he was speaking.

"You should tell them that sometime. You've kept yourself apart for too long." Órla's voice snapped him out of the moment.

He smiled wistfully. "You're probably right, but I wouldn't even know where to start. I said so many things to them last time we were together. I hurt them, Órla. I'm not sure they'd even want to be missed by me now."

"Declan, that might be the dumbest thing you've ever said, and you say a lot of really dumb things." She winged her way up to his shoulder. "They love you. They will *always* love you, no matter how stupid you are."

"I think my mother's right. You have the humble thing covered." He reached up and rubbed between her wings, chuckling as her eyes rolled back in pleasure and a *coo-purr* escaped.

Two hours later, the trio sat around (*on*, in Órla's case) the table in Kelså kitchen. Remnants of vegetables and cleaned bones littered their plates. The endless pitcher of wine sat in the center, challenging Declan to find its bottom, as everyone sat in silence, enjoying the peace that only comes following a good meal at the end of a long day.

Kelså broke the silence. "Tell me about your brother. You were both so small when I saw you last."

Declan stared into his wine. "What would you like to know?"

"Everything. What kind of man is he now? What does he look like? I only know the pieces fed to me by the Arch Mage over the years, and that was never very much."

"Well, he's tall, really, really tall, and he started training with the Guardsmen who protect the Guild when we were little, so he's grown muscular. Honestly, he looks like he should be one of those statues you'd see outside a palace —the idyllic warrior with his sword raised, poised to protect everyone from everything. Add his sharp blue-and-gold Guard uniform, and the statue really would be complete." He hadn't meant for bitterness to seep into his voice.

Kelså eyed him. "And he's an investigator?"

"No. He's not an investigator. He's *the* investigator. Early in his career, he solved a series of crimes that had stumped the Guard, and the papers ran with it, hailing him as the greatest investigator of our time. His Gift made it impossible for anyone to hide from his questioning, fueling even more success. He's twenty-six now and already second-in-command of the whole Guard. I don't think there's anything he's ever touched that didn't turn to gold."

Kelså's next question was tentative. "But what's he like? As a person?"

Declan absently ran a hand through his hair and scratched his scalp. "We've spent so little time together over the past few years, I really don't know. I guess we got to know each other a little on the mountain before we split up. He seemed really stern, inside his head a lot, always thinking, but there's a gentleness, a kindness to him, too. He wants things to be perfect all the time and thinks he can protect everyone from everything—or at least he tries to. Now and then, he'd let the old Keelan out, the one with the goofy sense of humor. That never went over so well with the boys in the Academy, but he always made me laugh. He's tough and quiet but commands attention and respect. I don't know. It's hard to explain."

"He sounds like a good man."

Declan refused to meet her gaze, and his voice was a broken whisper when he spoke. "He's the best man I've ever known. I could only hope to be like him one day."

She reached up and cupped his cheek with her hand, then smiled when his eyes finally rose. They searched each other for a long moment, each looking for something different, pleading in their own way.

Kelså finally decided to leave him with his thoughts and pulled her hand back. "You're probably tired. Let's get some rest and start early in the morning."

Chapter Thirteen

Tiana woke.

She'd been in a drug-induced sleep for more than fifteen hours, and it hurt to move. The compartment below the cart where they had her stored gave her enough room to roll over and stretch out, but there were no pads or blankets, and days of bouncing against the hard wood had battered her in places even a Healer wouldn't think could bruise. Thankfully, they had left behind the cold mountain air, replaced by a comfortable, temperate climate.

The drug they gave her kept her knocked out for all but an hour or two each day, and her head swam during those waking hours, still clouded by the powerful liquid. In a strange way, she was thankful for the drugs. They kept her from the uncontrollable fear she felt on that first night of her captivity. She couldn't imagine being lucid and making the long journey trapped in the bottom of a rolling coffin.

She lay on her back and searched for a crack in the boards wide enough to see out. If she craned her neck just right, she caught the bottom of a boot or robe;. She had better luck when rolling onto her right side. The slats that made the side wall were not as tightly fitted, granting her a slim view of the passing landscape. Gone was the smell of pine and steep slopes. Now, all she could smell were fields of grass and wildflowers.

One of the first things a new Healer was taught was to never Heal one's own wounds. The magical theory behind that sacred rule claimed that the Light of a person could not be "folded onto itself." Doing so would create a magical collision that would actually injure the Healer, rather than repair what ailed them. Five days in a bouncing wooden box convinced Tiana to test that theory. She wanted to ease the pain of her bruises, not actually Heal anything, so she placed her palm over her arm and closed her eyes. Her Light sputtered at her call, somehow inhibited by the sleeping drought. She pushed harder, and it brightened enough for her to send a trickle into her aching arm. The bolt that shot up her shoulder was magic's reprimand for breaking the rules, and she cried through star-filled eyes until the drug forced her back into a fitful sleep.

There would be no Healing.

She woke sometime later, and the shock of her failed Healing had somehow cleared her head, giving her time to think—something she wasn't entirely sure was a blessing. She'd replayed her capture a hundred times, blaming herself for walking alone or not fighting harder or a million other things she could've done differently. Her throat clenched as terror took hold, and she relived angry hands grasping and stuffing her into the cart's bed.

Then she drifted to her escape in the mountains. Fear mingled with desperation—and a sliver of hope—as she ran through the woods, stumbling to find protection in the wilderness. She saw the Ranger—Donny, yes, that was his name. His face was fuzzy in her mind, but she could still see his smile. He coaxed her from her hiding place and took her to the safety of his station.

His chivalry had been his undoing.

When sounds of furniture crashing jarred her away, Donny lay bleeding across the room, arrows protruding from his chest, and a look of pain and sadness marring his gentle face.

He'd died for her.

He'd died for nothing.

The bastards who'd killed him had recaptured her and continued their journey as if nothing had ever happened.

Hopelessness and guilt flowed through her, and tears fell freely.

Then she felt guilty for feeling guilty.

Oddly, that made her laugh.

Her father had raised a proud, strong, self-sufficient woman who didn't need to feel sorry for herself. When he'd died, it had been *her* strength that had kept his practice running. *Her* resourcefulness that had convinced the Guilds to grant her a building in the center of town for an infirmary. What was she thinking? Sure, she'd been kidnapped, drugged, and hauled to another country in a wooden box, but she could find a solution. She *had* to find a solution.

Think, Tiana, think!

She gathered her resolve and wiped her eyes. She would figure a way out of this mess.

Then *he* popped into her head. She pressed her hands to her face, rubbing her eyes to focus, but Keelan's brilliant blue eyes still stared back at her. In her mind, he smiled, and she shivered. She could see him walking across the parade grounds of the Guard Complex in his crisp blue uniform, so tall, so strong, so . . . perfect.

C'mon, T. Stop that. He's not here to save you. You're gonna have to do that yourself.

But he was there again, stumbling through her infirmary door with goofy Ridley under his arm. Ridley's visits to her infirmary over the most trivial injuries were comical. A woman knows when she's being flirted with. *Spirits*, a rock could've seen Ridley coming. It was flattering and sweet, and he was *really* cute, but Keelan was something else altogether. He filled a room simply by walking through the doorway, and not just from his massive frame and equally massive muscles. They were ok, if you liked that sort of thing—which she did.

Focus, T! Now's not the time to think about a stupid boy.

And then he'd smile, and the world would tilt. He didn't mean for it to. He wasn't even trying to flirt or impress, and maybe that made it more endearing. What was it about Keelan? He was so serious most of the time. Then, out of nowhere, he'd crack a joke or say something sweet . . . or just smile. He captured her more with that smile than anything the masked men had ever done.

She gave up on concentrating and opened her eyes to peek through the crack at the passing fields. In different circumstances, definitely with different company, this would've been a wonderful adventure. She'd always wanted to travel.

The cart slowed. She could make out a house off the road, surrounded by farmland. A few cows and a large wiry dog wandered in the fenced field nearby. It reminded her of home.

The cart pulled to a halt, and an old man in rough clothes hobbled out of the house, wandering in and out of her sliver of a view. The man in the bull mask with the angry bird beak hopped down to meet him. She couldn't hear what was said, but the farmer motioned around behind the house. A moment later, Bull-bird was back at the reins, and the cart were moving again.

They pulled into a large barn Tiana hadn't seen from the road, and a chill streaked down her spine as they squealed in their grooves and slammed shut. A few minutes passed before the cover to her prison was lifted, and dim light flowed across her face. The figure with the snarling wildcat mask helped her out and steadied her when she wobbled.

"It'll take me a minute to clear my head and get my legs under me. First Class isn't what it used to be." She'd decided to try to charm the beasts since nothing else had worked.

Wildcat didn't speak, but his eyes grinned at her quip.

She looked around the unremarkable building and found it was similar to ones found on every farm in every corner of the world. There were a few stalls for horses and a large pen for smaller animals when winter came. The opposite side was filled with bales of hay, stacked neatly to the bottom of a landing that wrapped around, forming an upper level.

Before she had time to look for exits, Bull-bird walked over holding a sharp knife. She tried to stagger back, but Wildcat held her firmly.

Panic flooded her body.

"Stop squirming." Bull-bird rasped as he sliced through the ropes binding her hands.

She rubbed feeling into the angry marks that scored her wrists. It felt good to be free of her bonds, but she doubted that would last.

Wildcat then led her to a set of rickety stairs and motioned for her to climb. Several thick pallets lay on the floor beside a wooden table and chairs, while brass lanterns with glass faces cast a warm glow. Tiana's stomach grumbled at the smell of seasoned meat that wafted from the table. She couldn't remember the last time she'd eaten a proper meal.

She startled when a frail voice spoke from a darkened corner.

"Please sit, Mistress, and I'll take care of those wounds."

The skeletal form of an ancient woman shuffled into the light. Back bent, she wore the brown robe of the Children but no mask. Several strands of milky hair fell into her eyes, and she swatted them back in annoyance.

"Usually keep this mess in a bun, but didn't expect ya 'til the morning. Sorry for lookin' such a mess, Mistress." She offered a rusty curtsey.

Tiana was baffled. The woman reminded her of a kindly old grandmother but wore the robes of her captors. Her mind told her to be wary, but her heart had run out of fear.

She cocked her head at the old crone. "Why do you keep calling me Mistress?"

Wildcat stepped between them and glared at the old woman. He shook his head once and stepped back to the railing to observe.

"Sorry, Mistress. That's not for me to answer. Come, let me look at ya. Ya must be starvin'. I scraped together some chicken and veggies. Sorry, there's nothin' more tonight."

Tiana sat where the old woman motioned and scanned the table. Her stomach wasn't shy and made its thoughts known again.

The woman shuffled around and knelt beside Tiana, wincing as her aged knees reached the floor. She shook her head. "Used to run for days. Now kneeling feels like a trip over a mountain. Don't get old, Mistress, whatever ya do."

Tiana returned a tight smile but said nothing. She wanted to like the woman, but how could she like anyone who helped keep her captive? She remembered stories from her training where kidnap victims would develop feelings for their captors. There were no magical treatments for mental conditions, but she'd learned to spot the signs so a vicar could be called to help. Now, *she* was feeling affection for the woman helping her abductors.

Don't be stupid, T. Stay on guard.

"I'm Bet. Just sit still, and I'll try to help ya feel a little better."

Bet took Tiana's wrists one at a time and placed a palm over her rope burns. The familiar Healer's glow flared from Bet's palms, and in seconds, the angry marks had vanished. Without a word, Bet placed her hands on the sides of Tiana's face and Healed her clouded mind and bruised body. She sat back and lowered her head submissively, waiting for a response.

Tiana rolled her neck, and probed the clarity in her mind. It felt wonderful to think and move without everything hurting. She braced herself with a hand on Bet's shoulder and stood, putting tentative weight on her legs.

"Feel alright?" Bet struggled to her feet, gripping Tiana's arms for balance.

"Much better. Thank you."

Bet turned toward the stairs, but Tiana reached out. "Wait. Please let me return the favor."

Bet quirked her brow but sat and watched as Tiana placed her palms above her withered knees. The brilliant Light that flared from Tiana's palms startled the old woman. It was considerably brighter than Bet's own Healing Light.

As she completed the Healing, Tiana whispered urgently, "Why are you helping them? Please . . . "

Bet's eyes darted to Wildcat and back. She shook her head quickly, and fear flashed in her eyes. Tiana thought she saw a tear forming and decided not to press.

"I can't return what age has stolen, but there was some arthritic damage I could Heal. Try standing now."

Bet accepted Tiana's hand and slowly rose to her feet. A smile burst from her lips as she bent and straightened her knees. "There's no pain when I bend, Mistress. Thank you. You're such a blessing!"

Bet squeezed the breath out of Tiana with a surprisingly strong hug before scampering down the stairs. Tiana smiled as she disappeared from view. There was nothing in the world like Healing to lift her spirits.

She noticed Wildcat staring at her from the railing and her heart sank again. He pointed to the food and made an eating gesture, then crossed his arms. She was a bite from finishing her meal when Bull-bird's head popped up from the stairs. He strode to the table and sat on the opposite side.

"When you've finished eating, change into the clothes on the cot." He pointed to a wooden cot in the corner she hadn't noticed before. Sitting on a colorful, fluffy quilt were a neatly folded pair of brown trousers and a light-blue shirt.

Bull-bird cocked his head. "Do you not like them? I was told blue comforts you."

The comment was so absurd that she laughed, spitting a little of her chicken onto the table. "A Healer's smock is blue. I suppose if that's what you mean, then yes, I like it just fine."

He nodded once, the matter settled. "Wear those tomorrow. Finish eating and get some sleep."

Before retreating to his pallet across the landing, he placed a vial of familiar liquid on the table and motioned for her to drink. By the time she'd finished her chicken and downed the potion, she could hear light snoring from behind his mask.

The drug wore off in the middle of the night.

Tiana scanned the loft with foggy eyes, trying to process where she was and how she'd gotten there. Reality was slow to return but felt like a punch to her gut when it did. She could see Wildcat and Bull-bird stretched out on pallets in front of the stairs that led down to the barn's floor. As she sat up slowly, she began to fear the spinning of her head as much as her captors.

No one stirred.

The men hadn't retied her wrists or ankles, so she decided to try standing. Her head swam again, and she nearly toppled over, bracing herself on the corner of her cot. She gritted her teeth and wobbled to the table, looking more like a newborn deer than a world-class Healer. They hadn't cleared the table, so she ate the few remaining scraps and found herself more thankful for the half-full pitcher of water than the hours-old chicken.

Still, no one stirred.

The water created an entirely different problem as her bladder pressed against places it wasn't welcome. There hadn't been cause to find a place for relief before now, so she had no idea where to even look.

It's a barn. Where would a horse pee?

She smiled at her ability to maintain some sense of humor in the middle of a kidnapping, but the same amusement that lifted her spirit also gave urgency to her bladder's call for relief.

She took a few careful steps toward the stairs, and the old boards under her feet groaned. She froze, waiting to see which of the men would wake. Fear mingled with her need to pee, and she had to resist the urge to dance the feeling away. The men hadn't been rough with her. In fact, other than tying her up and forcing her to ride in a rolling coffin, they had been almost respectful.

What are you thinking, T? They kidnapped you and are taking you who knows where to do who knows what?

She decided her fear was healthy and stoked its embers.

She took another cautious step, then another.

She stood directly beside Wildcat, only a few feet from the stairs. She could hear his slow, rhythmic breathing and was confident he remained asleep. She kept her eyes on him and took another step. This time, the blasted board screamed, and both men bolted into upright.

Wildcat cocked his head. "What are you doing, Mistress?"

Tiana trembled and did a childish pee-pee-dance. "I have to go. Please."

He stood and motioned for Bull-bird to go back to sleep, then led Tiana down the stairs and into a stall strewn with hay. The smell of horse dung wafted throughout, and she stepped cautiously.

"Pee here." Wildcat closed the stall gate and walked across to the other side, turning away to give her privacy.

When she called out, "I'm done," he walked back over and opened the gate.

An impulse struck and she grabbed his wrist, allowing the flow of Healing magic to burst from her palm. An expert Healer like Tiana could feel inside a person's body with her magic. It wasn't exactly like seeing what's in there, more like fumbling in a dark room with her hands. If she knew the room well enough, though, she could navigate it.

What happened next shocked her.

Her magic poured into Wildcat, but there was no dark room. No fumbling. No feeling. In fact, her magic found nothing but an empty shell. Then something flashed, and her magic bounced back like a ball rebounding against a wall, the shock knocking her off her feet. When the stars cleared, Wildcat was looming over her. He had barely budged.

"Thank you for trying, Mistress. As you could see, there's nothing to Heal." He stared that awful, blank, *amused* stare. "Time to go back to bed. Morning will be here soon."

Chapter Fourteen

The weeks that followed crawled as Kelså piled books in Declan's lap and spent hours forcing him to find his Light without actually touching it or doing anything useful. He was used to being active and roaming the wilderness all day, and sitting at a table, reading or focusing inward, was making him stir crazy.

Órla continued to surprise him, growing quickly and spending much of her time flying throughout the surrounding peaks. She had transformed from a relative hatchling to the human equivalent of a teenager in only a few weeks.

Declan sat in the stone circle, legs crossed and eyes closed. He could summon and dismiss his Light quickly now. He was about to release his concentration when Kelså's voice whispered his mind.

"Reach your hand into your Light. Touch it, but do nothing. Think nothing."

A thrill ran through him.

In his mind's eye, his hand reached toward the blinding ball and pierced its outer shell. Warmth crawled throughout his body, but it was more than warmth. It was a pulsing heat that flared each time his heart beat.

"It is *connected,"* he heard in his mind. *"You* are *magic, Declan. It is part of you, not something distant that you touch. Feel it course through your veins, pulsing in time with your heart. Breathe it in. Infuse it with your thoughts and desires. Become one with the Light of your magic."*

He had no idea how to do any of that—or what most of it even meant. How do you become one with a ball of glowing goo?

He took a mental step forward and allowed his Light to surround his body. He breathed deeply, as his mother had instructed, and was amazed he actually inhaled the *feeling* of power, not just its white plumes. The tiny hairs on his arms and neck snapped to attention, and an army of ants marched across his skin as intoxicating, majestic power filled him, and his senses expanded beyond human limits. With his eyes closed, he could hear the wind whipping across the neighboring peak. He heard the flapping of Órla's tiny wings and knew instinctively where she was, leagues away. His mind raced, and he heard the owl's thoughts and *felt* her joy as she caught a gust and was buffeted higher.

He opened his eyes and nearly lost his balance. He no longer saw through his own eyes; rather, he soared over trees and snow-covered boulders. Órla laughed in his mind, and her exhilaration filled him. She knew he was there in her thoughts—one with her—and she rejoiced at their union.

As he watched in awe, a voice echoed in the distance. He thought it was someone on the mountain below before realizing Kelså was calling out beside him.

"Declan, come back to me. Release the Light now," she commanded.

He struggled to step back as magic's grip resisted. He closed his eyes and released Órla's sight, focusing on his ball of white flame. A sense of emptiness flooded through him as he stepped out of its aura, and the last of the fiery breath fled his mouth and nose.

He blinked a few times and staggered.

"Easy. Sit on the ground for a minute." She helped him lean against the central stone pillar.

"*Spirits!* It feels like I just fell off the mountain rather than flew over one."

She smiled knowingly. "I would say it gets easier, but it doesn't. You get used to it, and I can teach you how to recover more quickly, but magic always exacts a toll for its use."

Declan looked up with bleary eyes. "I've never seen Gifted hit like this."

"You wouldn't. Magic works differently for them because they're only accessing a tiny portion of what's possible. When we altered the flow to limit each individual's access, we also limited the toll it would take. For those with only one or two talents, they might feel winded, tired, or hungry after using their Gift, but that's about it.

"You and I access the Well itself every time we touch our Light. It's like others are walking in a light rain, but you and I wrap our arms around a tornado."

"I guess that makes sense. My head sure feels like I went through a storm." He rubbed his temples. "But while I was in the center of the storm, it was the most incredible thing I've ever experienced. The raw power and . . . I don't know . . . passion? It still makes my skin crawl."

She turned and retrieved the pitcher of wine and a glass from the table. "Drink this. It'll help restore your strength."

He greedily guzzled the entire glass, realizing his mistake a moment too late. The wine sent a shock wave through him, and he dropped the glass.

"Easy now. You have residual magic flowing through you. Drinking this wine too quickly will make it react as though fighting an infection in your body."

"*Now* you tell me." He refilled his cup and sipped carefully, and the clouds in his head began to part.

Kelså chuckled, squeezed his arm affectionately, then returned with the pitcher to sit at the table. Órla floated down, circled the stones, and landed lightly on the table.

"Declan! I felt you in my head. Wasn't that incredible?" She scampered excitedly around the table.

"It was . . . *something*. Next time, can you please leave my head on my shoulders when we're done?" There was a smile in his voice as he turned in her direction. "Come here, little one. For some reason, I need to scratch your head."

"Spa time!" She darted from the table into Declan's lap. "Ooh! I can feel the magic oozing through your fingers. That feels tingly. You've gotta get drunk on magic more often."

Kelså chuckled again. "That's your bond. Declan, what you just experienced expanded the link between you and Órla. Magic flows freely between the two of you. Tomorrow, I'd like to experiment a little, see what you can do together."

"Wait. You don't know already?"

"I know more about magic than anyone alive, with the possible exception of the Arch Mage or Atikus, but there hasn't been another Mage with your connection, your abilities, in over a thousand years. If you lived another thousand years, you might never fully discover everything you can do with magic. This will be the adventure of many lifetimes."

"Okay." He thought a moment. "We know I can talk to animals, and they can talk back, and that I can See through Órla's eyes."

"Your bond with Órla is unique. It may not mean you can communicate with other wildlife. We'll have to test that." Kelså stood. "One step at a time, though. What you experienced today was the beginning of your understanding of magic and its power—*and its limits* as defined by the human body and mind. Tomorrow, we'll start with the Elemental pillar. That is the easiest to conceptualize and should give you plenty of practice touching and shaping your Light."

She put a hand on his shoulder. "Declan, it's about to get a lot harder. I know you've been bored and anxious, but as that boredom is ends, the risks will rise exponentially. When you were in the middle of your 'storm,' as you called it, I could sense the measure of your power, how much magic is at your call. My own Light is a candle next to your sun."

"You're kidding, right? I mean, you're *the Keeper* and one of the most powerful Mages alive."

Kelså took his hand and placed it on her chest. She focused, and a glow flared from beneath his palm.

"Look inside. See my Light," she said.

Declan cocked his head, confused, then closed his eyes and did as instructed. A moment later, he could see the flicker of flame before him. It was as bright as the one he'd seen within himself, but grew no larger than his palm as he approached. His own Light had far eclipsed his eighteen-hand frame and had grown well beyond that as he'd watched it.

"Now do you see? Your potential is beyond anyone since Irina, or anyone for millennia before her." Kelså's voice echoed through his head. *"That is why we* must *take care in your training. One mistake with such raw, untamed power could inflict immense destruction and pain—and not just on others, but on yourself as well."*

Kelså released her Light, and Declan snapped back to himself.

"Let's eat and get some rest. You can read more on the Elemental powers tonight if you can't sleep. I promise, that book will knock you right out." She chuckled and patted his arm again.

The next morning, Declan met Kelså and Órla outside by the stone circles. A light breakfast of fruit, cheese, and nuts lay spread across the table.

After they finished the meal, Kelså stood and took one of the bowls from the table, filled it with water, and set it on the stone circles' center pillar. Declan's eyes grew wide as her magic flared and a perfectly round ball of water rose above the bowl and hovered in place.

She turned and smiled at his amazed expression. "Today is all about Elemental magic. I think you'll enjoy this."

"Finally! I get to actually *do* something with magic." He hopped up from the table and raced to her side.

Órla settled onto the table and began cleaning herself but kept an eye on the lesson.

Declan watched the ball fall and splash into the bowl as Kelså released her magic. "You were raised reciting the four pillars: Elemental, Physical, Mental, and Natural. Within each lies many abilities that share commonality in their type, but produce very different effects. I'm going to introduce you to calling and shaping your Light in each of the four pillars, but there's no way to know how many abilities within each you will master—or even be able to use at all. Having a basic understanding of how each area responds to your Light will allow you to identify and control additional abilities as they surface."

Declan ran a hand through his hair. "So, you're saying that abilities will just show up? I'll just accidentally figure some of this out?"

She laughed. "I wouldn't put it that way, but it's not completely wrong. Emotion, need, and environment often call abilities to the surface.

"Let's try this another way. Forget magic for a moment. When I was a little girl, I remember my father telling me about a neighbor whose leg became trapped under his cart while he was fixing a wheel. No matter what he did, the weight of the cart was too great for him to escape. Worse, it was slipping off the road, threatening to crush him. His scrawny, fourteen-year-old son raced to his rescue. Somehow that child was able to lift the cart just enough for his father to roll away. Later that night, it took four men and an ox to pull the cart from the ditch."

"Was the boy a Physical with some kind of enhanced strength?"

"No. The boy never manifested *any* magic. His fear and panic—*his need*—drove him to do the impossible. No one will ever truly understand what happened that day, but magical abilities can be like that, even for Gifted with only one ability. The *need* in a single moment can drive power to the surface, though it once lay hidden or dormant.

"For you, this will be especially true. Your relationship to magic presents a limitless number of possibilities, most of which you will only learn when pushed or threatened. I wish I could arm you with training on every skill you'll manifest, but I can't. The best I can do is help you learn control and familiarity within magic's rules, and prepare you to recognize when new abilities surface."

"How many abilities do you have?" he asked.

"I only have four, although 'only four' is more than anyone alive today, except you. The Keeper is granted one within each pillar, not just to help protect the Well, but for *this* moment—the moment when *Magic's Heir* requires guidance."

Childlike wonder lit Declan's face. "Magic's Heir?"

Kelså grinned and nodded. "Enough theory. You wanted some action, so here we go. There are two ways to use Elemental magic. Either you shape something that already exists, or you call an element into being. We'll start with shaping something that already exists because it's much easier. I'll explain why in a minute.

"Water is the only element I can manipulate, but the basic principles should also work for fire, earth, and air. Different elements may be more challenging to mold than others, so you'll need to practice to master each.

"Alright. Your goal is to make the water ball you saw me craft earlier. Close your eyes, and I'll walk you through it."

Declan closed his eyes and, for no apparent reason, broadened his stance and squatted as if expecting a fight.

Kelså's chuckle echoed against the mountainside. "You're calling on magic, not wrestling a bear. Relax. Now, find your Light and approach it with both hands stretched outward, but don't touch it."

She watched as Declan mimicked her instructions with his arms and hands.

"Okay. I'm there."

"I want you to use your hands to 'shape' the Light, like it's a ball of clay. Just touch the outer edges with the lightest possible pressure. Don't let your hands sink into it. When it squirms out one side, gently guide it back into the shape."

His hands moved in stiff motions, and she could tell he was struggling to maintain a consistent shape. "Slowly. Smooth motions. Treat it gently, like you're stroking Órla's feathers."

His motions smoothed as his hands slowed.

"Excellent. Now, here's the hard part. You have to see both the water in the bowl *and* your Light at the same time. If you release one without the other, the water will drop or your magic will dissipate."

"How do I see them both? Beside each other?"

"No, overlay the image of the water. Not the bowl, just the water."

Declan's brow furrowed as he struggled. "I think I've got it."

"OK. Now imagine the ball of Light becoming the water. Merge the two images. It may look like the water is absorbed by the Light, but you should be able to see it there, as well as the flame."

Kelså smiled as the water in the bowl began to ripple and rise in an unsteady stream, forming into something not quite ball-shaped, more of a blob.

"Good. Shape it. Remember to use your hands to keep the shape."

Declan strained with concentration. Beads of sweat rolled down his face and tickled his cheek. Without thinking, he reached up to wipe it off. The water fell into the bowl and splashed loudly.

"I had it!" He opened his eyes and slumped in frustration.

"You did well, especially for your first time. Practice what we just did. When you think you have control, open your eyes and try to maintain the ball, but don't get frustrated. Think of it like sword forms. When you tried them the first time, they were stiff, almost mechanical, right? Just remembering the sequence and steps was hard, but with practice, they became instinct, and now you can execute them without even thinking. As you practiced and gained confidence, the rough edges smoothed, and you became one with your weapon. Learning magic is exactly the same. You'll get there, but it'll take practice."

Declan sat on the ground and leaned against a stone. He hadn't really moved during the exercise, but his breath was heavy, and sweat still dribbled down his face. Órla stirred and flew to the bowl, lapping up some of its water before ducking her head under, then shaking herself.

"Thanks for getting my bath ready, D," she said between splashes.

His tension released. "Anything for you, Princess."

"Again, with my title. You're getting really well trained, little Mage."

"You two!" Kelså snickered. "Enough rest. Let's switch to 'creating' water, rather than shaping what's in front of you. Before you get too excited, that's a terrible way to describe Calling an element. We can't actually create anything; rather, we call what is around us and assemble it for a purpose."

Declan's excited expression was replaced by a blank stare.

"I think fire might be easier to understand. An experienced Elemental with the ability to Call fire can hold out a palm, and *poof*! Fire appears floating above it. To the untrained eye, it might appear the Mage Called fire out of nothing, when in reality, he pulled warmth from the surrounding air and assembled it into the ball of flame."

"I guess that makes sense, but how would I even visualize that?"

"Perfect question. You're getting conceptualization, which is the most important piece of the puzzle."

He cut her off before she could continue. "But what if the Mage is on a mountain, in the snow? There's no heat up there."

"There's always heat around somewhere. It may just be highly dispersed or only exist in minuscule quantities. In your example, it would take longer, and the ball would be smaller or less powerful, but it would work. An inexperienced Mage might fail to create anything useful, but a powerful one could. In extreme situations, you could Call the heat from your own body to create flame, but that's dangerous and could kill you if you aren't skilled enough to stop in time."

He bolted upright, suddenly excited again. "If I can call heat from my own body, what about drawing heat from living things, like trees or animals? They're everywhere, and I'd never run out."

She frowned, and her voice became stern. "Drawing heat, moisture, or air from another living being is possible but would likely kill them. Imagine having the breath drawn from your lungs, being unable to stop it while you gasped and suffocated. Empress Irina used her power to do exactly that on the battlefield, drawing air and water from her foes, leaving shriveled corpses for leagues in her wake.

"Declan, those are the first steps down the path of dark magics that Guild law has prohibited since its founding. Sometimes a Mage must defend, but to use one's magic to harm another without cause is considered a violation of the Phoenix's most sacred principles. We were given magic to save and help life, not take it."

"Sorry. I didn't know," he mumbled.

"Why would you? Son, I'm glad you're asking questions, even those that stray into darker matters. We'll have to discuss those at some point if you're going to be fully prepared for what is coming. Irina has no conscience and will use all her abilities to crush anyone in her way, including you."

She walked over and kissed his forehead. "I'm going inside to work on a few things. Practice with the bowl. We can talk about what you learn over dinner later tonight."

He nodded but didn't meet her eyes.

"What is it?"

The dandelion-headed little boy spoke in a quiet voice. "What if I become like her? What if . . . what if this is all too much? The idea of drawing magic was so exciting that I never even thought about what it would do to the creatures or plants . . . or *people*."

She cupped his cheek in her hand until he met her gaze. "Listen to me, Declan. The man I see in front of me, the man I'm coming to know, is a good, honest, and *decent* man. Each of us chooses our own path, and you will choose yours. No one else can do that for you. No one.

"Irina chose a dark path that led to vengeance and death. She gained incredible power, but at what cost? There isn't the tiniest part of me that believes you would follow in her steps. You have a strong heart, and I'm proud of you."

She swallowed and glanced away before continuing in quiet voice. "For years, I dreamed what it would be like to be part of your life, to see you grow up, to watch what you'd become. I'm happier now than I've been in . . . in a *very* long time . . . because I'm finally getting to know you and play a part in your journey. I have always loved you and always will, and have never doubted your goodness, not for one moment."

Declan's throat caught, and his arms moved on their own as he wrapped Kelså in a tight embrace.

"Thank you, Mother. Thank you."

Chapter Fifteen

Tiana had barely slept when morning arrived. She sat numbly at the table as Bet served her a breakfast of biscuits with sausage gravy, poached eggs, roasted potatoes with peppers, and mixed fruit. Anywhere else, this would have been a breakfast to savor, but Tiana barely tasted the rich food. She sipped her tea and lost herself, staring at a stray bit of leaf swirling in her cup.

"Mistress, made you a bag of biscuits and fruit for the road." Bet placed a hand on her shoulder.

Tiana tried to smile. "Thanks."

"Time to go, Mistress." Wildcat strode over with another vial of the syrupy liquid. "Drink this."

She took the vial, perplexed at the amount, a dose that wouldn't even put her to sleep. Something in that made currents of alarm streak down her arms.

"I . . . I need to get my other clothes. They're on the cot." Tiana started to stand.

"Leave them. We need to leave."

The trickle of fear became a raging torrent, and she wobbled as she stood. Wildcat had to steady her.

When they reached the cart, Tiana braced herself to be stowed like baggage in the compartment below, but this time, an ornate carriage waited beside the cart. Wildcat offered her a gentlemanly hand into the main passenger section of the coach. Bull-bird was already settled on the cushioned bench opposite, and Wildcat joined them, sitting beside him. She was surprised when they left the curtains to the carriage's windows pulled back, but was thankful for the distraction. The strange, masked pair sat stoically, staring blankly and unblinking.

A half-hour later, the drug kicked in and Tiana's head began to swim. She was aware of the passing landscape but felt drunk enough not to care.

Around mid-day, they entered a village. A few houses and picketed farms appeared and vanished through the carriage's window before they stopped in front of a stone building that stretched as far as she could see. Other than one set of double doors, the face of the building was a blank wall of ash-colored granite.

Wildcat opened the door, stepped out, and motioned for Tiana to take his hand so he could help her down. Her head was clear enough for a small act of defiance, so she brushed off the proffered hand and stepped down. As soon as she was visible, masked figures walking nearby stopped and stared. The pair closest to the carriage bowed respectfully and uttered, "Mistress," in unison.

Wildcat walked her toward the building's entrance, as Bull-bird followed behind. The other figures they passed stepped back and offered space while bowing.

They entered the double doors, then strode down wide, sloping hallways before stopping in front of a gilded door. Wildcat opened the door, scanned inside, then motioned for her to enter.

Keelan reined in his horse and called for the others to stop, giving Sil a few minutes to try to reacquire the cart.

It didn't take long.

"The only thing headed to Irina's Seat right now is a carriage, and it's right about where we'd expect our cart to be at this point. My best guess is they swapped vehicles wherever they slept last night. They're moving just as slowly as before, so I don't think they know we're watching."

They mounted and resumed their trek to the village. The first time a group of men in military uniforms approached from behind, Keelan was so startled he nearly drew his sword. The trio pulled off and let the men pass, earning a salute in return. It seemed the Kingdom's call was being heeded by all corners of the country, as three more groups passed before Irina's Seat came into view.

"That scattering of buildings is the town? Sure doesn't look like much." Sil raised a hand to shield her eyes.

Atikus strained to make out details. "We'll stick out in a town that small. How should we play this, Keelan?"

"We could probably pass through, and no one would care, but we need to figure out what's going on and find our Healer. Asking questions will get everyone's attention, so I think we've got to be as quiet as possible and try not to be seen. We should find some place to lie low until dark, then find a way in."

Sil pulled to a stop and turned to face Keelan. "Give me a little time with the eagle to scout the town before we trot in. We're totally blind right now."

"Right. We're probably thirty minutes out, and I would guess we've been spotted. Let's turn off here and make them think we were headed somewhere else. Maybe they'll forget about us."

It took a half-hour of searching the countryside before they found a handful of trees thick enough to make camp. The rolling hills helped, but the trees would better hide them from anyone using a spyglass. Sil assumed her usual cross-legged pose and closed her eyes. This time, she remained still for more than an hour.

"We were starting to get a little worried there, kiddo." Keelan smiled.

"Keelan, Atikus, I saw her!" Sil's eyes darted between them. "I saw the Healer. They had just pulled up to the Children's main building when I flew past. Two robed men got out of the carriage and walked her into the building. She looked unharmed."

Keelan sat beside her. "That's a relief. What else did you see?"

"I got a good look at the town, as well as the Children's building. The village doesn't have much organization. It's just scattered buildings with a small market at one end of the street, but the Children's headquarters something else. That thing is *huge*.

"The front face looks like solid stone with a set of double doors at the center. There were no windows or markings. The sides were completely bare, no doors or windows, but the back had several sets of doors, as well as several long windows that overlook the lake. The back wall stands about fifty paces from the shore, and there's a dock with a few boats. Most looked like local fishing boats, but there were a couple that had a crest on the side. I couldn't get the eagle low enough to make out the crest."

"Did you see anyone coming in or out of the back doors?" Keelan asked.

"Yeah. A couple of masked figures went back and forth. One pair was unloading boxes from a boat and carrying them inside, probably supplies."

"Anything else?"

"No. There really wasn't much to see. The townspeople were going about their normal business, not even glancing at the Children as they passed by. I didn't see anyone who looked like an outsider or traveler. Now that I think about it, there weren't any soldiers either. Given all the activity headed east, doesn't that seem weird?"

Keelan nodded. "It sounds like everyone's avoiding that village."

Atikus finally stepped into the conversation. "It wouldn't be that unusual for people to avoid connections with Irina. Think about it. The town is called her "seat" and sits against a lake bearing her name. Fontaine has always been the Kingdom's capital, but Irina used this area as her staging ground during the war. Local legend, combined with the presence of the Children, may scare people away."

"Irina was *a thousand* years ago. You think that still holds?" Keelan looked doubtful.

Atikus's brows rose. "Never underestimate the power of a myth, especially one born from the reality of a great war."

"Whatever it is, we've got to get into that building. Unless either you have a better idea, we need to get our hands on two robes and masks. Sil, you and I will go inside while Atikus guards the rear and readies our escape. One of those boats should get us across the lake to Cradle. I wish we had some idea of the inner layout."

"When we get there, if I can find a mouse or rat, I might be able to get a look inside. Their sight isn't the best, but it's more than what we have now." Sil said.

"Alright. Let's try to get some rest. We'll need to be at our best tonight."

Tiana sat on the side of a sprawling bed and peered about the room. From the vine-etched pillars and ornate furniture, to the bed's stunning headboard engraved with an intricate Phoenix, the whole chamber looked like something out of a palace or children's tale.

None of it made sense.

She'd been snatched off the street, stuffed into the bottom of a cart, drugged, hauled for hundreds of leagues to who-knows-where, and now they treated her with respect and put her in a room made for royalty? This had to be some kind of game or trick— something designed to put her at ease, but to what end?

A side table held a platter of fruits, nuts, and pastries, and she didn't care that the largess came from her captors; she was famished. She poured a mug of steaming tea and greedily downed two of the pastries.

As she scooped a handful of nuts, the mirror caught her eye and she realized powdered sugar clung to the top of her nose. An instinctual chuckle slipped out, the first time she'd laughed in . . . well, she couldn't remember when.

The door's hinges screamed, and two masked figures she hadn't seen before entered.

Her laughter died.

A man in a snarling eagle mask set a vial on the table.

"Mistress, tonight you will attend a great ceremony in your honor. Drink this and rest. We will return to help you dress in a few hours." He stared unblinking.

When no one moved, Eagle motioned with an open palm toward the vial, then in Tiana's direction. Her shoulders fell as she realized there was no way around another dose of the drug, so she complied, returned to the bed, and waited for sleep to take her.

Eagle and his companion bowed and backed out of the room. She flinched as the locking bolt slid into place.

It felt like only a few minutes had passed when she heard the bolt slide back and the hinges groaned again.

Eagle was followed by a Child wearing the mask of a wolf's head with wings of some ancient predator. Wolf set a large box on a chair by the fireplace, then helped Eagle pour steaming water into a white basin.

"Come. It's time to prepare." Eagle held a hand toward her.

As she rubbed sleep from her eyes and sat up, Tiana looked up at Eagle. "What's this ceremony? What's going on?"

"All will be clear soon, Mistress. You will receive the highest of honors."

He sounds sincere, she thought.

An hour later, she was bathed, robed in a golden gown, and her hair was brushed to perfection. She turned and held her reflection, shocked at the regal figure staring back.

"You look like a queen, Mistress. The only thing missing is jewelry."

Her eyes widened as she turned to find Eagle holding a magnificent necklace whose every inch shimmered with inlaid diamonds. The teardrop at the chain's center was a sapphire nearly the size of her fist, surrounded by more thumb-sized diamonds. Tiana couldn't take her eyes off the sapphire as he raised the necklace toward her.

"Please allow me, Mistress."

She turned and lifted her hair as Eagle placed the wealth of a nation around her neck. She was amazed by its weight, then she recognized something familiar in the sapphire. It glowed faintly, and she could feel a magical aura pressing against her own power.

It felt *hungry*.

She heard the snap of a clip, and Eagle stepped back. "You are perfect, Mistress. Please come with us."

They led her down a series of hallways illuminated by magical flames, stopping before a pair of well-polished doors. Pearlescent Phoenixes stared down from their perch at the center of each door.

Eagle stood to her left. "Mistress, take my arm if you need it."

The doors crept open, and the rhythmic thrumming of drums echoed from the hall. Tiana cocked her head, unable to discern why their measure felt so familiar.

Then her eyes widened.

The drums were beating in time with *her own heart*.

Atikus, Keelan, and Sil knelt only a few dozen paces from the dock at the back of the Children's building watching two masked figures standing guard at the base of the dock. Two rowboats bobbed lazily at the pier's end. Sil had scouted the perfect spot behind a ridge crowned with tall grasses and scraggly shrubs.

"There's too much open land between us and those guards. We won't be able to sneak up on them like I'd hoped. Ideas?" Keelan whispered.

Sil patted her bow. "There's just two. From this distance, I can take them out before either can react. We just have to get them to step away from the edge so neither one falls into the water. That would make a lot of noise."

"Alright. I'll walk up like I want to ask them something, see if I can pull them toward me a few steps. Try to avoid hitting the tall guy with your pointy sticks." He smiled with a confidence his gut betrayed.

Before Sil could move, Keelan felt a hand on his arm and heard Atikus in his mind. *"You forget my Gifts. I can get them away from the water without either of you having to expose yourselves."*

"That'll work. Sil, Atikus is going to handle this for us. Nock and fire when ready. Atikus, we'll hide the bodies up here, then change into their robes. You secure those boats and be ready when we come out. There's no telling what might be chasing us if we're successful. Everyone ready?"

Atikus and Sil nodded. Keelan looked up at the guards, then turned and pointed to Atikus and whispered, "Go."

Atikus focused on the figure closest to the group. *"Intruders! Secure the door! NOW!"*

The man's head snapped up in confusion and alarm. He said something to his partner before the two started running toward the building's back door. Sil didn't hesitate, dropping the man Atikus had spoken to with an arrow in his neck. The second man froze as his head whirled about. His hesitation earned him a shaft in the chest, followed by another in the stomach.

Keelan launched from their hiding place.

Sil covered him from the bushes, scanning the area with a nocked arrow. By the time he reached the guards, they were dead. A few seconds later, he and Sil were hauling the corpses into the bushes and donning their robes.

"Wish we could've avoided holes in the front. Still, nice shots." He gave Sil an appreciative head bob.

"I think your height might be more of a problem than my holes. Nice calves." Sil smirked at his exposed legs. Neither of the guards had been very tall, nearly turning the robe into a skirt for Keelan.

He rolled his eyes and continued searching the dead bodies. He found a large metal key, then reached for the man's mask, a twisted version of a rat with horns. Sil donned the other mask, a lion with tusks.

Mask in place, Keelan glanced down at the two guards and froze.

They couldn't have been more than twenty years old. Seeing those boys, their eyes now vacant orbs, he wondered how kids could get wrapped up in a group like this.

Then Declan sprang to his mind. He'd avoided how much he missed his little brother and how much he wanted to make things right after their last conversation on the mountain.

Sil's touch on his shoulder snapped him back to the present. The unexpected mask greeting him as he turned nearly scared him to death.

The lion's eyes grinned.

"Atikus has the boat. Ready to breach?"

Keelan nodded, and the pair marched purposely toward the back door.

As the doors swung wide, a gasp escaped Tiana's lips. Her heartbeat quickened, and her eyes darted. Pillars of polished black and white marble swirled high, well beyond the magical light flickering from brass braziers standing before them. Her eyes followed the columns into the darkness, never finding the ceiling they supported.

Standing silently to either side were over four hundred masked and robed figures. The figures formed into lines that ran the length of the chamber and faced inward, creating the impression of a grand walkway. As soon as Tiana appeared in the doorway, the figures burst into a discordant hum that undulated in an odd, mystical pattern, sending a shiver down her arms and neck.

Eagle prodded her to walk forward, and her feet rebelled. She nearly tumbled to the stone floor. He gripped her elbow with one hand, and actually tried to *comfort* her by rubbing her back gently, but his touch made fear blaze through her.

With the next step, their procession began.

Keelan unlocked the door, and they crept inside. The hallway they'd entered stood empty.

"Do you hear that?" Sil whispered.

"Drums?"

"I hear those, but do you hear singing, too? Or *humming*? I can't tell. It sounds like a lot of people."

Keelan hadn't noticed the humming but couldn't get it out of his head now that she'd pointed it out. He motioned for her to follow and edged down the hallway.

This was a terrible idea, Keelan thought.

They passed a few doors before reaching a point where the hallway forked, the left side rising, while the right sloped downward. Keelan motioned to go up.

The humming grew from a discordant sound into a wave of force he felt press against his skin. They rounded a corner.

Keelan grabbed Sil and pulled her to the ground behind a half-wall. Eerie light flickered against the darkness from somewhere below.

"We're on a balcony overlooking a large chamber. Stay low," he whispered.

Keelan risked a glance over the railing, and his mind could barely process the scene before him. Hundreds of figures lined either side of the massive chamber. At the end closest to their hiding place was a two-tiered dais. On the upper level of the dais stood the statue of a woman in flowing robes, her chin raised, as if she sought the top of a faraway mountain. On her brow rested a glistening crown of gold and silver. In her right hand, she held a silver staff. Her right stretched far above her head and held an orb that pulsed a deep, bloody crimson.

On the lower level of the dais, a marble throne lorded over the throng.

One hand of a figure in blood-red robes rested on the back of the throne. Keelan squinted, but couldn't make out the animal on her mask. He wasn't even sure there was one. It looked *blank*, like skin stretched tight over her features.

Motion at the far end of the chamber caught his eye, and his heart lurched as *Tiana* emerged through the massive doors. He'd always thought she was beautiful, but in that golden gown, she stole his breath.

Sil nudged him, and he ducked back down.

"We're fifty feet up, and I don't think they can see us in the darkness up here. Sil, she's down there. Just walked in. Hundreds of robed men performing some kind of ceremony. I . . ."

He couldn't think, couldn't breathe.

Sil gripped his shoulder. "We can't help her if we get caught."

He nodded and drew a breath to gather himself, then peered over the railing to watch the spectacle unfold.

As they paraded past ranks of robed figures, Tiana could hear the hundreds mutter, almost hiss, "Mistress." They fell to their knees in cascading wave of masks and men.

She paused long enough to stare into the eyes of one of the humming figures before it fell to its knees. She searching for some sign of humanity, any shred of empathy or hope—but *nothing* peered through those irises, no shred of the individual who once was.

Only hunger and lust returned her gaze.

Her head was already cloudy from drought they'd forced her to drink, but those monstrous eyes sent a new wave of dizziness through her, and, before Eagle could catch her, her legs gave way and she fell face-first onto the lifeless stone. Horror filled her escort's eyes as they pulled her to her feet and resumed their endless march.

They made it halfway through the chamber before Tiana saw the figure in crimson behind the throne. Her eyes darted from the kneeling row on her left to the one on her right, then up to the faceless cardinal on its perch. Her breathing quickened and fear grew into panic. Her heart raced as Eagle's hand found her arm again, forcing her forward.

Three hundred paces felt like a million leagues.

When she finally stood before the throne, her eyes widened in awe at the magnificent statue reigning over the chamber. The woman's robes flowed in lifelike brilliance while the set of her jaw and depth of her eyes exuded strength and power. Tiana's view traveled up the woman's form to pause on her face. She was strong and proud.

The crimson orb in woman's hand flared, and Tiana sucked in a breath. It blazed in time with the drums—and *her* racing heart.

Her gaze dropped from the statue to the marble throne. Eagle stood to her left and Wolf to her right. On a plush cushion in the throne's seat rested a crown. Set in its golden band were seven thumb-sized diamonds, five of which pulsed a bloody burgundy in time with the drums.

Tiana startled when Eagle bounded up the steps and seized the crown, then stepped to the side and lofted it reverently for all to see. Wolf nudged Tiana forward and motioned for her to sit.

She scanned the assembled crowd in their silky robes and wild masks.

Their drug raged in her veins. Their humming and drumbeats thrummed in dizzying waves. Her vision danced. Her body swayed. As hard as she tried, she couldn't wrest control from the potion as the world to spun and blurred.

The bloody-robed figure stepped from behind the throne and clapped once.

Immediately, the humming ceased, and the figures gathered in a wide arc before the throne. Tiana tried to follow the movement around her, but her mind was adrift on a sea of sensation. Her head lolled as she scanned the masked figures, unable to fix on any single one.

Once in place, Skin-mask clapped once again, and the humming of hundreds became wails and cries.

The drums again bellowed, now faster and louder.

Skin-Mask chanted a staccato verse, then seized crown from Eagle's outstretched hands, raised it high, and placed it on Tiana's brow.

The flock fell to their knees.

Their song grew urgent and pleading.

The drums became cannon.

And they swayed as one.

They cried as one.

Skin-Mask drew a golden dagger from her cloak and plunged it with all her strength into Tiana's chest.

Tiana screamed.

She stared down in bleary disbelief, and her eyes glazed, and the horrors of the chamber faded.

Her head snapped up, confused to find her father's eyes. He cupped her cheek, and she pressed into his palm. His touch was the first comfort she'd felt that day.

"Baby girl, I've missed you so."

Tears fell freely at the sound of his voice.

Her vision faltered.

She reached for her father, but only darkness stared back.

The last thing she heard before drifting away was a familiar voice. It wrapped her comfort, though she couldn't remember why.

Far above, Keelan cried out, "TIANA! NOOOO!"

Hundreds of heads snapped upward as Skin-mask tore the crown from Tiana's head and slammed it onto her own. Tiana's spirit fled, and the sixth diamond on the crown's base flared to bloody life.

In a murderous rage, Skin-mask pointed to the balcony and bellowed, "Kill them!"

Keelan sat frozen.

Sil threw her arms around him and tackled him to the ground. "We've to get out of here. Now!"

She crouched below the banister and propelled him forward. Before he knew what was happening, they were sprinting through the hallway toward the back door. The sound of shouting and countless boots turned the quiet passages into chaos. As Keelan and Sil burst through the door, racing toward Atikus and the boat, masked faces appeared in the windows above the door. An arrow flew past Keelan and embedded itself into the wood of the dock.

More arrows followed.

"Atikus, untie the boat!" Keelan cried out.

The *whizzing* of arrows multiplied as more figures joined the fray.

Keelan had one foot in the boat when he heard Sil scream. He turned and gaped in horror at the arrow jutting out of her chest. Two more struck her in rapid succession. She locked eyes with Keelan, and the world slowed.

She drew her bow, then an arrow.

She turned and fired.

Her aim was true, and one stream of missiles ceased.

"Keelan, go! I'll hold them off as long as I can. Get Atikus out of here!" She dropped two more before taking another bolt in her thigh.

She sank to her knees.

Atikus grabbed Keelan and pulled him into the boat. The pair rowed for their lives. Arrows splashed around them, yet Sil's held the line.

Until she didn't.

Keelan shot a looked back. Sil launched one last arrow, then tumbled face down.

His granite facade shattered, and tears streaked down his face.

First Tiana, now Sil.

Atikus gripped his arm. "Row, son. Just row. There'll be time to mourn later."

Chapter Sixteen

It had been two days since Isabel's disappearance was discovered, and no one had see nor heard from her since. Alfred was beside himself with anger and fear.

She would never admit it, but Isabel knew she and Jess were cut from the same stubborn cloth. Isabel wanted to think Jess was the unruly child rebelling against her righteous and caring parents. The truth, at least as Alfred saw it, was that Isabel got the daughter she raised—and she was the spitting image of her mother.

But the same frustrating qualities that drove Alfred to drink were those that he cherished the most. Isabel was brilliant and savvy. Her unyielding backbone was one of the things that had made him fall for her all those years ago.

Everyone had known he would be King one day. He was the Heir. They bowed and scraped, telling him only what they thought he wanted to hear, complimenting his every word or deed. He'd grown into the crown and its unique challenges, but it was sickening back then, when he was new to it all.

Isabel—fiery, infuriating, beautiful Isabel—said *exactly* what she thought, damn the consequences. The first time they'd met, she'd insulted the doublet he was wearing, causing ripples in the rings of courtiers that tutted about them.

He fell in love on the spot.

And her strength ... He couldn't count the number of times she'd lent him her resilience, helping him through a difficult negotiation or political conundrum. She never wavered in her support for him. Her voice was nearly as strong as her backbone. She committed to a course and followed it to the end, no matter what. He knew that knife cut both ways, and that her strength, taken to excess, was a hinderance, but everyone had blind spots. He needed her. More than that, he loved her in a way only twenty years of marriage allowed.

Then there was Jess.

She was the one person in the entire Kingdom who could turn the King into a blubbering puddle of mush. Every time he thought of her, his mind flashed to her early days, holding her in his arms, watching her tiny toes curl then release. He could still see her toddling about the palace, terrorizing the family's bulldogs who'd wanted nothing more than to nap by the fire.

Why did the simplest memories captivate him so?

From the moment she drew breath, Jess was a handful. She'd refused to feed from her mother's breast, refused to sit while her parents tried eating in peace, refused the fineries of a princess, begging for wild adventures in the woods. Her whole life was one rebellion after another, most aimed at her mother.

Alfred chuckled at that thought.

They were cut from *exactly* the same cloth.

And here he was, King of the largest nation in the world, surrounded by the most powerful army ever assembled, *helpless* to protect either of them.

He was having trouble focusing. His mind was a constant swirl of emotion and pain.

"What the hell do you mean you don't know anything, Wilfred? It's your *job* to know what's going on. At least it is *for the moment*. Find my wife and daughter or start planning for your retirement." Alfred stalked the room like a caged beast.

"Yes, Your Majesty." The High Sheriff bowed and began to back out of the room.

Alfred stopped him with a raised hand. Pain creased the skin around his eyes. "Sebastiano, forgive me. It's been a tough few weeks. Just bring them back to me, please."

Wilfred eyed his old friend. "Alfred, I would give my life for theirs. You know that. We'll do all we can to bring them home safely." He gave another bow and walked out, leaving the King alone with High Chancellor Thorn.

Alfred unfastened his cloak and threw it against the wall before resuming his pacing. He had the most spacious room the inn could offer, but it felt more like a prison. All he wanted was to *do something*.

Thorn stood silently in the corner, hands clasped behind him, watching.

"Thorn, what do you know? You have eyes everywhere. You must know *something*."

The Chancellor remained still, back stiff against the wall. "Unfortunately, sire, you know everything I do. Her Majesty vanished. No one saw her leave, and she hasn't been heard from since. None of our men on the roads have seen or heard anything."

"If those Triad bastards harm my Queen, I'll burn their country to the ground."

"Your Majesty," Thorn hesitated. "Have you considered the possibility that the Queen *wasn't* kidnapped? That she left on her own?"

"Don't play your *Spirits-damned* games with me, Thorn. Not *now!*"

Thorn bowed his head. The King was practically a priest, never allowing cursing or even rude language at court. The Chancellor was stunned.

"Sire, I . . . it's just that . . . she talked about using an Enchanted item to Travel."

Alfred froze, and his eyes snapped to Thorn's. "She wouldn't dare."

Thorn raised a brow.

"Right. She *absolutely* would," the King admitted.

"I have no evidence to say that she did, sire, but it remains a possibility."

"We need to be certain. Is there something your Mages can do to test this theory? A spell? A charm? Anything?" Alfred sat on the bed and stared at his shoes. "She was *desperate* to help find Jess, and I could see her ignoring all of us and taking off. I hate to admit it, but it makes sense."

"She was quite desperate to find the Princess, sire. That's very true." The corner of Thorn's mouth quirked. "I'll talk with my Mages and see what can be done."

"Thank you, Danai." Alfred paused, then looked up. "Would you send Justin to me, please."

"Of course, sire." Thorn bowed again and backed out of the room, leaving the wounded king alone.

How had it all come to this? His daughter kidnapped. His wife missing. His kingdom on the brink of war. He missed the days, not so long ago, when their greatest worry was who Jess would marry. Everything had fallen into chaos since, and he didn't know how to restore peace and order.

Despite the mounting evidence provided by his advisors, he couldn't understand why the Triad had turned on them so quickly. The Kingdom had been a loyal friend to Melucia for centuries. The magical disparity was a fair point Thorn raised, something he'd have to address. But to kidnap Gifted? To attack the royal house itself? The Kingdom's army was ten times anything Melucia could muster, even if magic did thrive in their gene pool. Surely, they understood war would be inevitable with such provocation. Why? Why do it?

Something felt *wrong*.

A soft knock at the door interrupted the King's thinking. "Come."

Justin peeked tentatively around the door. "Dad? You ok?"

"Come here, son." Alfred looked up and motioned for his boy to join him.

Justin stepped into the room, closed the door behind him, then shuffled to sit beside his father on the bed. Alfred reached around him with one arm and drew him close.

Justin eyed his father. At fifteen, it had been years since he'd held him.

"I need to tell you some things—things that will be difficult to hear." Alfred drew a breath.

"Dad, you're scaring me. I could hear you yelling all the way down the hall. What's going on?"

Alfred pulled away and squared to his son. "We still have no word on Jess. There've been no sightings, not even a rumor vibrating in Thorn's web."

"You have the whole country looking for her and Danym. They'll find them. Right?"

"Son, as a father, I want that more than anything in this world. My heart breaks thinking of her . . . of what she must be going through. We're doing everything we can, including turning the Mages into investigators. But nothing's working, and it's been over a week.

"As a father, I can't give up hope, but as a king, as *the* King, I have to plan for the future of the Kingdom." The King's eyes met his son's, and he put a hand on his shoulder. "I know you never wanted to be my Heir, never planned for that life, but if we . . . if we can't find Jess, you'll have to start preparing to wear the crown."

"Dad, stop it. She's ok. She *has* to be ok!" Tears welled in Justin's eyes.

Alfred gripped him by both shoulders. "Listen to me, Justin. The Kingdom *must* have an Heir. Our duty—*your* duty—is to the Kingdom above all else. I need to know that you'll step up, that you'll be ready should that day come."

Justin tried speak. All he could do was nod.

"Good." Alfred held his grip. "I'm sorry, but there's more."

Justin's watery eyes snapped up.

"Your mother is missing."

Justin's gaze fell to the floor.

"Thorn thinks she might've used magic to Travel somewhere to find Jess. She hasn't been herself since your sister's kidnapping. She was . . . I don't know . . . desperate to *do* something." Alfred's voice broke as he released Justin's shoulders and sat back.

Justin's voice was a whisper when he spoke. "I'm not ready, dad—for any of this."

"I'll let you in on a secret: nobody's ever really ready, son." Alfred smiled wistfully. "Not for what we're facing with your mother and Jess, and definitely not to wear the crown. I pray we find your sister and mother, and you can live the life you choose, but Justin, if you must become the Heir, take some comfort in what my father told me when I was your age. 'The crown never fits when first placed on your head, but you'll grow into it.'"

Keelan couldn't stop sobbing.

Halfway across Lake Irina, both he and Atikus quit rowing. At the narrowest point between Irina's Seat and Cradle, the lake spanned nearly three leagues. They were sore, tired, and hungry, and Keelan couldn't stop replaying the nightmarish scene of Tiana's death. Her smile would flash into his mind, then be replaced by her pained grimace as the crimson-robed figure plunged a dagger into her chest. He couldn't shake the haunting sounds of those drums and that incessant humming. The murderous melody echoed in his mind. It made his skin crawl.

He would shake Tiana's image in time for Sil to fall face forward in his mind, arrows jutting out of her body.

He was there to save Tiana, to protect her, and he'd failed.

The guilt and grief threatened to shred his heart, but he was also *angry*. Angry at Sil, that she gave up, that she turned to face certain death rather than trust her team. Angry that she left them.

Then his anger turned inward. How dare he *blame her* for her bravery, for her strength, for her sacrifice. She died saving them. Saving *him*.

She'd saved him.

Keelan's eyes burned and his throat was raw, but he couldn't stop the sobs.

"Put the oars down a minute. We both need to rest." Atikus tucked his oars inside the boat then edged forward and placed his hands on Keelan's forearms. He helped him stow his oars, then wrapped him in father-ly arms. There, cloaked in the darkness of a moonless night, in the middle of their sea of sorrow, the two men became father and boy once more.

"I couldn't save her, Atikus. We were *so* close . . . but . . . there were so many of them."

"Oh, Keelan. My boy." Atikus gripped him tighter until the tears were exhausted.

Keelan finally sat back, wiping his eyes and nose with a sleeve. Atikus gave him a pat on the shoulder and head-ed back to his seat in the front of the boat.

"We'd best start rowing again. I'd rather get to shore before sunrise, just in case . . . " Atikus's thought trailed off.

An hour and a half later, Keelan spotted the shore and the dim lights of Cradle's dock. He spotted a few boats bobbing next to a long pier, much larger than the dock they'd left in Irina's Seat. Movement on shore caught his eye as several torches flared to life. He thought he could make out the silhouette of men holding a nocked bows, but the torchlight blinded his vision.

"This is the King's Protectorate. Bring your boat in nice and slow. We have bows nocked and ready, so don't resist." A strong voice, rich with authority, carried across the open water.

Keelan and Atikus shared a look.

The voice called out again, all friendliness gone. "Dock your boat. If you resist, we will shoot."

They rowed the last quarter mile and were greeted by heavily armed men. When they reached the dock, one of the men helped Atikus out of the boat while another boarded and tied it off. Two other soldiers kept bows trained on Keelan as he stepped onto the dock.

The soldiers slapped on iron cuffs and shoved them onto the land at the base of the pier. Keelan got a brief look at the other boats and noted two bore the crest of the Royal Protectorate on their hulls.

Must've been the ones Sil saw.

As soon as their feet touched land, a tall soldier approached, his gaze scrutinizing the pair. Silver officer's pins on his collar glinted off the torchlight. One of their escort leaned toward him and whispered, "Sir, they wear the robes, but their masks were in the bottom of the boat."

The officer's stare intensified.

Keelan towered over everyone, though the power of his frame was somewhat disguised by the robe he still wore. The officer met his eyes, and placed one hand on the pommel of his sword. "You're a long way from home, gentlemen, and from the looks of things, you had a rough trip. By the King's agreement, Children are to stay on the other side of this lake. Why are you here? I'll give you *one* opportunity to tell me the truth."

Keelan and Atikus shared a quick glance. Keelan shrugged and turned back to the officer. When he spoke, his voice carried authority born of years in uniform.

"My name is Lieutenant Keelan Rea of the *Saltstone* Guard. This is Mage Atikus Dani. We are here under direct orders from the Captain-Commander of the Guard and Arch Mage of Melucia investigating the kidnapping of a prominent Healer from our city that occurred approximately two weeks ago. We followed her kidnappers through the mountains to Irina's Seat, where we disguised ourselves as Children and attempted a rescue. We failed and barely escaped. A third member of our team, Guard Sil Wesser, didn't make it."

The officer's eyes widened. Keelan looked glanced around to see other soldiers within earshot also shaken by his tale.

"You say the Healer was kidnapped *from* Melucia?"

Keelan nodded. "That's right. She ran an infirmary near the center of the city, across from the Guard Complex. I saw her the day before her kidnapping."

The officer looked at the other men. "Take these two to the command tent and get them something hot to drink. Take whatever's in the boat with them." He started to turn. "Not a word of this to anyone. Hear me? Not … one … word."

"Yes, sir." They said in unison.

Not long after, Keelan and Atikus found themselves sitting on wooden chairs inside a marquee housing the leadership of the King's army-on-the-move. Their shackles had been removed, but the two soldiers who's escorted them to the tent stood guard a few paces away.

Atikus sipped his tea, savoring the heat and honey. "I think that officer recognized your name."

Keelan leaned toward the Mage and whispered. "Maybe. Or maybe the idea of a team of Melucians roaming the countryside while the Kingdom preps for an invasion threw him off. I can't remember getting this many sideways looks since you took Dec and me into the Guild all those years ago."

"Maybe they've just never seen anyone so big or ugly?" Atikus grinned with one bushy brow raised.

Keelan rolled his eyes. Even then, sitting captive in the middle of soon-to-be enemy territory, the old Mage joked. It was a wonder he hadn't asked for food yet.

The officer they'd spoken with walked into the tent and headed straight for them. The two guards snapped to attention, but the officer ignored them, pulled up a chair.

"Mage, Lieutenant, I'm Commander Evan Paul of the King's Protectorate. His Majesty wants to talk with you, so here's how this will work. The two men behind you, along with another six, will accompany us to the King. Out of deference to your rank and reputation,

Mage Danai, you will not be bound. Lieutenant Rea, I'm afraid your bulk alone requires shackles for the audience. I believe the story you told me was true and hope some good can come of this, but make no mistake, if you even flinch toward the King, I will personally put you down. Understood?"

Atikus nodded.

Keelan leaned forward and spoke in a low voice. "Commander, why does the King want to see us? We've already failed in our mission. It's time I got Mage Danai home."

Commander Paul shook his head. "You think I know how to read a king's mind? You'll find out soon enough. Let's go."

The two guards led them out of the tent with Commander Paul trailing. As soon as they exited, six additional men joined the procession, forming a box around Keelan and Atikus. Keelan knew immediately these weren't common soldiers. Their near-black uniforms with only a hint of olive and a gold braid across one shoulder set them apart, but it was their movement that gave them away. They flowed with the athletic grace and easy confidence of the elite. Their eyes never rested, scanning before them in predatory vigilance. These men were part of the King's elite personal guard.

As the group traveled through the center of town, Keelan noted soldiers milling about. Soldiers easily outnumbered townsfolk by three or four to one.

The group slowed as they approached a wooden two-story building. A roughly hewn sign bearing a painted parrot swung above the door. Script scrawled in crimson read, "The Perky Parrot."

A line of the Royal Guard stood like statues in front of the building, their heads unmoving, but their eyes never still. Passing soldiers in common verdant doublets gave their braided brothers a wide berth.

"This is where we leave you in the hands of our good friends of the Royal Guard. Lieutenant, one word of advice: no games. Their sense of humor was removed at birth." Commander Paul gave Atikus a nod, then he and his men marched back toward the command tent.

Their six escorts didn't move. Nor did they look at Keelan or Atikus. They simply scanned the surrounding area and stood in place. Atikus was about to say something when the doors to the inn opened and a behemoth in Royal Guard colors stalked toward them. His shoulders were wide, and his doublet barely contained the muscles that bulged beneath. Two daggers hung from his belt, one on either side, while the hilt of a colossal broadsword peered over his back. Keelan was speechless as he *looked up* at the man. He'd never met anyone who eclipsed his height by a full head. As he approached, the six surrounding them took a couple of steps outward, maintaining their perimeter but giving the giant space and deference.

He glanced at Atikus, then bored a hole through Keelan before surprising them with a polite bow. When he spoke, he sounded more like a courteous concierge greeting his guests than a fearsome warrior. "Gentlemen, welcome. I am Captain Marv Proctor, commander of His Majesty's Royal Guard. When we enter, you will bow to his Majesty and wait to be recognized. I will be with you every moment. Please do not speak unless His Majesty asks you to do so or step past where I stand. The audience will end poorly if you do, and my men hate cleaning up after *unfortunate* audiences. Questions?"

Atikus and Keelan shared a glance then shook their heads.

"Good. Let's not keep the King waiting." As he turned to ducked through the door while the perimeter guards tightened their box and edged forward. Keelan and Atikus took the hint and followed Captain Proctor.

They entered the common room of the inn and were surprised to find it to be . . . common. Seated about a round table in the middle of the room were the King, a teenager, and two men Keelan didn't recognize. Aside from the guards and those at the table, the area stood eerily quiet.

Captain Proctor turned and faced them, ten feet in front of the King's table, then rested both hands on the pommel of his broadsword. Keelan's eyes roamed the length of the blade that was now drawn with its point resting on the floor a giant's arm's length away. Two of the six guards blocked the door, while the others fanned out around the room.

Keelan and Atikus edged forward and bowed toward the King. The King's eyes never left Keelan.

Alfred let them stay bent for a long, uncomfortable moment before speaking in a stern, unwavering voice. "Rise and look at me, Lieutenant."

Keelan did as commanded.

"I have been briefed on your . . . *unusual* journey, but I would like to hear the tale directly from you—and Lieutenant, don't leave any details out. My friends here will know if you do." Alfred nodded meaningfully toward Chancellor Thorn and Sheriff Wilfred, while Justin shifted uncomfortably, unsure why his father insisted he join this conversation.

"Of course, Your Majesty."

Keelan spoke in the clipped, professional tone of a Guardsman, walking the King through the events of the past weeks, starting with the discovery of Tiana's disappearance. He detailed the search for Bel, the Gifted who went missing from the town of Freeport, and the second investigative team's failed efforts at finding her. Keelan left out any mention of his brother and the mission to Rea Utu but painted a detailed image of the rest of their journey. Emotion finally threaded its way into his voice as he recounted the events he witnessed in Children's ceremonial chamber.

"It all happened so quickly, and we were so far away. There was nothing we could do to save her."

The King leaned forward.

"All we could do was run. There were hundreds chasing us, and if Sil hadn't . . ."

Atikus rested a hand on his shoulder.

The King waited a moment before asking his next question. "And your investigations led only here? There were no leads pointing . . . closer to home?"

Keelan's head snapped up. "No, Your Majesty. All of our leads, in both kidnappings, pointed here."

"And when did you learn of *our* missing Gifted?"

"We passed through Rutin two nights ago. A man in your household livery stood on the base of a statue, whipping people up with stories of the Triad kidnapping the Princess. We picked up a flyer, one among many scattered about, that called for volunteers to avenge the kidnappings."

The King thought a moment, then turned to Atikus. "Mage, your reputation precedes you. Chancellor Thorn tells me you have been a friend to the Crown for many years, a voice of reason when tempers flare. What do you have to say?"

Atikus offered another deep bow to the King. "Chancellor Thorn and I have been acquainted for many decades, working together at times, opposed on other occasions. I suppose that is the way of things when you live as long as we do."

"I was referring to the kidnappings and the Lieutenant's tale. It strays from what our sources report," the King said impatiently.

"Forgive me, Your Majesty. We Mages wander and ramble when our lips move." A laugh escaped Thorn's lips, drawing a sharp rebuke from his monarch.

"King Alfred, I have been with Keelan since the beginning of his investigations. Mages in our Guild in Freeport were deeply involved in the search there and reported to me in detail. What the Lieutenant described is exactly as I recall it, and your Chancellor might have a word to say on my skill for recall."

"I am well aware of your Gifts, Mage," the King said, before staring at the table's surface. After a moment's reflection, his gaze rose to meet Keelan's once more. "I need some time to think and confer but wish to speak again tomorrow. For the moment, you will remain *guests* of the Kingdom. Captain, find accommodations for these men."

Captain Proctor stepped forward and bowed toward the King. "Of course, sire."

The detail was already closing in when Keelan and Atikus offered their own bows.

Once the room was cleared, Alfred turned to Justin. "So, what do *you* think? Should we execute them?"

"DAD! Of course not!" Justin caught Thorn grinning and remembered himself. "No, *sire*, I do not. Do you?"

Alfred put his head in his hands and mumbled. "No, son, I don't think so either, but I have no idea what to make of their story."

Wilfred's chair creaked as he leaned forward. "Sire, all our evidence pointing at Melucia is circumstantial. Added together, it seems like a lot, but there's no direct link and no witnesses. I hate to admit it, but I believe them."

Thorn rose and stood behind his chair, resting both hands on its back. "Your Majesty, the Sheriff may be right. Mage Dani is certainly well-known and respected. Perhaps their Gifted were taken and brought to Irina's Seat—but we *know* ours were taken across the mountains into Melucia. We *know* the Triad was involved, despite their best efforts to cover their tracks. We have *their* seal. This changes nothing."

Thorn shot Wilfred daggers, daring him to disagree.

Justin stood and placed a hand on his father's back. "Dad, what if they're right? What if the Children took

Jess and Mom? Can we ignore what they said just because it doesn't fit what the men of Council *know*?"

Alfred sat back and stared up at Justin. He finally gripped his son's arm, but spoke to his counselors. "Sheriff, Chancellor, I'd like to have breakfast with my son—and think."

Finally alone in the inn's great room, Alfred turned to Justin. "It's just you and me. What do you think we should do? This is your mother and Jess we're talking about—oh, and the Kingdom going to war, too. Don't forget that."

Justin sat and fiddled with his fingers so long Alfred thought he might not answer. "Dad, I know Thorn's been with you for years, but I don't like him. Something about him makes me want to bathe, and I really don't trust him. Jess despises him."

"I understand where you're coming from, but there's value to be found in unsavory places. Thorn has an underworld network that gives me insight into a very different side of our kingdom, and that's useful. As King, you need to know everything, not just what you like or want to hear—*especially* those things you don't want to hear."

Alfred let his statement hang before giving Justin a conspiratorial grin. "Son, sometimes a king has to do things no one expects. Information is more powerful than any weapon, and right now, our information is at war with itself. None of this makes sense. In Jess's words, 'It sucks!' What do you think we should do when that happens?"

Justin thought a moment before surprising his father. "Find a new source of information."

The King nodded proudly and grinned.

Chapter Seventeen

Declan tried seeing the water in his mind, shaping it into a ball. He tried using his hands to mimic molding clay. He tried putting his hands *in* the water and touching his Light. He tried for a week and only succeeded in soaking his trousers and boots. He'd been so confident after his early successes, but control was proving far more challenging.

Kelså watched from the table as he failed again, water splattering over the edge of the bowl in the stone circle. He let out a frustrated growl and flopped to the ground before realizing his mistake. He jumped up quickly and tried to wipe the water and mud off his trousers, but it was too late.

Kelså chuckled softly. "You might want to watch where you sit next time."

"I really am starting to see the depth of your wisdom, Mother." His sarcastic tone was accompanied by a sidelong glare. "I've never had such a hard time picking something up. The magic responds, and I can feel it flow into the water, make it ripple, but it's like trying to hold . . . I don't know . . . *water*. It slips between my fingers, and the more I focus, the faster it falls apart."

Órla had been soaring high above but descended to land in front of him when she noticed his practice end abruptly. She now stood a towering one hand, and the golden brown of her wings and body was fading to pure white. Oddly, the feathers across her chest were turning *more* gold. Part of him was sad to see the set of her eyes transforming from their perfectly round, perpetually wide-eyed look of surprise to a more oval, serious, predatorial presence. She hadn't lost her playful, childlike banter, but would now slip into moments of serious contemplation as often as she jibed.

She was growing so quickly.

"Declan, you think too much," Órla said. "Magic needs you to *react*, not think. It responds to your heart, to your needs—not your head—and that's a good thing, because I've been inside your head. It's a very scary place."

Kelså's eyes widened. "You should listen to her more often. She may be a better teacher than I am."

"You hear that, D? You should listen to me—and that's from your *mother*." Órla flapped into the bowl and took a drink.

Declan shot Kelså another glare. "You don't have to encourage her, you know? She may be growing fast, but she's still that perky little owl I found in the woods."

"Uh, Declan, I found you. You were hopelessly lost, as I recall. Well, I remember the hopeless part. You might not've been *that* lost." Órla giggled and splashed water on his head.

Kelså shot to her feet. "Declan, stand up and go to the inner edge of the ring. I have an idea."

He was startled by her change in tone but did as she asked.

She stepped just inside the outer ring of stones as he shuffled to the other side and turned to face her. Before he knew what was happening, a ball of water was streaking from the bowl toward his face. Instinct kicked in, and he threw up his hands. Magic flared from his palms, and the ball froze in the air a few inches away. He watched with wide eyes as the ball wiggled and wobbled but didn't break apart.

"I've got it!" he shouted. "Órla, are you seeing this? I've got it!"

Órla streaked by, poking her beak into the ball and splashing water all over Declan.

"Hey! What was that for?"

"Kelså told me to keep you humble. Looked like you needed your bubble burst," she giggled.

Declan scowled as he wiped his face.

"Órla, I'm glad to see you're taking your duties seriously." Kelså laughed and clapped. "Well done, Declan. Now, dry yourself."

Declan shrugged and turned to leave the circle, a proud grin plastered across his face.

Kelså raised a palm. "Where are you going?"

"You told me to dry off. I'm going to get a towel."

"You have everything you need in that circle. Now, dry yourself."

Declan glanced down at his dripping shirt and realized what she meant. He was working on controlling water. He *could* dry himself if he could just master control, but concentrating and trying to out-stare his magic hadn't worked. On a whim, he looked down again and waved his arm in a sharp motion, "yanking" the water out of his shirt. Droplets of water flew out of the fabric, across the circle, and all over Kelså.

Now it was Declan's turn to laugh. "How was that? Looks like *you* might need a towel."

Kelså chuckled as she brushed off her robe. "I'm ok with a little water if it helps you take the next step. What did you do that time?"

"I don't know. I didn't really think about it; I just did it."

Kelså's eyes smiled. "Good. Form a ball above the bowl."

Declan turned to the center pillar and formed a floating ball of liquid. He raised it high, then made it fly around the circle before accidentally smashing it into one of the outer stones.

"That's incredible!" He could barely contain his laughter and excitement. "What else? What's next?"

"Alright, let's make this harder." Kelså moved to the bowl and scattered its contents across the landing. "Now, you're in the woods, and there's no lake or stream nearby to pull from. How do you form the ball?"

Declan thought a minute then decided to try the same trick he used on his shirt, pulling the scattered water off the stone and dirt of the ledge. He motioned as though he was yanking a rope toward him, and the droplets flew toward him. When they were a stride away, he opened his palm and began "molding clay" to command the ball to form.

"Not bad, but you used what I scattered. That's like having a lake nearby. I want you to do it again, but *not* use the water that was in the bowl."

His smirk fell into a frown of concentration as he scoured the area to find anything that might contain water. Rocks, weeds, trees, birds—he couldn't use living animals—that was forbidden—but plants?

"Are plants part of the dark magic prohibition?"

Kelså nodded. "Off limits. What else?"

The mountain air was cool and crisp with virtually no humidity.

He looked down again. The inner ring rested on a floor of solid, unmarred stone. Something in the powerful magic of the circle kept nature at bay, but as his eyes traveled outward, he realized that a thin layer of settled dirt began with the outer ring and covered the areas outside of the stones, allowing growth of some wildflowers, weeds and shrubs. He walked to the edge of the outer ring, knelt, and rubbed a clump of dirt between his fingers.

His cocky grin returned.

He leapt back into the inner ring and focused on the surrounding dirt, careful to avoid the plants. Through his magic, he *felt* the moisture in the dirt. There wasn't much, but it was there. He began to pull it toward him, but quickly realized how much effort this would require. After a couple of minutes, a tiny drop of water shimmered in front of him. His pinky toe was bigger than the drop wobbling back at him.

The ball Kelså had asked him to form was the size of his fist.

He grimaced and returned his focus to the dirt.

An hour later, he fell against a stone of the inner ring with sweat pouring down his face. A ball of water meeting Kelså's request jiggled unsteadily above the bowl. His hands shook as he struggled to contain it, tired muscles rebelling after an hour of intense magical strain. He peered up to claim victory, but his concentration failed and the ball splashed into the bowl. He leaned his head back against the cold stone and sucked in labored breaths.

Kelså clapped from her seat at the table. "Very good. What did you learn?"

Declan lolled his head toward her, too tired to lean forward. "That I don't want to stray too far from a water source. That might be the hardest thing I've ever done."

She smiled. "What else?"

"I can't think right now. I can barely move. Can we take a break and talk about this later?"

"No. This is important, perhaps the most important lesson you'll learn today." She crossed her arms. "What else?"

He stared up at the sky. The Ranger corps put new recruits through physical trials that were meant to weed out the weak, but in that moment, he couldn't recall ever being so sore. He'd barely moved throughout the exercise, but every muscle in his body cried out.

"Magic hurts like hell."

Kelså laughed. "Not the most elegant answer, but I'll take it. When you use magic, you combine your own life force with your Light. It takes both to achieve a result. You pour them into the task at hand, draining yourself in a similar way you just drained the surrounding soil of its moisture. In this case, it's your endurance, *your health*, that's being drawn out. It's exhausting, but it can also be dangerous—even deadly. Draw too much, push yourself too hard magically, and you'll literally sacrifice yourself for your task."

"That makes sense. I sure feel it right now." Declan braced himself on the stone as he struggled to his feet. "What I don't understand is how magic users, especially Mages, can do such incredible things and not cross that line. I don't remember seeing Atikus get winded, much less wrecked like I feel right now."

"Think of it like physical conditioning. When you first joined the Rangers, were you as strong as you are today? Were you able to run as far? Climb as long? Did you have to work at it consistently to build up your endurance?"

"Of course. We worked out and practiced every day."

She nodded. "Swordplay, marksmanship, magic—the idea's the same. Your endurance is built in different ways, but the same principle applies. So, my strong Ranger son, not only do we have to boost your knowledge and skill, we also have to build your magical stamina."

He passed through the rings and flopped into a chair then poured himself a glass of the wine that now tasted like plumbs. "Do we have that long? I mean, the Kingdom's invasion could come with the spring thaw. How am I going to be ready to do any good by then?"

"How long have you been here?"

He thought a moment. "A couple of weeks, maybe a little more."

She smiled and nodded. "A full day hasn't passed back on the mainland. By the time spring arrives, you will have been here nearly three years. I wish we had a hundred more . . ."

"Three years?" His mouth fell open. "That's incredible . . . but . . . do you think we'll have enough time, even with the spells?"

She stared at her hands and spoke quietly. "No. I'll make sure you're as ready as possible. I just . . . I just wish I had more time with you."

They spent the next few days practicing Water skills. Declan mastered calling water from an existing source and shaping it into something useful or hurling it across the ledge. He particularly liked that skill and instigated several all-out water battles. Drawing water from secondary sources was still challenging and painfully draining. He hoped there wouldn't be much need for that particular ability.

Kelså expanded his training to include other Elemental powers: Fire, Earth and Air. After a week of exercises and diligent study, she determined Fire was absent from Declan's magical arsenal. She gave him books to read and tried visualization techniques. She'd even built a giant bonfire in the middle of the stone circles, but Declan's magic couldn't sense the element, much less do anything with it. He was equally blind to Earth, unable to sense or touch the most basic stone with his Light.

"I know it's disappointing. Fire, in particular, offers practical applications, particularly in battle, and Earth magic is what the Phoenix used to raise the mountains on the border," she explained. "There's nothing we can do about it, so let's move on to Air."

Declan's shoulders slumped. He knew shouldn't expect to be able to do everything magic had to offer, but was still disappointed.

Fire would've been really cool.

"Declan, are you listening?" Kelså had been talking while he daydreamed about balls of flame floating above his palm.

"Sorry, can you say that again?"

She shot him an annoyed glare. "Air may seem weak compared to the other elements, but I assure you, it's not. Do you remember calling a shield that blocked arrows in your trial with the Keeper?"

"Oh, yeah. I have no idea how I did it, but that was awesome . . . until it disappeared and Atikus got shot.'

"Focus," she chided. "Air is powerful, and, like water, it's everywhere. Up here in the mountains, where things thin out, you'll have the same issue as when trying to draw water from the dirt, but in virtually every other place, you should be able to easily manipulate the surrounding air.

"The biggest challenge with air is that you can't see it. You may see the effects of its passing, like blowing leaves or swaying trees, but seeing the air itself is next to impossible."

Declan cocked his head. "I couldn't see the water in the dirt. Shouldn't it be basically the same thing here? I just use my Light to reach out and grab it?"

"Inelegant, as always, but accurate." She chuckled. "Before we try practical exercises, one word of caution. Air is naturally connected to most everything. Think about it. It's all around you right now, and you're breathing it in. So, it's actually going in and out of your body. What do you think could go wrong?"

"Oh, I know where you're going. If I draw too much or am careless about drawing, I could suck the air right out of my own lungs."

She nodded. "Not a fun experience. I've done it and nearly killed myself. It's even easier to do to another person, because you can't feel *them* being out of breath like you could if it was your own lungs. A strong draw can happen so quickly that it could be too late by the time you realized you were killing someone."

"Does it matter how close the air is when you draw? I mean—if I draw from three hundred paces away, will it take longer to shape the air than if I drew nearby?"

"No, it really wouldn't matter. The draw is so fast that you wouldn't lose any timing or effectiveness. So, given that, how would you do a draw from three hundred paces away?"

"That seems simple." Her raised brow told him to think again. "I guess . . . wouldn't I just focus on a point three hundred paces away and draw?"

"Show me with your finger. Point to where you'd draw right now."

He scanned the ledge and pointed out across the stones into the wilderness.

"Alright. That would work, but what if there were people over there, and you couldn't draw in that direction? What if you needed to draw from, say, inside the cavern?"

"I guess I could do that, but I can't see in there right now. How would I know there's no one in there? How could I even know I was actually drawing from where I wanted to, since I couldn't see it?"

"Good. Very good. Here's the rule: You can only draw from a place you've actually visited, because you'll need to recall it in your mind to guide your Light. As for people being there, that's the risk you're taking by drawing out of sight. I would only do that in extreme emergencies," she said. "Questions before we try it?"

When he didn't object, she walked them back to the center of the stone circles. "Let's use the focus point you mentioned before, three hundred paces out there in the woods. Actually, it's above the woods from here, even better. Find your Light, then reach out and sense the air. This time, don't actually touch the air, just sense it. I want you to describe what you see."

The past couple of weeks had taught him confidence, and his Light came to him without having to close his eyes to concentrate. He squinted beyond the ledge to a point high above the forest and cast his Light in that direction. It was as if part of his own consciousness was sailing toward the clouds.

"This is crazy!" he laughed.

"Tell me what you see. What you feel."

"It's like . . . like part of me floated out of my body, and I'm in both places at the same time. I can feel my Light weaving in and out of currents of air, being pushed and pulled in different directions—but it's more than wind; I can see the air shimmering as my Light passes through it. It's as though I'm painting the air with a magic brush, so it's visible for a couple of seconds. There are so many colors. It's incredible."

"The colors represent temperature and purity. Cold air appears tinged with blue, while hot air flares yellow. As your Light passes through objects, like leaves floating in the wind, those things will flare with a color of their own. Living things will pulse and have an aura that varies with their nature." Kelså paused to let him enjoy the experience. "Now, find a place where the air is pure blue, or as close to it as you can get. I want you to use your Light like you did with water and shape the air. Form a ball again."

"Ok. I found it, but how will we see it? Air's invisible, right?"

"You're infusing the air with your magic. You'll see it. Trust me."

Seconds later, a ball of air materialized, swirling high above the trees. It pulsed with shimmering light. Declan's eyes widened, and he laughed as he forced the ball to rise and fall, then zip back and forth.

"I'm doing it! I'm really doing this!"

As his excitement grew, the ball expanded and pulsed brighter. Branches on the tops of the trees began rustling and pointing upwards, as if being sucked into the ball. A chorus of birds erupted below, and hundreds of took flight, scattering in all directions.

"Declan, release it now." Kelså's voice was suddenly stern.

He didn't act immediately, and the ball continued to grow. When Kelså placed a hand on his shoulder and shook him to break his concentration, the ball dissipated, and the trees drooped back to their resting position. A shock wave of air rushed over the ledge, kicking up dirt and debris.

"What was all that?" he asked.

Kelså turned his shoulders toward her. "You lost yourself in the moment—in the excitement. We call that the Thrill of magic. This is another cautionary lesson: The whole thing is intoxicating, having power . . . being able to do things few others can do. The way magic feels when you give yourself to the moment is unlike anything else, but Declan, listen to me now. If you lose yourself like that without me here to pull you back, you will cause incredible harm to everyone and everything around you. Your Light may save you, but you will become the eye of a terrible storm."

Declan's head drooped. "That was the most incredible thing I've ever felt. It was like I was full of power and energy . . . but you're right. When I got excited, it was like the magic took over. It *wanted* to grow. Wait . . . does that mean part of our role is to contain magic when we use it?"

"That's exactly our responsibility. Son, magic is a force. It's a tool. It doesn't have a mind of its own. As a Mage, you must remain in command of your magic, or it will run wild and consume everything around you, possibly even consume you if you can't regain control."

He peered over the ledge at the trees. The birds that fled were distant dots on the horizon. He felt himself deflate thinking about how close he'd come to harming the forest with so little effort.

As he stared into the distance, Órla's voice echoed in his head. *"Now you know why we were brought together. When the time comes for you to leave the safety of the mountain, I will be the one to ground you, to protect and guide you. You are my purpose, Declan."*

He scanned about for the owl, unable to spot her anywhere near the ledge. "Where are you? How are you talking in my head again?"

"Uh, hello! Powerful, wise, magical Owl. Daughter of Magic, remember? Here I thought we were making progress." She floated down and landed on the pillar beside him.

He tried not to laugh. He really tried, but when she cocked her head and raised one bushy brow, he lost it.

Kelså eyed them both, then turned toward the cave's opening. "I don't know what that was all about, but I think that's enough for one day. I'm going inside to work on dinner."

Declan whispered to Órla, "She couldn't hear you in my head?"

She spoke in his head again. *"Nope. I can choose who hears me. We had a moment. Moment's over."*

"I heard that!" Kelså's laughter echoed through the cavern.

Declan sat on the inside edge of the inner ring of stones juggling three balls of air, a proud grin plastered across his face. Without warning, Órla zipped into the middle of the flying balls and pooped all over his boot. The balls vanished as he stared down at the white goo splattered all over the leather.

"Hey! What was that for?"

"Kelså told me to distract you while you practice to see if you could maintain your concentration." She landed on the center pillar and placed both wings on her sides, mimicking a human with hands on her hips. "Looks like you need more practice. I'll work on making more poop."

"Maybe we can come up with a *cleaner* way for you to distract me?"

Órla cocked her head. "I don't know. Target practice is fun."

Declan didn't want to encourage her but couldn't stop himself from laughing. She was just so . . . *perky*.

He stood and turned to walk to the table for something to clean his boot to find Kelså smothering laughter with a hand. "Uh, Son . . . something on your boot?"

"Very funny. Is there a towel or something I could use to clean this off?"

"Nope. Guess you'll have to think of another way." She cocked a brow.

Órla flew over and landed on the table in front of Kelså. "Declan, I'm starting to think you really *are* as dumb as you look. You have magic, silly. Use it."

"Now Órla, no need to be cruel. He's still young in his magical journey."

"I guess," Órla said, ducking her head in deference before turning back to Declan. "Sorry, Dec."

He ruffled the feathers on her head. "Keelan's the only person who ever called me Dec. Makes me miss the big guy."

"Enough, you two. Time to clean that boot, Declan," Kelså ordered.

He called a burst of wind and directed it to blow across his boot. The runny liquid dried and hardened across the leather.

Kelså and Órla giggled.

"Guess that's not right," he said sheepishly.

He then drew water from the bowl in the stone circle and directed a careful stream back and forth across the boot. Once the poop was gone, he switched to air and dried the leather. When he looked up, Kelså clapped and Órla mimicked clapping with her wings. Declan offered an exaggerated bow.

"Alright. Elemental is the easy one. Time to dive into deeper water."

"*That was easy?* Spirits, I may not make it through the rest." Declan let out a huff.

Kelså ignored him and returned to the center of the stones. "Physical, Mental, and Natural are the areas we haven't covered. Like Elemental, there's no way for me to know what abilities you may possess in each area. It's likely you'll discover abilities over time—or, more likely, learn how to apply an ability in new and different ways—but you'll need the basics in each area if you're to recognize new abilities as they arise."

Declan joined her in the center ring and leaned against a stone. "Makes sense, I guess."

"There are four key abilities that fall into the Natural pillar. Animal Communication allows you to speak with non-humans. Depending on the strength of your ability, this could be one-way or work both ways.”

“Well, I already have that box checked. Right, Órla?” He nodded toward the little owl. She continued preening and ignored their lesson.

Kelså shook her head. “Remember, what you have with Órla is a unique bond. She isn’t precisely an owl, even though that’s how she’s chosen to appear in this lifetime. The two of you can communicate telepathically, you can ‘borrow’ her vision, and I would bet you’ll find other abilities you share over time, but that doesn’t mean you’d be able to talk to the squirrel that’s sitting on the ledge over there.”

Declan followed where she pointed. A black squirrel sat chewing remnants of nuts they’d dropped around the table.

“Hey, squirrel! Can you hear me?” he shouted.

The fur ball didn’t flinch or look up.

“I was going to say I doubt you’ll end up with this ability. It’s pretty rare and tends to surface in extremely introverted, socially awkward children. You don’t fit any of that description.”

“I don’t know, Kelså. He *is* pretty awkward. You oughta see him romping through the woods. Total klutz!” Órla squawked from across the ledge.

Declan rolled his eyes, then tried using telepathy with the squirrel. *"Hey! Look over here. Got some really good wine."*

"You know I can hear you badgering that poor thing, right?" Órla's voice echoed in his head.

He turned back to Kelså. "Alright, guess that one's a bust. You said there were four Natural abilities. What else?"

"Animal Husbandry is the ability to raise and care for livestock or other animals, extending life longer than normal, and granting greater health to the beasts.

"The third is Horticulture. Think Animal Husbandry, but with plants. I doubt you have either of those two, and testing for them would take months, probably longer.

"The fourth is an interesting one I hope you possess. We call it Spirit Interaction. At its most basic level, this ability allows you to speak to spirits or ghosts. More powerful, advanced Mages with this Gift may summon spirits, or even banish them from the living realm. I haven't known anyone with this ability in generations, but it would be extremely useful as you continue on your path." Kelså knelt and began drawing in the dirt at the base of the center pillar.

"Why do you think this one would be so useful? Seems cool, but kinda creepy." Declan's brow furrowed as he imagined ghosts everywhere.

"Well, think about the mission you were helping your brother with. What if he could've spoken to the spirit of the girl who was taken from Freeport and later killed. What could an investigator learn from their victim to help solve the crime or stop the killer from striking again?" She stepped back and examined at her drawing, then looked up at him. "Now, imagine you're fighting a war for the survival of your people, your country, and you could compel the spirit of an enemy to speak? What could you learn?"

"Okay, I get it. I see how that would be helpful, but it's still creepy."

Kelså pointed at the ground. "Look at this symbol."

Declan studied her drawing. A large outer circle contained a square whose corners touched the inside edge of the circle. Inside the square was another circle whose edges touched the inside of the square. Two perpendicular lines began at the inner edge of the innermost circle and formed a cross that intersected at the exact center of the drawing. The whole thing reminded Declan of a device he'd seen a sailor use once to sight the horizon.

"What does it do?" he asked.

"This is a summoning circle. It focuses your magic and creates a barrier between the world of the living and that of the dead. Mages who can summon, entrap, or banish spirits use the circle as the foundation for their work, and most have circles crafted or inlaid to ensure stability. It's critical the circles remain unbroken, or whoever you've summoned will escape and cause untold havoc. Spirits, especially of those long dead, are not generally friendly to the living, and some are outright hostile," she said.

"Great. Don't let dead people escape. Got it." Declan reached up and ran his hand through his hair.

"*Psst*, Kelså. He's nervous when he does that thing with his hair," Órla whispered.

Declan's hand froze. "The idea of bringing spirits around for a chat doesn't make *you* nervous?"

Órla laughed. "Good one, Dec. I *am* a spirit, returned to your world in the familiar form of a brilliant and beautiful owl for your comfort and viewing pleasure."

Declan turned to his mother. "One day, you're going to have to explain all of that to me."

She smiled and nodded.

"Let's stay on track." She shot Órla a glare. "Communicating with the spirit of a person who recently died is the easiest of these skills. As a general rule, the more recent the death, the easier the communication. If the person's body is nearby, that makes things even easier. Spirits gravitate toward their physical shell even after they are separated by death. An item of particular sentimental value to the person comforts the spirit and also makes communicating easier."

"I'm not going to sleep after this, am I?" Declan said.

Kelså ignored his comment. "Communicating with a spirit that is nearby is relatively simple. You just talk to them like you would anyone else. Unfortunately, if your Gift in this area is weak, they will probably ignore you or run away. The power of your innate Natural Gift compels the spirit to remain and converse. There's nothing you can really do to boost that, other than have use personal item.

"The most difficult end of the spectrum is to summon the spirit of someone long dead *and* where you don't have anything of sentimental value. In other words, you're summoning them blind, across hundreds of years or more."

"Why would I even want to do that?"

She thought a moment. "Let's assume the last person with your same power wasn't Irina, and you could talk with him or her about your abilities. Would that be helpful?"

"Of course, it would. That would be awesome. I mean, you're doing great teaching me, but you don't have all these abilities. If I could talk with someone who did, who knew how to use them, I could learn so much more . . . and faster." Declan surprised himself with his own enthusiasm.

"I'll just ignore you comparing my teaching style to a dead person," Kelså quipped. "The basic principle in summoning is picturing the person in your mind as if you truly believe they are standing in front of you. Once you have their image firmly in place, touch your Light. The summoning circle and your Light will do the rest. You'll then be able to release the mental image and communicate with the spirit. To release the spirit, simply release your Light."

"Sounds easy enough. What's the catch?"

"The catch is that we don't even know if you have this ability or not. I don't, and wouldn't be able to sense a spirit even if you summoned one. You'll have to practice on your own, and I won't be able to tell if you struggle because you're doing something wrong, or because you simply don't have this ability at all.

"For today, let's just have you practice drawing a summoning circle. It's a simple pattern, but very precise. If you get even the slightest angle off, your summoning won't work. Worse, if you fail to close your circles, the spirit *will* escape."

Kelså handed Declan the stick she'd been using, and he spent the next hour drawing and erasing the summoning circle. He was surprised how difficult the simple magical symbol was to draw, but twenty attempts cemented it in his mind.

When Declan stepped back onto the ledge, Kelså sat at the table with two glasses of wine filled to the brim in front of her. He walked over and sat, intrigued by an afternoon of exercises *and* wine.

She read his thoughts and chuckled. "Yes, you get to drink the wine. Down them both-and don't sip this time. We need you fully loaded."

"Yes, ma'am!" He grabbed the first cup and lifted it to his lips, careful not to let a drop spill. "How does this stuff never get old? I mean, it tastes better every time."

"Actually, that's an interesting observation. The magic in the wine senses what you like, what pleases and comforts you, then adapts to your changing interest or taste. We designed it as a healing drought and thought it would be more effective if the patient enjoyed the experience. I think we can both recall medicine that might've tasted worse than the injury felt, right?" She smiled as he downed the second glass. "Remind me never to get into a drinking contest with you."

"You wanted your boy to have skills, right?" He winked.

"Handling wine like a champ . . . just what *every* mother wants in her son," she snorted and some of her wine splashed onto the ground.

"Careful, mother. That's alcohol abuse."

Órla flapped onto the table. "Alright, you two. What does Declan getting drunk in the middle of the day have to do with Mental magic? Other than I'm going *mental* just thinking about it?"

Kelså snorted again and covered her mouth with the back of her hand. When Órla tottered over to her glass and dunked her head in for a drink, Declan lost any semblance of composure and snorted along with his mother.

"Snorting must be a family trait. Any other weird noises I should know about?" Declan heard Órla chirp n his mind. Her head popped out of the glass, beak dripping with wine. He reached across the table and gave her head an affectionate scratch, and she craned her neck to give him better access.

Kelså finally gathered herself and cleared her throat. "So, we're working on Mental magic this afternoon. There are more abilities in this Pillar than any other, but they're very specialized, which makes it nearly impossible to possess more than two—even for someone like you.

"Let's start with the ones I'm fairly certain we can rule out. Heightened Senses allows the user significantly improved hearing, sight, or smell. If you had this one, we'd know it already because it manifests at a very early age.

"Empathy is similar in that it usually manifests by the age of three or four. It's often overwhelming for small children, causing them to act out. If a Mage isn't consulted, parents often assume the child is disturbed or ill. Those cases rarely end well. Regardless, I think we can safely strike that off the list.

"Atikus is the best example of Enhanced Memory I've ever known. He may actually have perfect recall. If you had this ability, you would've only needed to try the summoning circle once. I've been watching for signs of this ability since you arrived and am confident it's not in your tool kit."

"You callin' me slow, Ma? Thanks a lot."

"That brings us to Enhanced Charisma. Spirits help me, I think you've overdosed on this one." Kelså stood and motioned for them to move to the stone circles. "Atikus reported signs of this one when you were very little, charming everyone in the Guild with a wicked smile. He couldn't sense your magic at that age, but believed you'd grow into a powerful Gift."

"It had to be his smile," Órla couldn't stop herself. "It couldn't have been his hair. That's a bird's nest—and I'm a bird. I would know!"

"Hey! Many people love my wavy locks." Declan flicked his hair off his shoulder and turned dramatically away from Órla.

"I believe that's a 'yes' for Charisma Overkill." Órla peeped.

"Class, back to me, please." Kelså shook her head at the never-ending banter. "Enhanced Charisma is a passive ability. That means it's not something you turn on or off with your Light. It's either present, or it's not, like Atikus's memory. I'm afraid there's nothing we can do about your painful likability, son."

"If it's my burden, I'll bear it." He placed a hand over his heart and bowed his head in mock solemnity.

Kelså rolled her eyes and stifled another snort. "That leaves us with Telepathy and Illusion. Telepathy is one of the easiest abilities to master, but Illusion ranks up there with Healing as the two hardest.

"Let's start with Telepathy. Once you've mastered the basics, you'll be able to speak into someone's mind without much effort, similar to how you speak with your voice. You ready?"

He nodded.

"Touch and hold your Light, and *think* as though you were speaking to me. It will help if you look at me. You should eventually be able to do all of this without the visual queue."

Kelså walked to the outside of the second ring of stones and turned to face him. He squared with her and began to concentrate, reaching for his Light. The wine in his belly served as an amplifier, and his magic flared brightly before him. He threw his hand into the pulsing flame and tried calling out to his mother.

"That wine sure makes my Light go crazy!"

Kelså replied in his mind. *"Those are the first words every mother hopes to hear from her baby boy."*

He giggled like his ten-year-old self. *"This is awesome! Órla can you hear this? I'm Telepathing!"*

"Great. You're talking in my head and *making up words. I'll never have a moment's peace!"* She leapt from the table, streaked by him, and pooped on his boot before soaring out over the neighboring treetops.

Declan's concentration snapped, and his Light winked out as he stared down. He shook his head and drew moisture from the air to wash away the poop. "I'm going to pluck that little owl one of these days!"

"Heard that!" Órla called from a league away.

"Telepathy is a yes." Kelså walked back to the stones' center. "Now, this next one is going to be tough. I believe you have the ability to create Illusions because of your Telepathy and other Gifts, but we won't know for sure until it works."

"What makes Illusion so hard?"

"With most other skills, like manipulating water or air, you're pushing your Light out, or using it to shape an inanimate object. With Illusion, you're actually reaching into another person's mind. You aren't creating an image in your own mind and pushing it out into the world for others to see; you're using your magic *in theirmind* to alter what they *think* they are seeing."

"Um, okay, that just made my head hurt."

"That's why I made you drink all that wine. You were right when you said it acts as an amplifier for your Light—at least when taken in large quantities. The stones are an even more powerful amplifier that we'll definitely need throughout the rest of your lessons. As challenging as Illusion may be, Healing is the *most* difficult of all skills. We'll need all the help we can get with that one."

"Great. Can't wait," he said sarcastically.

"Let me show you what a successful illusion looks like, and how it feels to the target." Kelså closed her eyes, and the stones of the circles began to glow. Nothing happened for a few seconds, then a white and brown dog appeared in front of Keelan. It spun in circles and barked up at him. His mouth moved, but there was no sound. Declan's eyes widened at how lifelike the dog appeared and decided to try petting it. As he knelt and reached out, his hand passed through the image.

He jumped back.

"Whoa! That was wild. It felt like my skin was going to tingle off my hand."

The dog vanished and Kelså's eyes popped open. "Now *that's* interesting. That was my magic you felt. I've never heard of anyone being able to feel another's magic like that."

"I keep trying to tell you, he's a weird one!" Órla's voice echoed in both of their minds.

Declan chuckled. "Just when you think we're alone . . ."

"I don't think you'll ever be alone again, son." Kelså's eyes smiled. "Back to Illusion. I know it looked like I was projecting the image of the dog onto the ground in front of you, but I wasn't. That was your mind *thinking* it saw a dog because I was casting the image into your mind."

"Sounds like there could be a lot of ways to abuse that power. What if I wanted to block you from doing that?"

"Great question. A Mage with enough skill can Shield her mind. I suspect that's in your bag of tricks, too, but we need to make sure you have the power of Illusion before we try to tackle Shielding. Another challenge with Illusion is that each person's mind is unique, so your magic will have to be wielded in a slightly different manner with each person."

"I'm starting to see why you said this one's so tough. If every mind is different, and I'm trying to cast an Illusion in a mind I'm not familiar with, it'll be like learning the skill all over again. What a pain."

"It's not quite that bad. Once you learn the basics, it gets easier, but you're right about always having to adapt to the target's mind, and if that person is a Mage, things get even more complicated. They might try to Shield or use some kind of counter on you. There are even Enchanted items that block mental intrusion."

He turned to follow her into the cave. "Enchanting? You haven't said anything about that power yet."

"It's coming. It's in the Physical family with Healing and a few others." She picked up the wine glassed off the table. "The sky's darkening. Let's get cleaned up, and you can help me make dinner. I'll teach you the power of Chopping Vegetables."

He stopped walking and cocked his head. "Chopping Vegetables? That's a power?"

Órla drifted down, landed on Kelså's shoulder, and whispered in her ear, "Please go slow. He's really pretty, but not that smart."

Kelså's high pitched laugh was punctuated with rapid-fire snorts that echoed off the mountainside.

"I really don't want to know, do I?" Declan raised a brow at Órla, then walked through the cavern's entrance.

"And he calls *me* perky!" Órla whispered.

Kelså's snorts bounced through the passageways, only ending as Declan reached the blissful quiet of his room.

Chapter Eighteen

"**S**o, what do you make of the King?" Keelan lay on his cot, staring at ceiling.

After their initial audience with Alfred, Keelan and Atikus were escorted back to the army encampment and placed in a small tent with two regulars assigned to guard their "guests." Aside from the cots, the tent was empty.

"He looked like the stress was starting to get to him. His daughter was kidnapped, his nation's going to war—I can't blame him for being on edge, but there was more than that. I could feel it. We're missing something important." Atikus paced between the beds, the only clear space that allowed more than a stride. "We've met before, the King and I, though he likely doesn't remember. It was more than twenty years ago. The Arch Mage sent a delegation to Fontaine to offer magical assistance rebuilding one of their port towns after a hurricane struck and blew everything to pieces."

"I didn't know we had good relations, other than through trade routes."

"We haven't, really. Velius thought reaching out in a time of need like that might lead us to a better place—show our good faith in building a stronger kinship," Atikus said.

"Did it work? Certainly doesn't look like it lasted very long if it did."

Atikus stopped pacing and sat on the edge of his bunk. "I don't know. The people of Cooper were certainly thankful for our help, but the men around the King were less enthusiastic. It felt like they were always suspicious, waiting for us to make demands in return for our aid."

"Did anything come of your work afterwards?"

Atikus shook his head. "No. I can't recall anyone even mentioning the visit again."

"That's a shame. Sounds like a missed opportunity."

Atikus was settling into his cot when the tent's flaps flew open, and Commander Paul appeared.

"Hope you gents are well rested. The King would like to see you again."

"That was quick. We've only been back here a few hours." Keelan sat up.

Paul chuckled. "Again, you're asking me to jump into the mind of royalty? I barely understand them half the time, but I know how to follow orders, and His Majesty requires your presence. I'll be right outside when you're ready."

A few minutes later, Commander Paul handed the pair off to the Royal Guard at the inn. They were surprised when the giant leader of the King's protection force opened the door and stepped back to allow them entry. He followed and stood near the table where King and his son waited.

"Lieutenant, Mage, come and sit. Would you like something to eat? Or a drink, perhaps?" The King's change in tone made Atikus's brows furrow.

"I'd love an ale, Your Majesty," Atikus said.

Alfred smiled broadly and nodded to Justin. "And Lieutenant?"

"Uh . . . the same, thank you."

Justin rose and scampered behind the bar, returning a moment later with three ales and a glass brimming with wine. Alfred cocked a brow when Justin set an ale down in front of his own seat but decided not to embarrass the boy in front of strangers. A smile of victory crept onto Justin's face as he sipped quietly.

"It's amazing what one can learn when he's the King." Alfred swirled his wine, eyeing Keelan over the top of the glass. "You are quite famous on the other side of the mountains, Lieutenant."

"I suppose. Crime stories sell papers, and I've been fortunate to solve a few."

Alfred turned to Justin. "Son, that's what true modesty looks like. You won't see much of it from the people swarming around court. Refreshing, isn't it?"

Justin met Keelan's eyes. "Are you really as good as they say?"

Keelan leaned forward. "I am, Your Highness."

Justin seemed thrown off by Keelan's directness and stared into his mug.

Alfred turned to Atikus. "And you, Mage, are known to us as well. I believe it has been twenty-two years since your last visit, though. Why have you avoided our hospitality for so long?"

Atikus's brows rose again. "Your Majesty, I had no idea you recalled my visit. It was an honor to assist in your people's time of need. I had hoped we could have found more opportunities to share with each other. It saddens me to think that our next engagement may be across a battlefield."

"I never dreamed my legacy would include another war." Sadness crossed Alfred's face. "Regardless, I have never forgotten your efforts, Mage Danai. Members of our Guild speak highly of you. They say you are an honorable man."

"I like to think so." Atikus's cheeks reddened slightly.

"Good. Very good." Alfred leaned back and paused a moment. "We need your help, and I have decided to trust you. You may refuse, but if you do, you will be considered prisoners of war and detained until our conflict ends."

Keelan and Atikus glanced at each other, dumbfounded.

The King spoke before they could voice their confusion. "You already know that my daughter and heir, Princess Jessia, was kidnapped some time ago. She and her captors were spotted on the King's Road headed in this direction but haven't been seen or heard from since. There have been no demands, and I fear she is being taken to Irina's Seat like your Healer.

"What only a few know is that my wife, Queen Isabel, also went missing a few days ago. She may have used an amulet to Travel in search of Jess. She and I argued about that option, and I forbade her from doing so, but she's never been one to follow *anyone's* orders.

"We also cannot discount the possibility that she was also kidnapped. If that is true, we have some serious issues with our personal security, because she would've been taken from the royal pavilion in the midst of our army while we traveled here, and I have a hard time believing that theory.

"Either way, the Queen and Princess are missing. I want you to find them and bring them back to me. Do this, and you will be free—and I will be deeply in your debt."

Keelan was stunned. "Your Majesty, I'm sorry for your daughter and wife. I truly am, but this is makes no sense. You're preparing to invade our country. How do you expect your people to cooperate with an investigation led by two Melucians? Based on what we saw with that crowd in Rutin, they'd rather string us up than help with anything. We wouldn't even be able to talk to people without raising suspicion, and I can't recall ever leading a successful investigation without interviewing witnesses."

Keelan sat back and ran his hand over his head while he stared at the King.

Atikus reached over, placed a hand on Keelan's arm, and spoke into his mind. *"Keelan, I know this sounds impossible, but what choice do we have? He'll just throw us in jail until the war's over. I get the impression he doesn't really want the war, so we may be able to prevent something terrible. Hear him out."*

"Keelan, let's talk this through. If you were to agree to the King's investigation, how would you go about it?" Atikus's fatherly tone caught the King's attention, but he remained silent.

Keelan turned. "Well, I'd need all the basic information. Someone who knows the facts would have to let me question them for as long as it took."

Alfred leaned forward. "What would you need to know? There can be no higher priority for the crown than finding the Queen and heir."

Keelan compiled a mental list, then spoke. "What happened? When? Where? Were there any witnesses? Who were they? Where are they now? Was anything found at the location where each was taken? I'll have a hundred other questions once we get into it."

"I can answer most of those questions. Begin," Alfred said.

Keelan cocked his head toward Atikus. *"I believe the King just gave you permission to question* him. *"*

This is going to be a long, weird day, Keelan thought.

"King Alfred, you said the Princess was taken from the road? How long ago was that?" he asked.

"Nine days ago."

"Were there any witnesses? Did your teams see anything?"

"Jess ran away with her boyfriend, Danym Wilfred, the High Sheriff's son. One of our teams tracked them from the town of Spoke up the King's Road. There were several units patrolling nearby, so the commander ordered a whistler to mark their location. That spooked the pair, and they fled. Our units searched the area but found no trace of them. They'd simply vanished."

"Tell me about Danym."

"You'd really have to talk with the Sheriff to learn more about his boy. I barely knew him. Isabel and I didn't even know they were seeing each other until a week or so before they disappeared. They were meeting secretly in the woods just outside the palace grounds."

Justin cleared his throat, and all eyes turned to him. "Uh . . . well, Dad, I can probably help with Danym."

The King's eyes widened. "You *knew*, didn't you?"

Justin nodded.

"I should've guessed. You and Jess were always close. Well, go on. Tell the Lieutenant what you know about him."

"I really like Danym. He's funny and smart, and he treats Jess like a queen. Well, she will be—you know what I mean." He fidgeted with his hands.

"Do you know how long they had been meeting in the woods?" Keelan asked.

Justin shot his father a glance, then looked back at his hands.

"Now's not the time to go quiet, Justin. Your sister's life is at stake," Alfred said.

"A little over a year."

The King leaned back so fast he nearly tipped his chair backwards. "A *year*? Are you sure?"

Justin's head rose, and he nodded.

Alfred threw his elbows onto the table and planted his face in his palms in a most un-kingly gesture.

Keelan studied the interplay between father and son without reacting but decided it was time to save the King. He clearly hadn't known his daughter was carrying on behind his back until recently.

"Justin, I need to know everything you can tell me about Danym and any conversations Jess may have told you about. Anything, even something small, could be helpful."

Justin turned to his father, then back to Keelan. He started to say something a couple of times but lost his nerve.

Atikus finally leaned toward the King. "Your Majesty, I know this is a difficult situation, but perhaps we should let Justin and Keelan speak alone."

Alfred started to object, but Justin chimed in. "That would be great. Perfect. Yes, let's do that."

Alfred blew out a breath. "Fine. You two go somewhere else while the Mage and I talk. The Royal Guard goes with you everywhere, understand?"

Justin bolted out of his chair and grabbed a surprised Keelan by the arm. "Let's go, Lieutenant, before he changes his mind."

Keelan grunted and gave the King a sympathetic glance before following the boy out of the common room. They were immediately surrounded by guards, all of whom eyed the Prince with curious gazes.

"The Captain is with my dad . . . er . . . the King. You are to accompany us . . . to . . . wherever we go." Justin shot Keelan a questioning eye.

Keelan leaned down and whispered, "They work for you. Remember that and keep your head up. You'll get the hang of this, *Your Highness.*"

Justin nodded nervously. "I guess you're right. Second sons aren't used to being in charge of anything. Everybody expects . . . I don't know . . . for me to be ready to fill Jess's shoes overnight."

"What was that about holding your head up, soldier?" Keelan grinned. "Now, where to?"

"Why don't we go down by the lake? I'd rather not be overheard talking about . . . *you know who.*"

"So, while we're walking, why don't we start with how *you know who* . . . met the other *you know who*?"

Justin chuckled. Despite talking about his sister's kidnapping, he couldn't help liking the giant Melucian. "I don't know where they met, just that Jess thought our mom would hate it if she found out. Dad started including her in Privy Council sessions and court when she was fourteen. I guess she picked up on something between mom and the Sheriff.

"Jess would go riding a lot just to get out of the palace, so it wasn't a stretch for her to ride into the woods. She and Danym found a clearing where they'd meet and have picnics. She took me there a couple of times."

When they finally reached the edge of the lake, Justin walked aimlessly along the shoreline, debating how much to tell Keelan, but once he started talking, everything came tumbling out.

He confessed that he *did* remember when they'd met.

"Try to remember how Jess described it to you," Keelan said. "Just take a breath and play back her words, how she told the story."

Justin nodded. "I'll try." Long moments of passed with nothing but the breeze and the rippling of the lake's surface to break the silence. Suddenly, in a faraway voice, Justin began Jess's tale, that began with the Queen's birthday ball held every spring, the social occasion of the year for Fontaine's elite.

Danym didn't want to attend, but his father insisted. How would it look if the son of a Privy Counselor refused to show his face at the Queen's favorite event? She already fought him at every turn in Council sessions. He certainly didn't need to fuel that fire.

For most of the night, Danym clung to the walls, desperate to avoid the eyes of the revelers. Most of the women wore ridiculous plumed hats with white or black lace covering their eyes. He watched as hundreds twirled about the floor in their lavish gowns and tailored long coats. The music was loud and the people were louder, especially as wine and ale flowed freely. The whole thing was a pompous, drunken circus to Danym, and he wanted nothing to do with it.

Then she noticed him.

In contrast to the ridiculous fashions of the courtiers, Jess wore a simple green gown that clung to her figure and shimmered as she walked. She refused to plume herself, preferring her traditional diamond-and-ruby tiara with matching earrings and necklace. The evening might've been held in our mother's honor, but I remember how Jess stole the show from the moment she arrived.

Danym later told her his breath caught when he noticed her looking at him.

Bachelors of all ages assaulted Jess, begging for a dance or a stroll. In her early teens, the attention had been flattering, but now she saw it as tiring, bordering on insufferable. She could never be sure if they were more interested in her or her crown. Deep down, she loved the attention, even craved it, but her heart wanted something more, something deeper, something she'd never really known.

Danym was so quiet, so shy, openly hiding from the swirling mass of socialites. Her ladies giggled as they mocked "the weird boy in the corner," but Jess thought that awkward shyness was his most endearing trait.

Other girls saw him as awkward, but she thought he was handsome. Years of training with his father's men added muscle and height to his already athletic frame. Jess would drone about his wavy shoulder-length hair and his chestnut eyes to match.

Danym was staring into his cup when she glided up beside him and commanded him to dance. After a painfully long moment, his head lifted, and their eyes met. Unlike so many others who wanted something from the crown—or feared it—he didn't act intimidated by her title or family … or anything. In that gaze, she found a boy who was quiet and thoughtful, one who wanted to know the girl rather than the throne. Her regal confidence evaporated, and she devolved into a timid, self-conscious fifteen-year-old girl.

They talked for a while, sipping wine at the edge of the ballroom. Jess finally tired of the constant stream of suitors begging to pull her back onto the dance floor and suggested Danym escort her through the palace gardens.

They strolled for hours.

The Sheriff interrupted their conversation as morning's hues began to paint the sky. She ran back inside and woke me, breathless as she described the night. She always thought it was funny that our mother despised the match born at a party thrown in her honor.

Keelan listened. Justin wasn't what he had expected of a royal son. He was humble and good-natured, almost shy, but there was also strength and intelligence behind his eyes. His memories were clear and vivid as he relayed his account with the skill of a bard. It was hard to not like the Prince, making Keelan wonder if his Gift involved Persuasion or Charisma.

"Did you ever spend time with them?" Keelan finally asked, when Justin remained silent.

"A few times, but hey were a lot to take. Jess turned from a strong future queen into a lovey, giggly girl so sweet my teeth hurt." Justin grinned.

"Tell me about Danym. What's he like? Not what Jess told you, but what you saw when you were together."

He thought. "He's quiet, kinda reserved, but once you get to know him, he can be funny. I like him."

Keelan waited. When Justin offered no more, he asked, "What else? What kind of things does he like to do?"

"Oh . . . well, being the High Sheriff's son, he gets to train with the palace's Armsmaster. I only saw him sparring a few times, but he's good. He's really fast, too. You can tell by watching that he's great at reading an opponent, anticipating their moves. I think he won a few local tournaments.

"Jess told me about how he wanted to go up into the Spires to get away from the city and just hike or camp. She loved the idea of getting away, but I don't think Her Highness would've loved the camping part." Justin chuckled at the thought of Jess sleeping on the ground without ladies to dust it for her.

"Did you ever see him get angry? Did she ever mention anything like that?"

"No, not at all. He really is the nicest guy. I was only with them a few times but never even heard him raise his voice, and if he'd been angry with Jess, she would've told me. I'm the one person she tells everything."

Justin resumed meandering along the waterline.

"You two sound pretty close."

"She's my best friend, always has been."

"What about the rumors that you want to take her place in the succession? I live hundreds of leagues from Fontaine in a different country, and I've heard those stories." Keelan watched him closely.

Justin actually laughed. "That's always been a joke with us. I don't know where it started, but I've *never* wanted the throne. Have you seen the life the King has to live? In a bubble? With petty little nobles nipping at his heels night and day? I don't want to be some wandering adventurer or anything, but I've *never* wanted to be King.

"Besides, Mom and Dad have been grooming Jess since she was old enough to talk. I think they actually put a tiara on her head as a baby so she could get used to the weight. She's really good at it, too, at least the parts she's been allowed to do so far." He bent and pick a rock off the bank, then tossed it into the water. "She sees a bigger picture. I barely know half of it exists until she explains it, and people like her when she's not being a . . . teenage girl." He gave Keelan a wan smile, then turned to continue aimlessly forward.

"Did Jess have any enemies? Anyone she mentioned who might want to hurt her?"

Justin's eyes widened. "She's sixteen and hardly ever leaves the palace. How could she have enemies?"

"Well, how do the people feel about having *a queen* next, instead of a king like they've had for centuries?"

"Okay, there is that. I guess that's where the rumors about me wanting the throne came from, too. From what dad says, there's a group of people out there who hate the idea of a woman ruling the Kingdom. It all seems so stupid to me, but I guess if somebody was angry enough about that, they might want her out of the way."

"And Sheriff Wilfred? What does *he* think about a woman on the throne?"

Justin spun around to square with Keelan. "The High Sheriff? You think he had something to do with this?"

Keelan shrugged. "Do you?"

"Of course not! He's my godfather and has been one of Dad's most loyal counselors since the day he took the throne. He's *family*."

"Family that your mom openly dislikes?"

"Mom hates everybody except Lord Sneak . . . er . . . I mean the High Chancellor."

Keelan grunted. "Why do you call him Lord Sneak?"

"It's probably not fair. He does a lot for the Kingdom and my parents, but something about him makes my skin crawl. It always has."

"Alright. What about the other members of Council?"

"Until Jess went missing, I never attended Council meetings. I've avoided the court as much as possible. Jess would know, though. She knew every little secret and enjoyed the games all those people play, even though she said she hated them."

"What about your mother? Anyone want to hurt her?" Keelan asked.

"Only half the Kingdom." Justin laughed again. "Mom can be . . . well . . . a lot. She's strong and stubborn, but what queen isn't? If people knew half of what goes on, especially around the Council table, they'd see her differently. Dad's the King, and he makes the final decisions, but he leans on her a lot. I've heard him tell Jess the most important decision she'll ever make is who she chooses to sit by her. It's ironic they tried to choose a husband for her after telling her that."

Keelan let that hang a second before asking, "So, tell me about that. Who did they try to set her up with?"

"I wasn't actually there for any of it, but Jess told me about it. I've never seen her so mad. That's why she and Danym ran away in the first place. I know Mom and Dad had dinner with Jess and the three men, but she left before she could tell me anything about that night. I tried but couldn't get Mom or Dad to tell me anything, either. Mom was in one of her moods, so I stayed out of it."

Justin stopped walking and stared out over the lake as he spoke. He described the day Jess was introduced to her potential suitors in the throne room. She had actually dressed for the audience, determined to show the Queen that she could rise above, be a monarch, even when she faced a terrible situation. Then Lord Parna had waddled into the room, and her facade had cracked. The arrogant, garish little man was disgusting. He might've commanded Fort Huntcliff and the eastern lands, but immense power couldn't overcome his immense ego. Then they ushered in Treasurer Dask and General Marks, two of the King's Privy Counselors. When General Marks, whom the royal children called "Uncle Ethan," was introduced as a potential suitor, Jess spiraled into a dark mood that carried over to the dinner that night. After storming out of the dining room, she ran away, leaving only a note on Justin's pillow.

"I can understand why Duke Parna was on the list, but why the Treasurer or General? Any ideas?" Keelan asked.

"You'd have to ask my mother, but I guess she wanted to offer Jess someone familiar. General Marks is a good man—one of the best. Jess might be a hundred years younger, but she wouldn't have to worry about him mistreating her or trying to take her throne. He'd actually be a good King-consort. Treasurer Dask is immensely rich. Mom might've wanted to tie that wealth more closely to the Crown, but that's just my guess."

Keelan switched tracks again. "Did Jess ever mention anything about running away? Where she might want to go if she did?"

Justin rolled his eyes. "She's sixteen. She talked about running away once a week. Nobody took her seriously. I mean, really. She's going to be Queen of the Spires. Who runs away from that?"

Keelan smiled. "You actually sound like someone who might run from the throne."

"Oh, I'd sure *want* to, but our family has a duty. It's hard for others to understand, but we believe in that duty. It's sacred. That's drilled into us before we speak our first words. I still can't believe Jess—."

"So, she never talked about somewhere else she might want to live? Just in a daydream?" Keelan pressed.

Justin thought a moment. "She's been on a few trips with Mom and Dad, but I can't remember her ever really mentioning anywhere special. She did talk about Melucia and the border states a few times, but we all talk about stuff like that. I never thought she meant anything by it."

Keelan turned and began walking back toward town, and Justin followed his lead. "We'd better get back before your father thinks I stole you away. Everybody's a bit jumpy these days."

"You can say that again. I can't wait to get back home."

"Oh, one more question. Have you ever heard of the Children?"

"Sure. They're the nuts who worship Empress Irina. Tutors mention them when they teach about the Kingdom War. I don't think I've ever seen one, though. They're supposed to be really secretive."

"Sounds about right," Keelan said.

As they reached the inn, they were passed from one group of Protectors to another. Keelan hesitated at the door, but Justin barely broke stride, used to being surrounded by the heavily armed guards. The King and Atikus were talking quietly when they entered.

"Come, sit. Was Justin helpful?" The King motioned to the chair beside Atikus, then looked to his son as if trying to read how their conversation went.

"You have a fine son, Your Majesty. He was most informative."

"Excellent. So, will you accept my charge? Will you help find my wife and daughter?"

Keelan looked to Atikus, then met the King's gaze and bowed. "Of course, Your Majesty. I am a Lieutenant of the Guard. My life is bound in service . . . to whoever may be in need."

The King smiled up at Keelan, then nodded his approval, as Atikus reached over and patted Keelan's shoulder.

Chapter Nineteen

The next morning, Kelså and Declan met for breakfast. Side by side, they enjoyed the simple pleasure of making a meal together. As she dropped bacon into the hot iron pan, he stepped back and smiled. He would turn twenty years old in a week, and this was the first time in his life that he felt at peace—*really* at peace. There was something about his mother's love, the way she looked at him, her smile, her gentle touch on his cheek; he couldn't quite understand its power, but he knew it to be a magic all its own.

She turned and caught him staring.

"Care to share?" She flipped the sizzling bacon.

When he didn't immediately answer, she turned and faced him. "Son, what is it?"

He smiled and glared at his boots as he spoke. "It's still hard to believe you're real sometimes. I mean, I always thought you were dead, that I'd never get a chance to know you, but here we are and it feels so . . . I don't know . . . normal. Okay, that's not right. You're teaching me magic to defend the world from destruction, and I'm being hounded by a talking owl. There's nothing normal about that, but you're my mother . . . and that feels . . . *right*."

She reached up and moved a curl from his face, then cupped his cheek. "I love you so much, Declan. I never thought we'd have this time together either, but I thank the Spirits every day that you were brought into my life."

"I wish Keelan could be here, could know you, too. He really needs this. We both do."

"We all need this, son." She turned away quickly as a tear escaped. "But, when you've lived as long as I have, you learn not to say the words *never* or *impossible*. Maybe one day we can all be together."

A loud *pop* made them both jump.

"For now, the bacon needs me more than you do. Go get the table ready." She swatted him playfully with her spatula.

An hour later, the table was cleared, dishes washed, and Declan sat sipping wine by the stone circles. Kelså walked out with Órla perched comfortably on her shoulder.

"I've enlisted a little help for your lessons this morning." Kelså gave Órla an affectionate scratch as she walked to the center of the stones, where the owl hopped off and began splashing about the bowl on the center stone.

"You gonna teach me how to turn Órla into something big and scary?" Declan grinned as he stood and set his glass on the table.

"Careful, Big D. Those boots look very inviting this morning," Órla said before ducking her head under the water.

He chuckled and turned back to Kelså. "It's never boring here. I'll give you that."

"This morning we should be able to learn if you have the ability to cast Illusions. If you can, we'll spend the next month, possibly longer, working on that skill."

"Why so long? I mean, I know you said it was hard, but is it really that important?"

She raised a brow. "Of course, it is. Just think about your time in the mountains before you came here. You said there were scouts searching through the forest, right? What if you could've made them believe there were tens—or *hundreds* of Rangers in those woods?"

He nodded. "We might've scared them off, made them report misinformation. I see where you're going."

"Let's figure out if you can even cast an illusion, then we can worry about applications." She took Declan's hand. "Alright, close your eyes and touch your Light."

"Got it."

"Now, let's use something very familiar to you. Hmm . . . picture Órla in your mind. See every feather, every tiny detail. Don't let go of your Light while you're doing this," she instructed.

"Alright. I see her."

"This is the hardest part. Hold both her image and your Light, then reach forward and find the Light in my mind. If it helps, imagine yourself walking toward me and then search my mind," she said.

Declan's brow furrowed, and sweat trickled down forehead. "I . . . think I see a faint glow. I'm reaching out to it."

"Good. Don't touch it. Take the image of Órla and 'push' it onto the glow, onto my Light."

When several minutes of silence passed, Órla spoke in Kelså's mind. *"Anything?"*

"I see him. His Light…" She paused a few seconds. *"I think I see…something. It's faint. It's…gone."*

Declan blew out a huge breath and opened his eyes. "That's so hard. It feels like juggling balls that have a mind of their own. You have to focus on so many things all at once. Did I do it?"

Kelså opened her eyes. "I saw something, but it wasn't clear, and it disappeared quickly."

"Go take a few sips of your wine, and we'll try again. This time, Órla, whisper something Declan should make me see, but don't tell me what it is. That should be a better way to know if you're actually projecting the image into my mind, or if I'm creating the image on my own."

Declan was more than happy to comply, stumbling to the table and downing another glass of wine in a few gulps.

"Show her me again," Órla whispered in his mind.

Declan grinned at his clever little friend. "Ready when you are."

The second time, Kelså could make out the silhouette of an owl, but the image shimmered and failed before she could positively identify it as Órla.

Declan slumped back against one of the stones, his shirt drenched in sweat and his chest heaving with each breath. "Spirits, I thought I had it that time."

"You did well for your second attempt. Illusion is extremely difficult. I'm surprised you were able to conjure much of anything. What you proved is that you *have* the Illusion Gift. We just have to help you master it." Declan saw a hint of pride in Kelså's smile. "We'll try again. This time I'm going to raise my mental wards so you know how a Shield looks and feels."

"Alright, but I need a break. It's crazy how drained I feel from just a few minutes." He hobbled back to the table and filled yet another glass.

"We've been testing your abilities and learning a few useful skills. Tomorrow we'll test for Healing aptitude, but the rest of our time will be spent building up your magical endurance through practice. Get used to that tired feeling."

He wasn't sure he liked the glint in her eye. "You might be enjoying this a little too much, dear mother."

Órla shook the water off her wings and glided to the table. "Not nearly as much as I'm enjoying it. You're kinda cute when you're tired."

"Thanks for the support, little one."

"Of course. Always happy to help."

After a few minutes of rest, the trio made their way back into the center circle. Declan and Kelså held hands and closed their eyes. This time, when Declan tried to reach out to her Light, his mental presence bogged down before reaching it.

"Ack! That feels like I'm trying to shove my way through syrup."

"That's my shield." Kelså squeezed his hands. "Try pushing through."

He drew in a breath and added a magical shove, only to be swallowed by the gooey barrier. Frustrated, he pulled his presence back and tried a different tactic. He waited a few seconds, then sprinted as fast as he could, trying to catch Kelså off guard. The shield gripped him even tighter than before.

"Don't get frustrated. Keep trying." Kelså gave his hands another squeeze.

So, going fast just got me tangled up faster. Hmm . . .

For his next attempt, Declan moved as slowly as possibly, trudging his way into the spongy wall. He barely broke the surface of the shield this time, as his forward momentum halted when he made contact.

He tried spinning into the wall again. This time, the sticky web wrapped itself around him with every turn until he was completely enveloped and immobilized. Kelså released him, and he stumbled backwards.

"I take it you need help?" Órla chirped in his head. *"Be a hummingbird, not a horse."*

"That's supposed to be helpful?"

"I can't just give *you the answer, silly. At some point, you have to use your brain and figure things out,"* she giggled.

Alright, think, D. Hummingbirds versus horses?

Hummingbirds are tiny. Horses are big. Hummingbirds fly. Their wings go really fast, but flapping my arms doesn't sound like a good idea. They suck nectar. They . . . buzz? That didn't sound right either, but maybe sound was the answer. What do hummingbirds even sound like?

Be the hummingbird. Be . . . the hummingbird. Hummingbird.

Spirits, this is stupid!

Declan was about to break contact and head for the wine again when an idea struck. H

Hummingbirds are tiny and fast and have a sharp beak, at least, I think they do.

He imagined his magical presence as a hair-thin arrow, honing its tip into a sharp point, then he stepped back as far from Kelså's barrier as he could without losing contact and sprinted forward. The arrow flew true and struck the barrier, piercing it with its tip. Its momentum slowed but didn't stop as the arrow poked through the other side and tumbled into Kelså's Light.

"Got you!" Declan hooted, squeezing Kelså's hand before raising them in victory. In the excitement, his concentration failed, and everything winked out.

Kelså laughed at his happy dance, then shook her head. "You were supposed to use Illusion once you got inside my shield. Forget something?"

"Oh, come on! I just made it through the Mighty, Mushy Wall of Doom. Give me a little credit!" He beamed as he bounded to the table to pour more wine.

"You sure he's not hopeless? I think he's hopeless," Órla said.

"Órla, be nice!" Kelså snorted and joined him at the table. "You did well. Next time, though, I was to *see* something."

"Yes, ma'am." He grinned sheepishly between gulps.

"Declan Rea, the Badass Hummingbird. The Hummingbird Heartthrob. The Hummingbird Hero. Oh, yeah! That's it. Hummingbird Hero! Although, heartthrob isn't bad either, if ya know what I mean." He flicked his hair dramatically.

Kelså cocked her head in confusion as Órla landed on her shoulder. *"Sorry. I think I started something. You really don't want to know!"*

Weeks became into months.

And crafting illusions became the bane of Declan's existence.

He and Kelså worked exclusively on Illusion for three weeks before she realized he might need a mental break.

She decided each day would rotate between other skills as she pushed him to grow in strength and endurance. Besides giving his mind a break from the grueling demands of Illusion, she wanted to stretch his creativity in applying his other Gifts to different situations.

The sixth month began with a book. Kelså walked onto the ledge carrying a massive leather-bound tome whose flowing script had long since faded. Declan nearly leapt out of his boots when she dropped the book on the table with a loud *thud*.

"What's that?" He edged away as if the book had fangs.

She chuckled. "It's a book on human anatomy."

He groaned. "A whole book about body parts? Please Spirits, save me—or kill me—whichever's easier."

"We still have a lot of work to do with your endurance, but you've learned most of what I can teach in the other areas. Now it's time we work on Healing, the most important ability you may possess."

Declan leaned forward, intrigue replacing dread. "How do we test for it?"

She reached into her pocket and pulled out a small knife. Before Declan could say anything, she winced as she scored a deep line across her palm. Blood rushed to the surface and dribbled onto the table.

"Mom! What are you doing?"

"Quickly, don't think. Place your palm over mine and call your Light."

Declan grabbed her hand and shoved his other palm above hers.

Nothing happened.

"Now what?"

"Focus your Light. Narrow it, shaping its tip into a point, like a quill. Then use it to seal the cut. Visualize using your quill to 'write' a line of magic along the wound. Don't rush. Healing takes time." Blood was pooling under her hand.

His heart pounded faster as he watched the angry cut weep.

In his mind, he formed the image of a quill, then pointed it at the wound and trickled magic to its tip. His palm began to glow, and he nearly lost concentration as it flared brightly.

"Focus. Don't let go of your Light. Now, seal the wound." Kelså's voice was calm and reassuring.

A thin stream of magic flowed through the quill and out the tip onto Kelså's palm. It took a moment to figure out how to guide the flow, to aim the quill, but fifteen minutes later, the wound was Healed, and Kelså's skin bore only a faded pink line of new flesh. Declan slumped in his chair and wiped the sweat from his face.

Kelså smiled broadly as she examined her hand. "Very nice. Tell me what you just learned."

"That took more concentration than anything we've done so far." He poured a glass of wine and took a long sip. "I made the quill in my mind, like you said, but it was hard to direct it at first."

"Oh, I know. I felt you tickling all around the cut."

"Sorry about that. Once I got the hang of pointing the quill, the rest was easy. I just had to stay focused and keep the magic flowing into the wound."

"Perfect. That's exactly how it should work." Kelså poured herself a glass. "But that was a simple, superficial cut. Imagine someone seriously wounded with internal bleeding and multiple damaged organs. Speed would be critical to save their life. How do you think you would Heal that person?"

Declan thought a minute. "I wouldn't even know where to start, how to identify everything that was wrong, or which problem to attack first. I'm trying to visualize that person on the table and think through what to do, but all I see is blood and a dying man."

She nodded. "In that case, you'd never actually see the damaged organs unless the man's belly was split wide open. And then, you might have more on the table than magic could handle.

"Now, do you understand the need for that book? Unless you're happy with only the most basic Healing skills, you'll need to be able to identify internal parts of the body, their functions, and how they interact with all the other parts. Only then could you begin to Heal someone with internal injuries. I'm afraid this is the first of many books you'll need to study before your Healing lessons even begin."

He groaned again. "Great. I was never very good in classes at the Academy. The Mages always told me I wasn't applying myself. Guess it's time to change that."

"You'll get there." Kelså stood. "I have a few things to take care of. Why don't you get started on the first chapter, and I'll quiz you later."

Declan pulled the book toward him and dusted off the cover. It crackled when he opened it, and he had to pry some of the ancient pages apart. He flipped the first few pages until he reached the first chapter: *Levels of Organization*.

"This is going to be *awesome*." He deadpanned as he leaned back and stared blankly at the chapter title.

Órla made her first appearance of the morning, landing on the table and dunking her head into Kelså's wine glass before it was stolen away. When Declan glanced up, she had settled by the pitcher and was staring at him. He couldn't believe how much she'd changed in only a few months. The brown-speckled feathers of her wings and body were now snowy white, not a spot of color remaining, while those of her breast shimmered in brilliant gold, as if someone had painted the polished metal onto each feather.

"What are you staring at?" Her voice had also grown from a perky, high-pitched little girl to the husky notes of a fully-grown woman who might've smoked a bit too much in her early years.

"Honestly? Anything but this book." He grunted. "I was just admiring how you've grown. You were always cute, but now you're . . . beautiful and . . . majestic. I've never seen an owl with your markings or color."

She cocked her head. "You come from the mainland and are surprised the Daughter of Magic wears gold?"

"I supposed that makes sense. Still, you're stunning, and you're the best friend I've ever had. Thank you for bonding—for taking a chance on me before . . . before I even knew I was worth taking a chance on."

She tottered toward him and hopped onto the open book. "Listen to me, Declan Rea. You were *never* a chance. There has never been a more worthy heir, and I count myself lucky to have you in my life."

Declan was stunned by sincerity and ferocity in her voice. His eyes misted as he reached down to stroke her feathers.

"C'mon, dude. Don't make this weirder than it just was," she squawked.

He laughed and shook his head, then stroked her feathers anyway.

She pressed into his palm.

"Love you, too, Dec."

"It's hard to believe I've been here nearly two years. Feels like I just popped through the gate last week." Declan took another bite of his eggs.

Kelså's smile was sad. "It really doesn't feel that long. I've cherished every minute."

"Even when I was making a muck of your lessons?"

"Muck? Bit of an understatement there, Mage Mishap. Care to talk about your good friend, the squirrel you blew off the ledge?" Órla said, then cocked her head.

"Hey! He was trespassing. I was *protecting you*."

Órla rolled her eyes. "He did have really pointy teeth, and that bushy tail—how would I have survived without you? He might've dusted my feathers or something."

Declan and Kelså laughed as he reached across the table and scratched Órla's head. He'd lost track of how old she was now—in people years. Her voice and coloring might have changed, but the spunky girl he met on a mountain still kept his feet on the ground. He couldn't remember ever loving a creature so much.

His gaze lifted to Kelså, and his smile broadened.

He finished with Órla's knobby head and took Kelså's hand. She smiled, surprised by the gesture.

"I have a *mother*," a small boy whispered. "I have a beautiful, strong, amazing mother who loves me, who taught me, who thinks I'm something special."

"Declan?" She placed her other hand on top of his.

"Let me get this out. This is important." He looked down to gather himself, then back up into her eyes. "I was so lost, so very lost, and I didn't even know it. I mean, I probably knew deep down but couldn't admit it. So I ran from Atikus, and Keelan, and everybody who ever cared about me. When I joined the Rangers, I kept running, grabbing any assignment that kept me far from people. I hid in the woods, wandering day and night, never going anywhere. I thought I was numb to it all, but the pain was unbearable.

"I'd been in the mountains for months, content as could be. I don't remember what happened, but something reminded me of Keelan and our life in the Guild. Memories flooded back, one after the other. I couldn't make them stop. Keelan was in every one of them, watching . . . *judging*. He was everything I dreamed of becoming but knew I could never be, and in those memories, he stared down and shook his head at his useless, lost brother." A tear slipped free as pain creased his face.

"A pair of other Rangers came to relieve me later that day. They found me in a pool of my own blood in the station, a bloody knife on the wooden floor beside me."

Kelså freed her hand and wiped her own tears, then scooted her chair around so she could be closer.

Declan continued, "One of the men had some basic Healing skills and closed my wrists. He even managed to erase the scars. It still took weeks for my body to recover its strength. I stared up at the ceiling in the infirmary wondering why the Spirits wouldn't just let me go, let me have peace. I was so lost.

"They sent me back out because there wasn't anything else to do with me. I wanted to go. I wanted to be alone, to run away again.

"The trees . . . didn't stare."

Kelså took his hand again. "Then Keelan showed up. He *actually* showed up. I couldn't believe it was really him when he walked through the door, but there's no mistaking his monstrous frame." His lips quirked upward at the memory.

"Never in a million years would I have seen that coming. It felt so good to see him and Atikus, that crazy old man. In that first moment, when I looked into Kee's eyes, I realized how much I'd missed them and hadn't even known it.

"I was such an idiot. They both tried to talk to me. They saw through my mask and didn't buy the smiles I offered. They just wanted to help, but I was too wrapped up in my own . . . whatever . . . to show them anything but contempt and bitterness. I don't know what came over me, but I said awful things to them, even to Atikus. They didn't deserve any of it, and I didn't mean it, but it just came out, and I couldn't stop it. Then they were gone. I watched them walk away, disappear into the woods. I've dreamed that moment a hundred times, desperate that it wouldn't be my last with them."

He stared at their clasped hands, unable to meet her eyes.

His tears fell freely.

"Then the Path led me here, to you—and to Órla." He smiled down at the little owl. "I don't know why I'm telling you all this, but I think . . . I just need to."

"Son, go on. I want to hear." Her voice was soft as she rubbed the back of his hand.

"Being with you these two years, it's changed me. I can feel it deep inside, and I'm not talking about the magic. I mean, you've changed *me*. I see how you look at me, and I've tried to challenge your stare, make it something other than what it really is, but I know now that nothing will ever change what I see in your eyes."

"What do you see?"

"The purest, most boundless love I've ever seen. I never knew a love like that could exist, much less come my way."

Squeezed raised his hand and pressed her lips against his skin. "Son, I love you more than anything. Please know that."

He nodded, but pressed on.

"It's more than that, more than just love. I could see it before, but it took me a long time to understand it. I struggled even longer to accept it."

"What—?"

"Pride . . . and confidence, I guess. I've never had either of those things for myself, but you've never been without them . . . *for me*. Before you even really knew me, when I first got here, those feeling . . . Sometimes I still can't believe it's real. It's overwhelming.

"I guess what I'm trying to say is thank you . . . for believing in me when I couldn't believe in myself, for always lifting me up and never judging . . . and for loving me so fully and unconditionally. *Thank you.*" His voice trailed off.

Kelså did the only thing in her mother's toolkit that make sense. She stood, wrapped her son in her arms, and wept with him until there were no tears left. The little boy who'd never known what he'd lost so many years ago held on for dear life. He clung to her, a desperate man gripping the edges a life raft amidst a raging sea—but in that moment, he knew he wasn't desperate, or lost, not anymore.

Then he heard the strangest sound. Coughing? Tiny, squeaky . . . coughing?

"Uh . . . hello? Can a sister owl get some hugging, too? I mean, what does a mystical, magical being have to do to get some lovin' in this place?"

And just like that, laughter replaced tears.

Later that night, the trio sat around the table on the ledge, enjoying the night air and wine. After two years, Declan still couldn't get enough of the garnet liquid. He took a long sip and sighed contentedly.

Kelså set her glass down. "Son, it's time."

"Time for what?"

"Time you went back to the mainland. I've taught you everything I can, and I sense shifts in magic's currents. Your true trial begins soon." She folded her hands and looked down.

"My trial? I don't understand."

Kelså hesitated. "I have dreams, son, dreams that offer hints of possible futures. They're never clear and only offer a glimpse into what *may* come to pass, but they're often near the mark. We've been preparing you for battles to come, and I fear they've arrived sooner than we expected. You have to go back."

There was fear in her eyes.

"What have you seen?"

"The end . . . of everything. A woman in gold carrying a long silver staff burning everything in her path. You stood before her. Declan, I saw you—"

"You saw her point her staff, sending magical flames into my chest?"

Her eyes widened. "How . . . How did you know?"

"That was one of my visions in the Keeper's Trial. I've dreamed it several times since, but I just assumed my mind was reliving the Trial."

Her hand flew to her mouth and drew a sharp breath.

Declan reached across and took her hand. "Like you said, it's just a possible future. One that *may* come to pass. I'm going back to stop it, right?"

She nodded, unable to speak.

It was Declan's turn to leave his chair and wrap her in his arms. "I'll be ok, Mom. You taught me well, and I have Órla to watch my back."

On cue, the owl floated down and landed on the table. "Somebody order a magnificent, magical creature? Wait . . . *more* hugging without me? I'm starting to get a complex."

Declan pulled her into the hug, though it only took a few seconds for her to squirm and squawk for her freedom.

Kelså sat back and smiled at Órla, then up at Declan. "Tomorrow, we'll go down into the village. I'd like you to spend the day practicing your Healing. There's always fish hooks in places they shouldn't be."

Declan's brow creased, and she chuckled.

"I love this place, but it really can be weird at times."

Declan barked a laugh. "Said the timeless woman guarding a mystical well of unending magic, a woman who pretends to be a cranky old man wearing a turban."

"Okay, point taken," she chuckled and slapped his arm playfully. "Get some rest and pack your things. We'll need to leave at first light."

She stood and gave him a kiss on the cheek, then gave Órla an affectionate scratch. When she disappeared into the cavern, Órla spoke into Declan's mind.

"I know how hard this is for your, Declan, but she's right. I feel the world changing—and not for the better. This is what you've been preparing for."

He nodded. "I know. It's not what lies ahead that has me sad, it's what I'm leaving behind. I'm really going to miss her."

Órla tottered across the table and nuzzled his hand. She had no words for what tomorrow would bring.

The next morning, Kelså ushered Declan out of the cave toward the mountain Path. He offered his arm, which she took gladly, and the pair began their trek into town. Declan was so wrapped up in his own thoughts that he didn't notice Kelså release his arm as they passed the Keeper's cottage. When he turned to search for her, the wrinkled old face of a wizened man stared back at him.

"What are you waiting for, young man? One foot in front of the other or we'll never get there." The man prodded him with his staff.

"Wait. Where are we going?" Declan looked around, feeling a little dizzy. "And . . . who are you?"

"You came to me seeking answers." The man laughed. "We had breakfast in the cabin, and now we're headed into the village to work on Healing skills before you head back home across the sea. Did you bump your head on the way out the door?"

Declan couldn't shake the feeling that he'd been here before, but nothing looked familiar. He vaguely remembered the Keeper and some sort of test, but everything after that was blank. It felt right that he should be challenging his powers, learning how to use them, but the old man seemed such an unlikely teacher. Before he could turn to resume their descent, Órla flapped into view a few feet in front of him.

"You ok, Dec? You look like you've seen a ghost—and we still don't know if you *can* see ghosts." She flew up and perched on his shoulder.

"I don't know. Something seems really . . . strange, like my brain is trying to remember something, but it's just out of reach. It's a really weird feeling. Maybe I've just been up here in the thin mountain air too long. The hike down should do me good."

Órla nuzzled the crook of his neck. As he scratched her neck, he realized that she was taller and heavier than he remembered.

"You sure are growing fast, little one."

She whispered in his head, *"I'm fully grown, silly. Two glorious, feathery hands—taller than any Saw-whet ever! I'm a record-breaker!"*

An hour later, they reached the first few buildings of the village. Gulls called in the distance, accompanied by the constant roar of waves. The fishy scent of saltwater greeted them as the coastal breeze cooled their now sunburnt skin. Declan drew a deep breath and smiled at the peacefulness of the island. He chuckled when Órla did the same, her tiny exhale carrying a throaty trill.

Two burly, shirtless men carrying fishing nets spotted the pair. They dropped their nets and ran toward them, one man hobbling as he ran. Declan reached for his bow, but the Keeper placed a hand on his forearm. When the men stopped a few paces away, puffing heavily from their run, they dropped one knee and bowed their heads. One of the men winced as he knelt.

"Keeper! What a blessed day!" a deep, rumbling voice said. "What brings ya down t' the village after so long, Honored One?"

The Keeper stepped forward and placed his palm on the man's bald crown, and a trickle of magic flowed into the fisherman.

"Rusty, that should help your knee a bit. I know it's still bothering you." The Keeper bent and helped the man stand. "Now, run to the village and let Larinda know we're coming. We need to spend the day with her. It's good to see you again, my friend."

"Yessir. And thank ya fer the Healin'." Rusty bobbed and gave them a toothy grin before grabbing the other man and sprinting toward the village.

When the men were out of earshot, Declan turned to the Keeper with a raised brow. "Honored One?"

The Keeper's high-pitched chortle caught Declan by surprise. "Being ancient and mysterious has its advantages. They think I'm something special. Just wait 'til you see how they treat us in the village."

They walked another few hundred paces into the center of the village. Declan was stunned to find them quickly surrounded by kneeling men and women. People rose and followed when the Keeper continued toward Larinda's home.

"Uh . . . *Honored Keeper*, sir, the whole village is following us." Declan looked nervously behind at the growing throng.

The old man nodded and smiled broadly, humming to himself. HeHHeHe never broke stride or looked back. By the time they stood on Larinda's steps, more than a hundred villagers huddled around and were humming the tune with the Keeper. The old man turned and faced the crowd, switching from humming to singing words in a lilting language Declan didn't recognize. He didn't recognize the melody either, but it carried an upbeat, happy feel with a catchy tempo that inspired a few to clap in time with the words. Several others tapped staccato counter-rhythms with walking sticks and fishing rods. Laughter and joy swelled when the voices broke apart in rich, exuberant harmony. When Órla started tooting along and bobbing her head, Declan laughed and released the tension he'd held since arriving.

Larinda appeared in the doorway and joined in the final chorus. The chorus swelled so loudly Declan felt the porch vibrate. When the last note sounded, the crowd roared with laughter and applause, and many turned and hugged the man or woman beside them. Larinda stepped forward, spun the Keeper around, and wrapped him in a warm embrace.

The crowd erupted again.

"Honored One, been too many years since ya led us in song. Ya be a sight fer t'ese tired old eyes." When she released him, Declan saw tears of joy flowing from both of their eyes.

"Did we walk into someone's family reunion, little one?" Declan whispered in Órla mind.

"Oh, this is definitely *a family like no other,"* she giggled in his thoughts. *"Isn't it wonderful?"*

Larinda turned from the Keeper, noticing Declan and Órla for the first time. Her eyes widened, and she covered her mouth with both hands when she saw the not-so-little owl.

"DAUGHTER! You're grown!" She laughed and stretched cupped hands before her so Órla could hop down and receive a proper nuzzling. The owl's giggle mixed with a deep *coo-purr*, creating an odd, vibrant sound of pure joy.

Larinda pulled back from the nuzzle and stared Órla in the eyes, listening to some private mental conversation. A few seconds later, she laughed and peered up at Declan.

"Ya been up t' a whole mess since I saw ya last, Ranger." She winked at him. "Órla say somet'in' about poop on yer boot?"

Declan stared openmouthed as Larinda cackled.

She then turned to the crowd. "The Keeper has returned t' us. T'night, the family feasts, t'gether again, at last! Go, git us ready!"

The crowd roared a final time then drifted apart, many humming the tune as they strolled away.

Larinda led the trio into her garden. Órla flew from her hands, dove into the pond, and began bathing herself, while Declan and the Keeper pulled chairs close to Larinda's throne-like seat. A lanky man wearing nothing but brown linen pants offered everyone a glass from a wicker tray, then disappeared back into the villa.

The Keeper spoke first. "Larinda, my beautiful sister, it's good to see you again after so many years. There is much I wish to hear, but it will all have to wait until the feast. For now, Declan needs your help."

She turned and eyed Declan thoughtfully. "How can I help ya, young man?"

"Well . . . uh . . ." Declan fumbled, unsure what his mother wanted him to ask the island's caretaker.

Before the Keeper could respond, Órla called out cheerfully from the pond. "He needs to practice Healing. He kinda stinks at it."

Declan shook his head and smiled. "She's right about the Healing. I haven't had many people to practice on, and I'll be heading back to the mainland tomorrow."

Larinda leaned forward. "So soon?"

"I'm afraid so. It's time I headed back. My... brother needs my help."

"Fine, fine. Let's get ya down t' the street an' find some hurt folk t' work on." She looked back at the Keeper. "But ya watch him. Can't go makin' anythin' worse!"

Declan and the Keeper spent the rest of the day working on one injury after another. The old man had been right; the village seemed to be crawling with hurt people. By the time the sun began slipping behind the mountains, Declan was exhausted and his brain felt like runny oatmeal—but he'd mastered many of the simpler Healing skills. He'd need to train with a Master Healer to develop the mental dexterity required when Healing serious internal wounds, but his skill at intermediate injuries progressed well.

As they climbed back up the steps of Larinda's porch, the old woman appeared in the doorway. She wore a brightly colored robe stitched with images of parrots and lush island plants. She smiled broadly and waved for them to follow.

"We be feastin' by the water t'night."

They strode around Larinda's pavilion, past the ring of huts that surrounded it, to where the path vanished into the sandy beach. Torches stuck into the sand flickered with magical flame, revealing dozens of long tables already set with plates, glasses, and silverware. Men and women bustled back and forth carrying platters of fish, pork, chicken, and more varieties of vegetables and fruits than Declan had ever seen in one place.

"How did they do all this since this morning?" He could barely believe what he was seeing.

"Magical island, remember?" Órla's voice crept into his head.

Larinda led them to a table that was shorter than the others, with seating for only a few people. It faced the other tables, allowing a view of everyone with the ocean in the background. As she motioned for Declan and the Keeper to sit, a boy struggling with a pitcher nearly as tall as he was approached.

"Wine, Mother Larinda?" The squeaky, high-pitched voice made Declan smile.

"For all of us. Thank you, Lobo." Larinda ruffled the boy's unruly mane.

Before long, every seat was filled as more than two hundred villagers ate, drank, and laughed together. Young boys and girls carrying platters were greeted with "Ooos" and "Ahhs." First were soups and several kinds of still-warm bread. Declan's mouth watered as he lathered butter onto a slice and took his first bite. Then came an endless stream of vegetables. Beans and peas, greens with little bits of pork, peppery roasted potatoes, and strange little bananas fried to a golden crisp. After the bananas, Declan lost track. It was overwhelming, but in the best way.

When the meats arrived, he nearly fell out of his seat. The chicken and pork he'd seen earlier were placed on the long tables while a massive roasted pig appeared in front of Larinda.

Then came the fish, platter after platter. In all, Declan counted ten different kinds, each cooked to perfection in its own style.

By the time chocolate arrived, Declan wanted to cry for mercy. Larinda cackled and grabbed every chocolate within reach.

Declan sat back, rubbing his overstuffed belly. Everywhere he looked, people smiled and laughed. A few even broke out in song, causing neighboring tables to start their own tune in friendly competition. The ocean breeze carried a feeling of contentment and joy.

"Feel it, do ya?" Larinda leaned over, smiling at him.

"Feel what?"

"'Tis a magical place in more ways than ya know." She winked and turned back to her chocolate.

When the last plates were removed from the tables, Larinda rose and everyone turned to the head table and conversations hushed.

"'Tis been many years since the Keeper returned to us. T'night he comes t' send off t'is young man." She pointed her open palm toward Declan. "Declan Rea, Ranger of Melucia, Bond-Mate of the Daughter of Magic."

The crowd sucked in a collective breath, astonished at the pronouncement, the depths of which they clearly understood better than Declan himself, then the beach fell completely silent. No one stirred. Even the waves and wind quieted.

Eyes followed as Órla launched herself into the air and flew beyond their sight. When she resolved into view once more, iridescent brilliance lined her body and shimmered each time she flapped her wings. Magic dripped off her like molten lava dribbling down a mountainside. She landed on the table before an open-mouthed Declan and whispered in his head, *"Wait for it..."*

She let out a screech, and the starry night sky exploded with magical light that shimmered from the mountains to the sea. The entire island glowed, and the crowd rose to their feet and hummed the song from earlier in the day. As their humming grew into words, the light of the island pulsed and faded, leaving only Órla—*and Declan*—aglow. Declan stood and gaped down at his hands, startled by the azure flames swimming across his skin.

"Not bad for a coming out party, is it?" Órla giggled in his head.

The song ended and every voice cried, "DECLAN REA! HEIR OF MAGIC!"

The villagers raised their palms toward the sky, and the glow of magic flared upward from every hand. The glows flared, then vanished, and the people erupted in cheers and applause. Larinda hooted and clapped, egging the crowd on.

When Órla laughed, this time aloud, Declan lost himself in the unimaginable joy of the truly magical celebration.

Chapter Twenty

Keelan and Atikus before at a table in their new room on the upper floor of the inn. Once they'd agreed to enter his service, the King had welcomed them into his fold . . . unless one counted the lone guard assigned to follow them everywhere.

"That's where the constables say the Princess was taken. The road makes a slight bend at this rise. The other teams were positioned here and here." Keelan pointed to the map splayed across on the table.

"Looks like they had Jess and Danym surrounded," Atikus said.

"The team behind them fired the screamer. According to the report they gave the King, it took no more than five minutes to get to where the Princess was spotted, but she had vanished. Neither of the other teams reported seeing them before or after the screamer was fired.”

“And they found the Triad’s seal exactly where the Princess was spotted? Pretty convenient, don’t you think?” Atikus crossed his arms, brows raised.

Keelan thought a moment. “If I’m going to do this investigation right, I can’t rule out that the Triad—or anyone else—might’ve been involved, but no, it doesn’t make sense. Set aside that we have high confidence that Melucia wasn’t behind this kidnapping; that seal was precious, worth a small fortune. I have a hard time believing someone just dropped it, even a kidnapper in the heat of the moment.”

Keelan then stepped away from the map and paced a few times. “Do you remember where they took that seal? Who has it now?”

“No. The report didn’t say. I would assume the High Sheriff’s people have it, but who knows?” Atikus cocked his head, curious where Keelan was leading.

“We need to examine that seal. It’s our only real clue right now.” He stopped pacing and looked up. “I want *you* to inspect it, see if there’s anything unusual about it, if it’s been altered.”

“What are you thinking?”

“I don’t know. Something doesn’t feel right, and that seal keeps popping into my head. It may be nothing, but it’s worth checking out.” He stepped back to the map. "Something else, all these other kidnappings can't be a coincidence. The Kingdom is huge, but this kind of crime is rare. I think we need to pay the Children another visit. Do you think the King's men kept those robes and masks?"

"Probably. Assuming the soldiers who arrested us didn't destroy or keep them for themselves," Atikus said.

"I don't even know where to start looking for the Queen. If she used an Enchanted item to transport to . . . somewhere, she could be anywhere." He reached to his cot and retrieved his scabbard. "I can't help thinking her disappearance is wrapped up in all of this somehow."

"You don't buy the frantic mother story?"

Keelan shrugged. "It's possible. What mother wouldn't move mountains to find a lost daughter? But for a Queen to disappear like that, with no guards or anything? That feels wrong. My Gift isn't much help without meeting her, but my gut says we're missing a lot that's important." He started toward the door. "Let's ask our shadow to take us to the High Sheriff and get our robes and masks back, then we can figure out how to take another look around the Children's headquarters."

As they entered the common room, they were surprised to find the King, Justin, and the High Sheriff sitting at their usual table. Captain Proctor took two steps toward them, cutting off their path to the table.

The guard escorting them bowed hastily. "Your Majesty, forgive us for disturbing."

"It's alright." Alfred said, motioning them to approach. "Come, sit. We were just finishing breakfast. Are either of you hungry?"

Atikus looked up at Keelan and spoke in his mind. *"He sure is friendly now. Tread carefully."*

They sat, and the innkeeper appeared with fresh rolls and steaming tea. Atikus lost any sense of caution when the fluffy rolls and butter landed on his plate. Keelan shook his head and smiled. When he looked up, Justin was chuckling.

Keelan broke propriety by speaking first. "Your Majesty, is the Triad's seal your men found at the kidnapping site here?"

"Sheriff?" Alfred turned to Wilfred.

Wilfred nodded. "We have it secured here in the town."

"Good. I'd like Mage Danai to examine it for alterations or magical enchantments. There's no evidence to suggest either, but I want to rule them out."

The King nodded. "Fine, but I want to be present when you do this. Understood?"

Atikus's eyes widened, then he nodded. "Of course, Your Majesty."

"Sheriff Wilfred, one other thing, do your men still have the robes and masks we were wearing the other night when we escaped the Children's compound?" Keelan asked.

Wilfred's face gave nothing away. "I believe so. Sergeant, go find out."

A man Keelan hadn't noticed sitting at a table by the fireplace leapt to his feet and scurried out the door.

"What are you planning? What do the Children have to do with the Princess's kidnapping?" Wilfred asked.

"We don't have any direct evidence to link the Children to her, but kidnappings are rare in the Kingdom, right? Now you've had what? Four? Five? In the last eighteen months? After what we witnessed, my gut tells me there's a connection here, and I want to check it out."

Wilfred thought a moment before turning to the King. "I don't like it, but it's worth ruling out. If our evidence is correct, the trail will lead much farther east than the Children's complex, but we're here now and may as well let them take a look. I'll send some of my men to assist."

The King started to nod, but Justin's voice turned his head. "I want to go with them, Dad. If Jess is in there, I want to be part of the group to rescue her."

Alfred's nod turned to a stern shake, but he was again preempted, this time by Keelan. "Absolutely not, Your Highness. Those people killed a member of my team last time and nearly slaughtered us all. It's too dangerous to risk another member of the royal family, especially the potential heir."

"He's right, Justin. Sometimes the hardest thing for a king to do is let other people do their jobs."

"And sometimes we have to lead from the front. That's what you've said since I was little, isn't it? I want to be there, Dad. I *need* to be there." He sat up straighter. "You keep telling me to think like a ruler, to make strong decisions. I *choose* to go. Will you let my decision stand?"

Alfred eyed his son. "I was stubborn when I was your age, too. Issy says I still am." Deep lines creased his forehead, and a long moment passed before he conceded. "Fine, but three of the Royal Guard go with you."

Alfred addressed the Captain, "If this one comes to any harm, you'll answer to me."

The giant nodded once.

"Sir, this isn't a good idea—" Keelan stammered.

Alfred cut him off with a wave of his hand. "Noted. Now, do as I command, Lieutenant."

Keelan started to protest again, but Atikus cleared his throat.

"He's decided. Let it go."

Keelan nodded, more to himself than the King. "We should breach their compound after dark. Sheriff, can someone repair those robes, make them look undamaged?"

"We'll see to it. Our men will meet you at the dock at midnight. I'd suggest landing on the southern end of the lake and hiking up the coast. You won't be able to approach directly by boat without being spotted."

"Agreed. Atikus, why don't we go take a look at that seal. Prince Justin, you may want to get some rest. It's going to be a long night." There was no joy in the tight smile he offered the Prince.

Jess woke to the sound of horses snorting nearby. One of them leaned down and gave her a slobbery kiss, his tongue making the trek up her neck to the top of her ear. She reached up and wiped the slime before realizing some had made its way down into the crevices of her lobe.

"Ugh. I know you're my only friend out here, but really? Was that necessary?" she whispered. He returned her stare, then whinnied and stomped away as far as his tether would allow.

"Good. You're up. We need to talk about a few things." Danym's voice spoke through his raccoon mask. He stood a dozen paces away, on the far side of the camp. "We've been here five days and believe it's safe to continue on our journey. From this point forward, we will not wear the robes of the Children, nor our masks. If asked, you and I are young lovers running from our family who wants to keep us apart. Sounds familiar, doesn't it?"

She glared at him, unable to come up with a sharp retort. Anger seethed in her eyes.

He removed his mask for the first time since her capture. He ran his fingers through his hair, then scratched his scalp.

"Actually feels good to get out of that thing."

She couldn't speak. She could barely breathe. She'd known Danym was one of her kidnappers, but the mask somehow muted the pain of that wound. It wasn't *really* him if he was wearing a mask, was it? There could be no mistake now that Danym, *her Danym*, had revealed himself. She turned away and threw herself on her pallet, fighting a swelling storm of tears. How had her life come to this terrible place? What had she done to turn him against her? Her heart writhed as she struggled for strength.

Danym watched for a moment before closing the distance and kneeling beside her. He paused, then placed a hand on her shoulder. She wheeled around and shoved him as hard as she could, knocking him backwards.

"Don't you *dare* touch me. Don't you *ever* touch me again! I believed in you—in *us*! What made you do it? Was it some sick joke to you? Or some plot to get rich ransoming the Heir? Was that it? Was I worth so little to you that you'd sell me to the highest bidder?" She was practically screaming the last few words.

He stood and brushed off his pants, his eyes betraying hollow words. "Stay quiet. You have no idea how much bigger all of this is than you. This has nothing—"

The other robed man, the one still wearing the mask of a snarling lion, cut him off with a harsh whisper. "Enough! Keep talking and we'll make you sleep the rest of the trip."

Danym stepped away and folded his robe. There was a reverence in how he handled the garment. He placed it in the bottom of his saddle bag, along with his mask, covering both with a blanket and other items. Jess watched as Lion removed his mask and robe, then repeated the folding and packing ritual exactly as Danym had done.

Faces visible for the first time, she studied her captors. Lion looked to have seen forty winters, seasons that had not been kind to his weathered skin. His scarred and cracked face was lean, almost skeletal, and most of his hair had retreated, leaving him with only a few scraggly patches along the side and back of his head. Jess couldn't stop staring at was his bony, bent nose that veered almost completely to the left. She'd seen broken bones before, but this was . . . she didn't know *what* this was. Accidents happen. Fights happen, but why live with that? Any Healer worth their blues could fix his nose without much effort. Did he wear his imperfection as a badge of honor? Or maybe he knew the mask would cover it and didn't care anymore?

Danym finished packing his bedroll and returned to Jess's side. "We're headed east, just like you and I had planned. Please don't make this difficult. He's serious about drugging you if you fight back," he whispered, nodding over his shoulder to Lion.

Jess couldn't look meet his eyes, so she just nodded, stood, and brushed herself off. He rolled her pallet and secured it to her horse. She didn't have anything to pack, so she a few paces into the woods to relieve herself. Danym watched but didn't follow.

When she returned, Lion joined them by the horses. "I have Illusion. No one will recognize you. Got it?"

"You've said that three times now. Yes, I've got it." She huffed a long breath before turning to mount her horse. Danym chuckled as she muttered, "Stupid Lion," to herself.

They'd ridden a few hours before passing another group of travelers headed west on the road. A woman crowned in silver hair peered out of the riding compart- ment of her carriage while an elderly man steered. Two bored-looking teenage boys rode alongside the coach, each on piebald horses.

Lion and Danym reined in their horses and greeted the family, who explained they were headed to Fontaine to get away from the heat of war. They seemed to think Lion was an elderly man and were shocked he was riding a horse "at his age." Jess wondered what insane face she must be wearing. When the small talk subsided, Lion asked what they'd seen on the roads, learning about troop movements and encampments ahead. He was surprised to learn that the King himself was staying in Cradle.

Hope flared through Jess.

The exchange ended, and the family disappeared beyond the hills on their way to a better life in the capital. Jess dreamed of being back in the palace, safe and comfortable with her brothers. It wasn't that long ago that she'd dreamed of being a thousand leagues away, but now she couldn't get her bedroom out of her mind. What demon had possessed her, convinced her to run away? She looked up and realized that demon was staring at her with his mesmerizing green eyes.

She looked away quickly.

He would *not* see her cry again.

The Sheriff had appropriated the manse of a petty noble to use as his center of operations while Jess remained missing. Atikus and Keelan arrived around noon, and Wilfred led them next door, where six heavily armed men surrounded a long tent. When they entered, High Chancellor Thorn rose from a chair at the far end and greeted the Sheriff with a perfunctory bow.

"Chancellor, the King is allowing these men to inspect the Melucian seal we recovered from the Princess's kidnapping site. When His Majesty arrives, would you please do the honor?" Wilfred indicated for Keelan and Atikus to sit in the remaining chairs.

Alfred arrived a few minutes later, and Chancellor Thorn retrieved a small silver box from a footlocker in the corner. He set it on a folding table by Atikus and placed his palm on the lid. Magic flared from his palm and the box *clicked*. Thorn spun the box around so it faced Atikus and stepped back.

Atikus leaned over and stared at the highly polished silver seal nestled in its velvet pillow. He held his palm a few inches above the seal, careful not to touch it, and his own cerulean magic flowed toward the seal. Several minutes passed before he sat back and turned to Keelan with wide eyes.

"That *is* our seal. It belongs to Guildmaster Burner. There were several layers of magical protection placed on it by the Arch Mage himself, but I can't sense any of them now. It's as though they've been removed . . . or hidden. I can't tell."

"What did those protections do?" Sheriff Wilfred asked.

Atikus struggled with how to answer, not wanting to give away too much to their soon-to-be enemy. "I'm not familiar with all the protections the Arch Mage may have placed on this item, but I know one was designed to alter the seal's imprint if anyone other than Guildmaster Burner used it. The person wouldn't know anything was amiss, but anyone in the upper levels of government would recognize the mark as a fraud. I believe your King is aware of this protection from his own correspondence with the Guildmaster."

Alfred nodded. "Yes, I am familiar with that particular Enchantment. Anything else?"

"As for protections? I don't know what else Velius might've added." Atikus scrutinized the seal again. "I can't find anything odd, at least nothing magically unusual, but I do find it strange that the seal doesn't show any damage. I couldn't even find scratches. Something made of soft gold, if taken on a difficult journey, then dropped onto the road, would surely show scratches or some other damage, don't you think?"

Chancellor Thorn spoke before Wilfred could answer. "Not necessarily. If the item possessed wards, it may have been protected from damage. An entry level Mage could cast that spell."

"Anything else?" the King asked, his patience thinning.

"No. I believe that's all we're going to learn here."

Wilfred had their ever-present shadow escort them back to the inn, where Keelan immediately flopped onto his bed and stared at the ceiling. "I could feel something wasn't quite right but couldn't tell if Thorn was lying or is just creepy. He didn't directly lie about anything. My bees would've gone berserk at that, but he just feels *off* somehow. I don't know. That whole thing may have been a waste of time."

Atikus closed the door behind him and sat. "Not necessarily."

Keelan bolted upright. "Out with it. I know that look."

"Don't get too excited. It's nothing earth-shattering." Atikus's eyes sparkled. "There was a trace of magic on the seal, something I'm sure *wasn't* cast by the Arch Mage."

Keelan shot to his feet. "Really? Who cast it? What was it for?"

Atikus chuckled at Keelan's sudden enthusiasm. "Easy there. I know who *didn't*, but I never said I knew who *did* or what the casting was supposed to do. We'd need an Enchanter to untangle that mystery, if it's even possible. It's as though the Enchantment eroded over time and had nearly dissipated. I could only sense a faint hint, like reading faded ink."

"That's not very helpful." Keelan deflated, flopping back onto the bed.

"I taught you better than that. It's not a breakthrough; but information is *always* helpful. Someone tampered with the seal . . . or tried to. Now we know that for sure."

"Right. Well, I'm going to do what I told Prince-Tag-Along to do and get some rest. Tonight's going to be interesting." Keelan closed his eyes and was asleep before Atikus could respond.

It took the better part of five days to reach the shores of Lake Irina. Lion forced the group to maintain a slow, plodding pace, blending in with other travelers along the King's Road. They even had to step off the road several times to allow passing military units space. Jess tried calling out once, earning a dose of the sleeping drought. It wasn't enough to make her pass out, but she was foggy headed the rest of that day. Danym played it off as "hitting the ale a little too hard" when a passing mother offered to help with whatever illness afflicted the poor girl.

When they were a half-day's ride to Cradle, Danym and Lion got into a heated argument over the best route. More concerning than the monarch's presence was the significant military and security complement surrounding the Kingdom's ruler. Danym wanted to take the risk, contending the increased chance for exposure was worth shaving two days off their trip, but Lion disagreed, arguing their mission's importance was so great that every measure to minimize risk of failure should be taken, even if it meant delays. Apparently, Lion outranked Danym, and the trio avoided Cradle altogether, plodding along the countryside a few leagues outside the western border of the town. When they reached the main road that led south to Rutin, Mr. Paranoid made them wait until dark to cross.

Around midnight of the seventh day after leaving the shelter of their wooded camp, Lion found the rowboat hidden inside a stand of tallgrass on the lake's shore. He and Danym donned their robes and masks, then loaded their packs onto the boat. Lion removed the saddles from the horses and set them free, claiming they'd either find their way home or someone would claim them. Before loading Jess onto the boat, he forced her to drink a full dose of the sleeping syrup. The world spun as Danym and Lion hauled her into the boat, and laid her flat so only the two men would be seen if someone spotted them rowing across the lake. The last thing Jess remembered before her eyes fluttered shut was the twinkling of the stars in the cool, clear sky.

Keelan, Justin, four of the Royal Guard, and four Protectorate officers assigned by the Sheriff stood at the dock staring at each other. Keelan had wanted a nimble team that could slip in and out without being detected. Now he had a small army that included a prince and his paranoid bodyguards.

After a lengthy debate, Atikus agreed to remain behind. He hated the idea of watching his adopted son sail off to meet his fate but had to admit that this was a young man's game—and he was *far* from young anymore.

Keelan and the Prince donned the Children's robes. The King thought Justin would be safer in disguise, arguing that he could blend in with the other Children if trouble arose. Keelan thought that was ridiculous, but let that fight go. He'd already lost the battle over Justin joining them; if the boy wanted to play dress up, so be it. All the other men wore pants, long-sleeved shirts, leather vests, boots, and masks with eyeholes—black from head to toe. Glancing around, Keelan wasn't sure if they were going on a mission or to some weird funeral.

He eyed each man as he spoke. "Alright, listen up. Our goal is to get in, see if there's evidence of the Queen or Princess being held, rescue them if so, and get out. We're *not* there to start a battle. Protectorate will take out the guards at the dockside entrance, but the King wants as few casualties as possible. The boats will leave the landing point by sixth bell, no matter who is still in the building. Don't be late.

"When we get inside, the hallway will fork almost immediately. The right fork leads to a balcony that over-looks the ceremonial chamber. That's where Atikus and I witnessed the last . . . ritual. I think the left fork leads down to an antechamber behind the stage. I want you three to take the right fork while I go down and search that room and the stage. If there's trouble, get the Prince out and don't look back. His safety is your highest pri-ority."

One of the Royal Guard growled. "Lieutenant, the Prince's safety is our *only* priority. The rest of this mess is on you."

Keelan returned his stare, then nodded once.

There were two boats waiting for them at the docks. The Protectors boarded one, leaving the Royal Guard, Justin, and Keelan huddled in the other, then the teams began rowing across the calm, moonlit lake.

Jess put her hands to her head as she woke. Her temples throbbed, and it hurt to just open her eyes. What had they given her this time?

She sat up in the bed and rubbed her eyes before realizing . . . she was in a bed! She looked down at the luxurious linens stitched with the finest needlework. She'd grown up in the palace, so being surrounded by ornate furnishings wasn't new or shocking, but after weeks of running from her mother, then running from kidnappers, she was a little thrown by the surrounding extravagance. The woodwork on the bed and headboard was remarkable, but she couldn't figure out who might want the Phoenix staring down at them while they slept.

She sat upright for a moment, scanning the room without becoming dizzy, so she sucked in a breath and threw her feet off the side of the bed.

She glanced down at the scratches crisscrossing her legs. When had that happened?

The last few weeks were a blur. None of it felt real. She should be back in Fontaine with her parents learning the finer points of diplomacy and Queenship, readying to rule, yet here she sat, captive, alone, and afraid.

Her mind drifted to Danym, the square line of his jaw, the sparkle in his eyes, his infuriatingly flawless hair. Fear twisted into bitterness, then anger. She was *sure* they were perfect together, sure they were building a life together . . . and then he'd betrayed her. The look in his eyes when she'd recognized him behind his mask made chills claw their way across her skin. The kind, gentle adoration she'd fallen in love with was gone, but that wasn't what fueled her anger. The arrogant *amusement* that replaced those emotions boiled her blood. He hadn't felt bad about deceiving her, about breaking her heart. On the contrary, he'd enjoyed it and was entertained by her shock and pain.

And for what? What did these people even want? She scoured her memory for any lessons on the Children or some private information her parents might have shared. All she could remember was the group traced their roots back to Irina, the woman who'd tried to take over the world—but that was ten *lifetimes* ago and no one cared about a long-dead queen.

Did they?

She set her feet onto the floor and tried shifting a little weight onto her legs. They were wobbly but didn't buckle. She shuffled her way to one of the chairs by the fireplace and allowed its pillowy cushions to engulf her, then she noticed a tray of cheeses, meats, and fruits on a nearby end table. She reached for a pastry, but the door burst open, and a figure in deep maroon robes and a strange, featureless mask entered.

The mask looked like it was made from— *sweet Spirits!*

"It's nice to see you awake. You'll need to eat to regain your strength." The husky voice grated in her ears. "I'll have a Healer repair those scratches and any other damage that might have occurred. Rest and recover. Your coronation will take place later tonight, Mistress."

The woman—Jess assumed she was a woman—bowed deeply as she said the last word, then turned to leave.

"Wait . . . What? What coronation? What happened to my father?" Jess pleaded. She would only be *coronated* if—.

"Oh, Mistress, you are Heir to so much more than one *man's* kingdom." She reached out and cupped Jess's cheek, her ring pressing into the tender skin of her face. "All will be clear when you ascend the throne. We—*You* are so close, Mistress."

The red-robed woman darted out of the room before Jess could ask anything more.

Her head spun with questions, but it was no longer cloudy.

There's nothing like the ice bath of "your father may be dead, but I'm not going to tell you" to wake you up from a drug-induced haze. Despite everything, she chuckled.

Jess attacked the charcuterie and emptied the crystal pitcher of wine, then she stalked from one end of the room to the other, again and again. It felt good to move, but she quickly tired and threw herself back onto the bed. Her dreams were troubled by scenes of her father being shot by an assassin . . . or being trampled by his horse . . . or being run through by a swordsman in a grand battle. She couldn't stop dreaming ways he might've died, each more gruesome than the last.

Hours passed before the door rattled again. Two figures entered, one carrying a silky, golden gown bearing the crest of the Phoenix.

The moon settled behind a veil of murky clouds. The stars, having lost their leader, retreated as well.

Keelan stared upward. "Darkness favors our plan."

Justin's nod was rapid, a child wishing a thing to be so, whether or not it was.

Around two o'clock, the boats struck land. They gathered weapons and supplies, hid the boats in the brush, then assembled one last time before the mission began in full.

"Any last questions? The hike should take about an hour." Keelan made eye contact with each team member as he'd done before. Each shook his head at the inquiry.

"Good. Remember, we're here for *information*. Lethal force is a last resort, but if you see us running from four hundred fanatics in masks, shoot anything that isn't us!"

The men chuckled quietly, appreciating the break in tension, then headed out. Two of the Protectors fanned out and scouted the surrounding area for anyone who might compromise their approach. The rest of the team crept in single file, the Prince securely in the middle of the line.

Forty minutes later, the two Protectors, Keelan, and Justin huddled a few hundred paces from the dock. The other team had split into pairs, one circling around the building to a position equally distant on the north side. The other sneaked to the shoreline and nocked their bows. Four Children paced between the dock to the back door.

"They've doubled the guard since we were here last." Concern crept into Keelan's voice as he whispered to the Prince.

Justin started to respond, but a bird's shrill call cut him off.

That was the signal.

The Protectors had insisted that kill shots from a few hundred paces were easy, despite Keelan's concerns about overconfidence. As it turned out, the constables won the bet as all four robed guards dropped simultaneously, a perfectly synchronized volley streaking from both teams. The Protectors were moving before the figures hit the ground.

Within seconds, the kills were confirmed and offending arrows retrieved. The Protectors dragged the bodies to the shoreline and hid them under the dock. They'd be discovered as soon as the sun peeked out, but hopefully not before the team completed their mission.

Four men assumed positions on either side of the rear entrance, and Keelan took his cue, motioning for the Prince and his guards to follow. When they reached the door, one of the men held out a key while the other three nocked arrows and stood to the side.

Keelan held his breath as the lock clicked.

Two masked faces poked out and were greeted by arrows from the remaining Protectors. Keelan stepped over the dead figures and entered the dark hallway.

As they approached the fork in the hallway, eerie, harmonized humming drifted on the still air from somewhere ahead.

Keelan glanced back and saw terror in the Prince's eyes. He placed a hand on his shoulder and whispered,

"Think about your sister. These men will protect you. Just stick to the plan. Okay?"

Justin's eyes swelled as he nodded.

The massive doors cried on their hinges, and discordant droning clawed across Jess's skin. She had been nervous before; now, terror seized her mind.

The Child in the fox mask nudged her forward as her head swiveled from one horror to the next. Hundreds of Children lined either side of the enormous chamber, bathed in the otherworldly light of magical flames and darkness. Their robes shimmered as the flames danced. Their asks growled and snarled as they hummed.

At the far end rested a seat of power, much like the throne of her father—like *her* throne. A spike of sadness and regret raced through her.

The woman in the scarlet robe peered across the hall, one hand resting possessively on the throne. As Jess edged forward, the woman raised her arms above her head and the slow, steady thrumming of distant drums added rhythmic vibrations unsettled to her already heart.

Jess's eyes darted, desperate for any possibility of escape. The woman had said this was her coronation, but something deep inside screamed otherwise.

She could barely breathe.

Keelan crept slowly down a long empty hallway. Aside from the incessant humming, there were no sounds. The only light bled faintly from the gap beneath two doors, one immediately to his right as he entered the hallway, and the other at the passage's midpoint. He remembered seeing a door near the corner of the chamber when he and Sil had watched from the balcony. He assumed the middle door to be his target, the entrance to the stage.

He reached for the knob and was surprised when it turned without protest.

Gently, *slowly*, he pulled, dreading a cry from the ancient hinges.

None came.

He cracked the door and peered in. The sound of the humming swelled, drenching him in the excitement and anticipation of the assembled throng, but there was no antechamber, as they'd expected, only a small open space behind the massive statue that reigned over the ceremonial chamber. The base stood above his head, preventing him from peeking over, but it also concealed his entrance from those beyond.

Motion flashed in the corner of his eye, and his eyes darted up to find the Prince and his guards entering the balcony, beacons in a sea of darkness. The guards were pulling at the Prince, trying to get him to duck down, but he was frozen in place, eyes locked onto something below.

Then it happened.

Time slowed.

Keelan's breath stilled.

His heart froze.

"JESS!" bellowed from the balcony, as the Prince's guards finally wrestled him from view . . .

A moment too late.

Hundreds of heads snapped toward the balcony.

The cry shook Jess from her daze, whipping her head upward in time with the Children around her.

She *knew* that voice—better than any other in the world.

She followed Fox's gaze as two figures in black pulled another masked figure from view. She was sure she'd heard Justin. The Children in the chamber all gaped upward. It couldn't have been her mind playing tricks. It *had* to be him.

The woman in scarlet screeched, "STOP THEM! AND BRING ME THE HEIR— NOTHING WILL STOP THE CEREMONY!"

Justin didn't even have time to chide his own stupidity.

The guards' training kicked in, and they dragged him from the balcony, racing toward the exit. They made it two steps before the first arrow dropped the guard on Justin's left, a perfect shot through the eye.

The other guard hesitated, stunned by the sudden loss of his partner.

It was his last mistake.

Three arrows flew from the balcony where a dozen robed men lay in hiding, waiting for any intrusion.

The masked beasts could learn and adapt.

Justin panicked and fled down the hallway. He'd forgotten the plan, that he still wore the mask and robe that he could blend in. He'd forgotten everything. All he could think of was the exit and escaping the missiles streaking around him.

The magical flames that lit the hallway winked out, and Justin fumbled forward in utter darkness, trying to feel his way with his hand against the wall.

He could feel the thundering of boots behind him.

They were getting closer.

He tore off his mask and threw it behind him.

And then he fell.

Keelan righted himself and strode around the statue's base, determined to maintain his disguise as one of the assembled Children. He stopped cold when he cleared the statue.

The room writhed with motion.

Robed figures scattered in every direction, pouring through doors on the sides like angry ants fleeing their home.

A young woman he assumed to be the Princess stood frozen at the center of the chamber, her gaze locked at the balcony. Her escorts gripped her arms and tugged her forward. On the stage, behind the throne, the red-robed leader screamed.

The scarlet woman stretched her hand toward Jess, urging them forward.

That's when Jess saw it.

The woman's ring.

Her *mother's* ring!

"Mother . . . MOTHER?" Jess cried as the truth enveloped her and consciousness fled.

Fox scooped her up and stepped toward the dais.

Keelan sprinted forward, seizing a heavy golden goblet he'd spotted on the floor behind the woman. He closed the gap in two strides and clubbed the woman in the back of the head.

She toppled to the stage in a heap.

His eyes rose.

A robed figure cradled the Princess in his arms. The Child strained at her weight but continued forward at a slow, steady pace. His eyes focused on Jess and hadn't seen his leader fall.

Keelan leapt over the steps and sprinted toward them.

Fox's eyes flew up as Keelan's meaty fist drove into the center of his mask, overwhelming strength and momentum crushing the man's nose and dropping him to the floor. Keelan lifted the Princess and began walking toward the stage, mimicking what he'd seen Fox do before his untimely blackout.

Within a heartbeat, the chamber stood empty. All the figures fled, either in panic or anger, desperate to catch whoever dared interrupt their sacred ritual. Keelan climbed the stairs and retreated to the hallway now drenched in darkness.

Somewhere ahead, a man called out, "I've got him!"

The sound of countless boots striking stones receded as the mob hauled their prize from the exit.

Keelan waited.

He could feel the Princess breathing. She thrashed, trapped in some horrific dream. He held her close, hoping his strength would comfort and keep her quiet.

The passage remained still and silent, so he inched toward the exit. As he stepped outside, he was greeted by bodies of robed men strewn everywhere, arrows protruding from shoulders and backs and chests.

Two men shot forward and whispered urgently. "We have to go. NOW!"

"Where's the Prince?"

The Protector shook his head and began tugging at Keelan. "We haven't seen him or his men. We'll all die if we don't get out of here! We can't hold off hundreds of them."

He was right.

They had to get the Princess to safety.

Chapter Twenty-One

The sudden flare of healing magic sent a wave of shock through her body.

Isabel jolted awake.

Her mind raced as she tried to piece together how she'd ended up on the floor with a Healer looming over her. Three masked men stood nearby, guarding her with loaded crossbows.

She reached back to rub her aching scalp and was shocked as her hand returned coated in blood.

"Please, Honored Vessel. Do not move. The Healing is complex." Bony hands pressed her back down.

"How long have I been out? Where is the Pri—I mean Mistress?" She asked as she scanned the hall.

Ferret shook his head and struggled to maintain his Healing focus while answering. "Our men are still searching for her."

Her mind raced.

It would take at least two hours to cross the lake, probably more. She could beat them there, but it meant using the last of her Traveling charms. That couldn't be helped. Everything hinged on the next few hours.

"Finish quickly. I leave within the hour." Her voice left no room for debate.

"Yes, Honored Vessel." Ferret's hand began to shake. "Your head . . . will still hurt. The Healing will not be complete, and there is no way to know what else you may experience."

"You can finish when I get back. Get on with it," she snapped.

A half hour later, Isabel stood in her private chamber, angrily wringing the blood out of her hair. She couldn't understand how Jess had been stolen from the watchful eyes of *hundreds* of her people.

A timid knock pulled her back to the present. "Honored Vessel?"

"What?"

A broad-shouldered man wearing the mask of a Hawk entered and eyed her naked form, then quickly lowered his eyes to stare intently at a crack in the marble floor. "Honored Vessel, we captured one of the intruders. He's in the royal chamber, dosed and asleep."

She grabbed a towel and began drying her hair. "Wait outside. I want to see this man."

"Yes, Honored Vessel." He bowed and backed out of the room.

As she dressed, Isabel thought of all the ways she would shred the skin from this wretched man. She scooped up her last Traveling amulet and stormed down the hallway.

When the door opened and she saw Justin, *her* Justin, nausea nearly consumed her. His face was more purple than pale from the bludgeoning he had taken. She winced at the sight of her boy's battered face. Two robed figures stood silently against the wall.

She strolled to the bedside, careful to not show recognition, a task that took more self-control than she would've anticipated. She peered down and nearly lost her composure, suddenly thankful that everyone in this blasted place wore a mask. The idea of sacrificing Jess, of seeing her killed, wasn't something Isabel relished, but it had been necessary. She'd never been particularly close with her daughter and had recently come to resent her constant rebellion and petulant attitude.

Justin was another story altogether.

Since the day she'd first held him, he'd become her world. As he grew, their bond deepened and strengthened to levels she barely knew were possible.

He was smart, kind, loving, *respectful*.

Jess was only respectful when she wanted something, even on her best days, but Justin craved any wisdom or guidance Isabel offered. In her mind, he was perfect—the Heir the Kingdom *should* have had, rather than some insolent girl who dared think herself capable of ruling, a girl who could barely command the respect of her own family.

Isabel's hand grazed Justin's cheek in a gentle, motherly gesture, then she remembered her audience and pulled it back. "He's so young. How did this boy get into the temple?"

Ferret stepped forward. "Honored Vessel, he was one of four. Our men killed two. The fourth is the man who struck you and fled with Mistress."

The other figure spoke. "Honored Vessel, this is Prince Justin Vester. Second in line to the throne."

"Of course he is, you idiot. Do you think I don't recognize him?" She glared at the Child who now cowered in place. "Get out, both of you. NOW!"

The men scurried out of the room, leaving Isabel, Justin and Ferret alone.

"Heal him . . . gently. I want him kept here and well-treated until I return and decide what to do with him."

"Yes, Honored Vessel." Ferret bowed.

Isabel's mind raged as she returned to her chamber. Justin?

How could that idiot Alfred allow our boy to go on a military mission?

She slammed the door to her chamber and stalked to the dresser, inspecting herself in the large, oval mirror. She forced herself to take deep breaths and brush out her hair, something that had calmed her since she was a girl. It also gave her time to think. If her calculations were right, Jess and her rescuers still had an hour or more before they arrived in Cradle.

She still had time.

Her memory of the events in the ceremonial chamber was fuzzy, but she thought Jess called out to her, called her "mother." That would definitely complicate things.

A spike of pain shot through her head, and she realized she was pressing the bristles into her wounded scalp.

Breathe. Just breathe, nice and slow.

She set the brush aside and checked herself in the mirror. She didn't want to look too perfectly made up for this performance. Satisfied, she gripped the amulet and muttered a few words.

Her chamber shimmered, and she vanished.

Keelan cradled the Princess as the two Protectors rowed. His first trip across the lake had felt long, but this one was eternal. They had only been pursued by two figures in a small boat who were quickly dispatched by the expert marksmen-turned-rowers.

At least their escape went somewhat according to plan.

Noting else had.

Keelan replayed the night in his mind. Why had the King insisted Justin be there? Sure, he was a Prince and possibly the next Heir, but he was also a fifteen-year-old boy with no military training or experience. They knew this would be a dangerous mission. Taking Justin made no sense.

Jess stirred.

Her eyes fluttered open, and she peered up at Keelan, confusion clouding her face.

"Who . . ." She tried to turn her head, to look around, but a wave of nausea held her still. "Oh, Spirits. That hurts!"

Keelan spoke softly. "Princess, your father sent me to find you. We're headed back to him now. Please, we have to keep quiet. Sound carries across the water."

"Water? What water?" She forced herself up onto her elbows, her eyes widening as she took in the surrounding lake. "I don't understand. Where's Danym?"

"Princess?" Keelan cocked his head. "What's the last thing you remember?"

She struggled to think. Her head hurt so much. "We were sitting at a table. There was an old couple . . ."

He'd seen trauma cause memory loss before, but to reset so far back was unusual. He waited, not wanting to disturb her attempt at recall.

"No . . . we left that place. There were men . . . chasing us." She couldn't hold herself upright anymore and fell back a little too quickly. "Ow!"

"Just rest. We probably have another two hours before we reach the other side. Here, drink some water." He held that canteen to her lips.

She took a long sip before spitting the liquid all over the boat. "That's not water! Tastes like whiskey."

Keelan gave her an apologetic shrug and pulled the canteen back.

Her hand shot out and the canteen was back at her lips before he realized she'd snatched it out of his hand. "Oh, no you don't! This is *exactly* what my head needs right now."

Despite everything, Keelan chuckled.

Jess watched him as she drank. The last thing she saw before sleep overcame her were his crystal blue eyes.

Isabel materialized along the coast of the lake several hundred paces northeast of Cradle. She threw herself into the water and ran her hair through the mud. It took a few minutes of struggling, but she managed to rip her dress in several places. She tossed one shoe into the lake and hobbled back onto shore. When she got within a hundred paces of the outer buildings, she forced herself to sob loudly and force tears to streak the last vestige of her meticulous face paint.

"HELP! Please, somebody help me!" she called out, more wail than cry. She didn't want to look too weak—Alfred would never buy that—so she Called a ball of flame and sent it high into the air.

Men in uniform, bows nocked and ready, poured out of the town. When the first one recognized Isabel, he called to the others, "It's the Queen! Get a Healer!"

She allowed herself to be swept away by a brawny soldier with a handlebar mustache. He kept asking if she was alright, nearly knocking her out with his putrid breath. She winced every time he spoke and covered her mouth and nose, feigning exhaustion. A few malodorous moments later, the man laid her out on the King's bed.

Alfred hovered. A desperate, worried look creased his face.

"Issy!" He dropped to his knees and gripped her hand. "Issy, are you ok? Talk to me."

Spirits, this might actually be easier than I thought.

She feigned disorientation. "I'm—where am I? Alfred?"

"You're here with me in the inn. You're safe, thank the Spirits." Tears dribbled down his cheeks.

What a weak little moron. Time to twist the knife.

"Alfred . . . I'm so cold. Where's Justin? Where's my baby?" She ran her fingers down his face, wiping the tears from one side.

The King choked up even more. "Issy . . . he's . . . I . . . I didn't stop him. Oh, Issy . . ."

She bolted upright and threw off his hand, her voice now stern. "What do you mean, 'you didn't stop him?' *What have you done, Alfred?*"

The King lost all control.

Isabel reached into a pocket sewn on the inside of her robe and removed a vial filled with clear liquid. "Here, sweet husband, drink this. It will calm your nerves and let you sleep. I'll find our boy."

Alfred barely glanced at the vial as he downed the potion and rubbed his eyes. Before she could stop him, he wrapped her in his arms and held her for several interminable minutes. She was only able to free herself when his arms finally went limp.

Lifting Alfred onto the bed proved more challenging than anything she'd done that day. She removed his shoes and coat, then positioned him on his back as though he'd decided to nap.

Now, she needed to find a way back across that blasted lake. She crept to the door and peered out. Two guards flanked either side.

"The King is sleeping. Get me High Chancellor Thorn. Now!"

The guards startled, and one ran to fulfill her wish.

When the door creaked open, and Thorn entered, Isabel rose from her chair by the fireplace. Thorn bowed, then glanced toward the King with a questioning brow.

"He can't hear us." Fire raged in Isabel's eyes. "I need you to get a message to the temple. Tell them to prepare again, *immediately*. I will return in three hours to complete the ceremony. Then I need you to get me on a boat and across to the other side."

"Yes, Your Majesty. Right away." He made to turn.

"No, Danai. Do the communication here. Speak your Telepathy. I want to hear every word."

He was stunned.

She had never questioned his loyalty before. He nodded and reached out to the mind of the chief priest in the temple, then spoke her message, both aloud and in the cleric's mind.

"Good. I need that boat and two men we can trust. I'll be at the docks in fifteen minutes."

"Forgive me, Your Majesty. Won't that look suspicious?"

"Not nearly as much as what the world will see *after* this ceremony." Her grin chilled his soul. "The time for sculking in the shadows has passed. Now, go!"

Thorn fled the room.

He would do her bidding. He was the only man alive who knew what she was capable of—what she would actually do for power. He would never cross her, the pompous little weasel.

She gathered a few things from her dresser, straightened her hair again, and turned to walk out. Her eyes drifted to her husband's prone form.

It would take these fools hours to realize he wasn't asleep.

Plenty of time to change the world.

Isabel straightened her crimson robe and donned her mask of flesh, then stormed into the ceremonial chamber. The hall had been thoroughly cleaned and reset. Only a handful of high-ranking priests attended her now, as every other Child was armed and positioned outside the building, ensuring there would be no interruption this time.

She turned to the priest standing closest to the base of the stage, "Get him in here. Now!"

The man scurried to the corner of the room and yanked a tasseled cord. A heartbeat later, the doors at the far end parted, revealing the outline of three figures.

Isabel's throat clinched at the sight of Justin's head hanging limply to the side. She'd never wanted to involve him, but there was no choice now. Between Alfred's stupidity and her people's incompetence, Jess was no longer in her possession and nothing, not even her baby boy, would stand in her way.

The men hauled Justin forward at a deliberate pace, minding the ritual's mandate to the letter. Isabel tapped her fingers impatiently against her arm. The priests' humming swelled, and the ceremonial drums beat faster and louder. Moments later—moments that felt like hours—Justin and his escorts stood before the throne.

The Prince's eyes opened.

"Where am I? What's going on?" He looked down to find himself dressed in a golden robe with the Phoenix stitched across his chest.

Fox, the traditional escort for every ritual, spoke. "Honored Vessel, the Heir. E vesh Irina!" Those assembled stopped humming and repeated the phrase, then returned to their discordant melody.

"Heir? I'm not the Heir to anything. What's going on?" Justin struggled against his escorts as they forced him onto the throne. Fox shoved a crown on his head and stepped back.

Isabel circled to stand before him. Her voice was that of a scholar instructing an ignorant child. "The King is dead. Your sister is Queen. *You* are the Heir."

Justin's mouth fell open. His eyes darted about, then widened as the voice—

"Mother?" he gaped. "What—"

Before a sob could take her, she whispered, "I'm so sorry," then plunged the ceremonial dagger it into his heart.

He shuddered and gasped, then stilled.

Isabel stared down at her hand still gripping the blade buried inches deep in the flesh of her son.

What have I done?

Her eyes found Justin's vacant stare and waves of anguish gripped her soul. She pulled the wrenched the dagger from his body and flung it across the hall, then drew her bleeding boy to her heaving chest. His lifeless weight fought against her, but she clung to him with a mother's ferocity.

Her hand pressed his head into her shoulder.

She stroked his hair.

The scent every mother remembers, learned from her child's first breath, drifted into her. She drew it in, held it with all her strength, willed it to never leave. With an exhale, it was gone, and her sobs grew.

The world froze as she held the limp form of her son.

After an eternity of tears, Isabel tore herself away, seized the crown from his head, and turned away. As Justin's spirit drifted away, she lowered the crown onto her brow, and the seventh diamond flared to life.

Isabel raised her hands above her head and screamed, "E vesh Irina!"

Wind swirled and whistled throughout the room. Drums beat louder and faster. The refrain of the Children became cries of wicked ecstasy.

Massive gears that hadn't budged in a thousand years began to grind, groaning through the stone hall, and the ceiling far above crept open, revealing a bright, moonlit sky. Isabel tossed her son's shell aside and claimed the throne as the entire stage uprooted and began to rise.

The priests stumbled back.

The dais rose high above the building's roof before grinding to a halt. Isabel surveyed the robed figures gaping up at her, and she screamed down, "E vesh Irina."

They answered her call, repeating the phrase again . . . and again.

Their chanting froze when the orb held aloft by the statue flared, its crimson light coating the night sky in blood. It shattered, and the glow within flared brighter, then streaked from the statue's palm to hover before Isabel. She spread her arms wide and opened her mouth.

The scarlet flame rushed in.

Her head snapped backward, and she released a primal shriek.

The figures below echoed her cry.

When the glow faded and she gazed down at her sycophantic mob, the woman *formerly* known as Isabel, Queen of the Kingdom of Spires, bellowed three simple words.

"I am returned!"

If you loved Ungifted, please take a moment to leave a review filled with stars. Your feedback inspires us to write more, and helps other readers discover our work.

Don't forget your gift, a free copy of *The Rise of Irina*. Click here to tell me where to send it.

THE
RISING
SON
JD RUFFIN
ISLES OF JADE & FIRE · BOOK I

J.D. Ruffin is the author of
multiple bestselling novels, including the epic fantasy Kingdom War series.

Ironically, he never really enjoyed reading until a friend
loaned him a dog-eared copy
of J.R.R. Tolkien's Fellowship
of the Ring. From that day, he
was hooked, discovering fanta-
sy authors Robert Jordan, Brandon Sanderson, R.A.
Salvatore, Terry Goodkind and many, many others.

Becoming an author was never part of the master plan,
but...

As a fourteen-year-old bespeckled and befreckled boy,
J.D. and his friends would gather around the D&D dice
for hours on end, trading reality for fantasy, if only in
their minds. In his quest to "stump his friends" with

an impossible campaign, he dreamed up a storyline that captured his imagination.

Then... well... nothing happened.

He grew up and went to work in a completely different world. Too many years later, that story pulled at the corner of his mind, demanding to be heard... to be written. Hence, an author was born.

J.D. lives in Florida with his three Australian shepherds. In his spare time, he enjoys playing amateur chef, hitting the tennis courts, traveling, and watching Survivor.